A JIG BEFORE DYING

A JIG BEFORE DYING

The First Sweeney & Rose Mystery

Danny Carnahan

Copyright © 2008 by Danny Carnahan.

ISBN: Softcover   978-1-4363-0833-5

All rights reserved. This book may not be reproduced, in whole or in part, by any electronic or mechanical means, without permission by the author.

This is a work of fiction. Names, characters, places and incidents either are the product of the author's imagination or are used fictitiously, and any resemblance to any actual persons, living or dead, events, or locales is entirely coincidental.

To contact the author about any of his novels or recordings, please visit www.dannycarnahan.com

Lyrics in Chapter 1 from "Summer Nights", Copyright © 1980 by Mick Fitzgerald. Used with permission.

Lyrics in Chapter 5 from "The Rose You Wore For Me", Copyright © 1989 by Danny Carnahan

This book was printed in the United States of America.

To order additional copies of this book, contact:
Xlibris Corporation
1-888-795-4274
www.Xlibris.com
Orders@Xlibris.com
46036

Many thanks to
Alex, Claire, Mareev, Mike, and William, who made me write and then write better.
And boundless thanks to the lovely Saundra, my daily inspiration.

Chapter One

•

Brighton, England, 1992

"Tell me again why you're serving hand-ground French roast in china cups to the idiots upstairs while we have to squeeze this umbrella water out of a Coffee Max machine," complained PC Jarvis to the hotel concierge.

"Don't ask me," shrugged the pouting, sloe-eyed young Indian woman leaning against the machine. "I wanted nothing to do with this summit deal. You can blame that wanker Weldon as usual. He's the one who insisted it be held here. Brilliant timing, too, with half the office being renovated and most of the front desk out with the flu. You're lucky the Coffee Max still works."

Jarvis felt bored and left out. He'd only been in the grand meeting hall long enough for the last security sweep. Then it was back to his crummy desk in the command center long before the escorted limousines pulled into the marble entryway. The Brighton International Hotel's plush suites and spidery, arched corridors might well be among England's most acclaimed architectural wonders, but the staff facilities were positively Dickensian in their unfinished confusion.

"So what do you suppose they're up to now?" he asked, not really caring.

"God only knows," replied the concierge. "Just so they stop scaring away our regular clientèle. Can't wait to see the back of them."

Jarvis nodded his head of tousled blond hair and tried to balance four paper coffee cups on his clipboard. The young Brighton Police constable had never drawn security duty at any government meeting before, let alone one as highly touted and publicized as this Commonwealth Economic Summit.

But besides a couple of crank IRA bomb threats, it was all just long hours and three nights in a row without seeing his girl. And bad coffee.

"Well, I guess it's back to the nerve center," he said sarcastically. "Maybe next time we can get a room with a jacuzzi."

"Not with Deputy Secretary Weldon running things, you won't," smiled the concierge. "High-handed old so-and-so. Where do they dig up these old government fossils? What was it the *Guardian* said about him yesterday? Nothing he attempts is ever well done? Ha. I only hope he doesn't bore them all to death before the press conference. What is it? A couple hours yet?" She glanced at her watch.

Jarvis just grinned darkly and maneuvered his luke-warm coffees down the service hall toward the room off the main lobby where the police security post had been set up. As he pushed through the door he was nearly knocked over by another uniformed policeman lunging for his radio.

"Where's the fire, Fred?" he cried, slopping coffee halfway across the nearest desk.

"It's Doomsday Paddy callin' again," snarled Detective Sergeant Crook with his hand clamped over the telephone mouthpiece. "Jerrold, do you think you could manage a trace this time?"

PC Jerrold vaulted cat-like over the back of the desk to begin tapping expertly at the computer terminal.

"Just keep him talking this time, damn it," snapped the thin young man at the computer under his breath. The room grew suddenly quiet, with all three uniformed officers intent on the Sergeant's half of the conversation.

"Yes, I recognize your voice," he drawled comfortably. "I can't say I appreciate those last two calls much, though . . . What do you think I told 'em? I mean, why ring to tell me there's a bomb in the hotel if it's just a load of bollocks? Why'd you ring again this morning? Just to yank my bloody chain? . . ."

"Almost . . ."

"Yeah, yeah, very clever . . . But what was all that about it all goin' up at three fifty-six? Maybe your watch needs winding . . ."

"Almost. Close by, wherever he is. Just another few seconds."

"Nothin' yesterday, nothin' today . . . Get your story straight, man. Think we got nothin' better to do than sweep the same damn conference room every four hours for imaginary bombs just for you?"

"Got 'im," hissed the policeman at the computer. "Right in the building. Car park phone box, street level." Jumping out of his seat, he spun around for orders to see that the Sergeant's face had suddenly gone deathly white.

"Sir? Go for him, sir? Car park?" The young man looked over in disbelief as Sergeant Crook placed the handset back in its cradle. The sergeant sat for a long moment as if set in quick-drying cement, then leaped up and bolted for the door.

"The bastard knew they'd changed rooms. Forget the car park. Clear the street! Now!" he shouted as he ran out jacketless into the wide hotel foyer and sprinted for the escalator while fumbling for the radio at his belt. The three constables scattered toward the east, north, and west entrances where a few more officers lounged along the barricades, keeping the public and press at a comfortable distance from the five cabinet ministers and twenty-eight industrial leaders meeting for another numbing harangue over trade barriers between Commonwealth members and the new, improved European Community.

Jarvis stumbled onto the pavement and shot glances quickly left and right before running across four lanes to the ITV crew gathered around the remote television van.

"All of you—move away from here at once," he shouted, sweeping his arm toward the far street corner. "No questions," he barked at the open-mouthed reporter holding a microphone. "Just move. Leave the van. All the way down there. Now!" The few scattered pedestrians not involved with newscasting took the cue and began hurrying away, shooting worried looks over their shoulders.

Jarvis looked back nervously at the five-story hotel, its sleekly modern stone and glass façade stretching the width of the city block. What had the Sergeant said? He knew? The cold, Irish voice on the phone, the voice that had taunted the Brighton police with empty bomb threats for two days since the summit meeting began, knew that the final session had moved. Impossible. Nobody knew. But had anyone swept the other conference hall since yesterday? Damned if he had the slightest idea.

His eyes counted the windows on the top floor from the left—five, six, there it was—the curtained room where the final agreements were being signed. Sergeant Crook would be there by now.

As he reached down for his radio the entire street blossomed in a searing yellow flash. The blinding shock wave lifted him off the sidewalk as if he were no more substantial than a leaf and drove him splintering through a display window a bare instant ahead of a shower of rubble and glass and the sound of worlds ending.

Screams echoed through the whirling dust. Jarvis couldn't see. As he choked on acrid smoke he was almost shocked to realize that he was still breathing. Yet with this realization came another. He couldn't move either of his arms. With a stab of white-hot agony he strained to turn his head. His left arm was a mangled, red mass. Quite useless. And the blood was pooling quickly.

Blinking away the pain he turned to his right. Across the street he could just make out the hotel, the top two floors entirely ripped away as if by some gigantic clawed beast. The last thing he focused on was the bulky object that had landed on top of him, crushing his right arm. It was Sergeant Crook—or most of him—judging from the uniform and shirt sleeves, anyway. Funny, thought Jarvis as he lost consciousness, the sergeant sailing all the way across the street without his head.

Two blocks away from the seafront carnage a neatly dressed man stopped casually in front of the Anglo-Irish Bank and inserted a card into the automated teller machine. Ignoring the choices offered, he entered ten digits, then held down the pound sign and hit "1." The words "Priority Transfer" appeared. He entered eight digits. The numbers vanished. He entered eight more. The screen asked "Would you like this transfer in U.S. dollars?"

"Bloody well right, I would," he muttered, touching another few buttons and retrieving his card. Expressionless he turned, lit a cigarette, and ambled down the street away from the rising wail of sirens.

•

San Francisco, one month later

Sweeney slammed his foot down onto the brake and squealed to a stop four inches from the tail lights of a wet black Chrysler.

"Blasted city drivers," he grumbled, reaching down to retrieve first his fiddle case and then the upended brown leather valise, now emptied onto the floor in a hopelessly scrambled pile of music sheets and a dozen or so compact disk jewel boxes. The traffic's headlights paraded jerkily through the wet, streaked windshield as Sweeney blinked into yet another soggy San Francisco evening. He tapped the steering wheel, annoyed.

Several blocks away there was a warm pub full of people he knew playing tunes he knew and drinking beer he could almost taste. And he was stuck in traffic behind some brain-dead New Age driver who had forgotten which pedal would move his car forward. And the guy was probably a teetotaller in the bargain. Sweeney leaned his head back and closed his eyes, shutting out San Francisco and trying not to tap his fingers.

> *Dublin is a pencil drawing*
> *Quayside fading, twilight falling*
> *Oh, summer nights*
> *Clean shirt well worth waiting for*
> *The bus is late but so's the hour*
> *Oh, summer nights*

The song he'd first heard in Flannery's Bar two years before popped in out of nowhere and proceeded to unravel itself in his head. It was as though a soft voice had spoken up, reminding him to relax a little.

"You've got to learn to enjoy being late, Niall." Brian Patrick Byrne's advice floated back to him. Of course, his Dublin friend's counsel was accompanied by a pint of Guinness two hours after closing time. Yes, at least in Dublin there were demonstrable advantages to procrastination.

"You've got to relax," said Byrne. "No point in feelin' guilty. That's right out. And it's your fiddlin' that'll suffer first, ye know," he exhaled a slowly uncurling helix of smoke through his dark, randomly arranged teeth.

"How's that?" said Sweeney with a bemused expression as he lowered his pint and wiped the untrimmed ends of his sandy moustache. He had never considered himself to be one for needless suffering.

"Sure, it's the soul of the man as comes out in his music, as you very well know. What consumes the player? What passions are breathin' in him? Why does he bother playin' a tune in the pub at all? The music comin' out the fingers is the music in . . ." he paused for effect, taking another drag from the pinched cigarette end held between square, calloused fingers and staring off into space. Tinker's light blue eyes in a dark face. " . . . in the soul. It's the music'll tell a man's passion as if it was carved on his forehead."

"Assuming there's any passion there to express in the first place."

"Well, so there ye are. But if there's none, it isn't music then, is it? It's just a lot of notes. Like your man sawin' away all summer at the sessions and festivals in Doolin and Milltown and Ennis. You're safe, mind. There's somethin' of the honest session man in ye."

Sweeney coughed rather than commenting in the face of this parade of sage pronouncements. "Come now, Brian. You telling me you can pick a man's driving passion by hearing him fiddle? Christ, you'd never know.

There'd have to be thousands of driving bloody passions . . . at least as many as there are fiddlers."

"Not at all." Tilting his head sideways, Sweeney's companion watched as another blue-gray spiral of smoke worked its way up from his pursed lips to the shadows above. "I figure there's only six. As make any difference, that is." He leaned back and counted on his fingers.

"Ye got your love and hate. Ye got your madness and faith in God—which may in actual fact be the same thing. Then ye got your whiskey. And finally ye got your guilt. Now a man can generate some lovely music wit' a push from any of the first five, but your guilt'll come out soundin' sour every time. Bloody Cat'lic intrusion in the sensible pagan scheme o' things. No use for it at all."

Sweeney suppressed the urge to dissect Byrne's little speech in any of the three or four obvious ways that leapt to mind. But a poor American visitor to Dublin hadn't a prayer of winning an argument with the likes of Byrne, who had spent the better part of his life learning to wield English like a switchblade in the pubs along the Liffey.

"So that's your point, is it? It's enjoy being late and lighten up or sound the guilty fiddler, eh? Oh well, we can't have that."

"I was makin' no point," Byrne tossed off vaguely. "But that's about the size of it. It's like from little acorns, boyo. My advice would be to avoid it entirely."

"Then what about a motivating passion? I suppose I should have one, shouldn't I? That is, if I can manage to avoid guilt when in the clutches of my Muse. What, oh what shall it be?"

"Well now, I'd say your choice is either love or whiskey, since ye ain't quite mad enough to make it sound inspired and we both know that faith in God hasn't done much for ye." He winked.

"Although," he added quietly, "I'll own I've heard men as have played for plain hate so's you wouldn't ever forget it." He dropped the pinched cigarette end from between his amber colored fingers and ground it dead under the toe of his shoe. "They just don't seem to be able to play that way for very long."

Sweeney pulled himself back to the here and now of the drizzly San Francisco evening. The windshield wipers flipped back and forth in soft, six-eight jig time. He opened his eyes, noticing that his fingers were drumming complex counter-rhythms to the soft sound. He gripped the wheel tightly and stared out at the evening, thinking how similar were the faces of San Francisco and Dublin on nights like this.

Come to think of it, the whole day reminded him of his year in Dublin. Wetter than expected. Colder than expected. Business appointments missed and little things left undone. In Dublin one always missed appointments and left things undone. He remembered being amazed initially at the casual Irish grace with which the urgent could be indefinitely deferred. And urgency had supposedly been the whole reason he and his colleagues had been sent to Ireland.

It seemed merely silly in retrospect that some financial hotshot had convinced the Anglo-Irish Bank that they should try a daring, if fleeting leap ahead of the Americans into the forefront of the banking industry, installing automated teller machines on Dublin street corners that could not only spit out ten pound notes but could handle foreign stock trades and mutual fund investments for American tourists. Of course, these corners had historically been reserved for the nuns brandishing their Catholic Charities collection cans, as Sweeney could have told them, had they bothered to ask. But Sweeney was only a mid-level engineer whose views on what was needed on Dublin street corners were neither solicited nor considered, even though he had logged more time wandering around Ireland than had his entire Board of Directors.

So, Sweeney and a knot of fellow engineers had been flown in for a projected month of installation, system tweaking, and training. When little had progressed in three months the conviction grew in Sweeney's admittedly contrary mind that automated tellers catering to Type-A Americans would never catch on in Ireland. Still nothing had progressed in six months and he was certain in his heart of hearts that he knew why: the Irish people were born with an innate, fundamental resistance toward any business transaction that did not offer an opportunity for lengthy conversation. Teller machines of any kind, efficient and taciturn, didn't have a prayer.

Sweeney had tried once or twice to impress this idea upon the home office. Failing in this, he decided instead to spend as much time as possible playing music in Flannery's Bar, awaiting inevitable failure and the call to come back home. His colleagues never did get the hang of Irish ways, sad to say, nor were they that keen on pubs. So, while Sweeney came to accept the speed at which things didn't get done in Dublin, the others degenerated into an unhappy collective lump of sheer exasperation. Finally, as Irish techniques of deferral began to take on aspects of high art to Sweeney, the bank gave up, the contract was scuttled, the engineers were sent packing, and the street corners were left to the nuns.

So now here he was, back home in traffic, doing exactly what he'd promised himself he wouldn't do any more. Wound tight after a bad day at work, willing to surrender to his Muse, and yet feeling guilty. And for what? Accomplishing virtually nothing all day . . . again? Fighting Old Man Berenson's antiquated decision-making system to two falls out of three . . . again? Being late for a session . . . again? How silly. Upstairs at Flannery's Brian would have had him shrugging off such a thought in no time as an amusingly alien concept. But that was two years ago, and that was Dublin. Well, it had been a hard day. Now more than anything he needed a beer.

The black Chrysler still stood frozen in the street ahead under wet, twinkling lights. Sweeney closed his eyes.

How he hated driving in San Francisco. But he put up with it as a grueling necessity. Not so in the Irish capital. He'd flatly refused to sit behind the wheel anywhere in Dublin's sweet chaos. The apparent Irish shortage of brain-dead New Age drivers had not made the looming menace of traffic measurably less harrowing for him. Whenever possible he'd opted for the company and imagined safety of the crowded sidewalks. In and out, through the wide selection of rotten weather, he'd march to the bank offices in Grafton Street or flit across the footbridge to the pub sessions and home again after closing time, fiddle case in gloved fingers, cap pulled down to his fair, bristling eyebrows, white breath dancing ahead of him over the cobblestones.

The windshield wipers had somehow shifted into hornpipe rhythm. Sweeney opened his eyes.

Looking again through the bleary glass he saw the door of the Chrysler open abruptly and a figure emerge to raise the hood. Craning his neck sideways, he saw that the rest of the traffic had cleared, leaving only the dead Chrysler between him and the session. Sweeney felt his impatience get the better of him. He pulled around the now double-parked car a little faster and closer than was absolutely necessary, and glowered toward the figure now looking up from the engine compartment. A elderly woman with a sagging neck and bleached Tammy Faye Bakker hair gazed over toward him in blank bewilderment. New Age? Not a chance. He shook his head and drove off.

Sweeney angled around the corner of Clement and Tenth and nosed into a parking space halfway down the long block. He nudged forward, kissed the bumper of the next car, stopped and surveyed the legality of his work. Only a foot of his car extended into the driveway of a pink Art Deco row house. Painted to resemble an attentive regiment of pastel peppermints, the house and its nearly identical neighbors faded as far as he could see on down the street.

"Close enough," he nodded to himself, kicking the bumper for good measure. Truly a stroke of luck at nine o'clock on a Friday night.

Emerging into the chilly evening he inventoried his pockets, dropped his keys into one of them, and reached back in to tidy the pile of CDs onto the seat. His own face stared up at him from each jewel box, below the lettered name "Niall Sweeney" and above the title *Among the Nightingales*. The youthful, almost unlined face on the booklet made an attempt to smile and look sincere as hell at the same time. The photographer had made Sweeney's well-trimmed sandy moustache appear a little bushier than it really was. He'd missed the eyes, though. In the photo they appeared several shades darker than their actual cornflower blue. Proudly, he patted the CDs; all shrink-wrapped, shiny and new. He'd taken to having a few with him most of the time, just in case . . . well, just in case. He kicked the door closed, tucked the untidy black fiddle case under his left arm and stretched to his full six-foot height until his neck gave a pleasant little pop. A couple of deep breaths of the refreshing, lightly-salted air and he found himself entertaining friendlier sentiments toward his fellow human beings.

Clement Street was growing indistinct as the evening fog crept up through the Avenues. The fog painted the street in a wash of quiet grays as it did every night. Armed with fiddle case Sweeney had strolled up and down that fuzzy gray street hundreds of evenings watching the moisture gather under the bay windows to drip down the necks of people coming out of cafes and restaurants. Now he walked on briskly past the bright windows and darkened shops, through bands of aroma that licked out across the sidewalk. Pot stickers and pizza and fog. Stuffed grape leaves and fish and fog. By the time he got to Eighth Avenue the knees of his jeans were soaked through and he was humming a jig the name of which he couldn't remember.

The Maids of West Clare? Nah. *The Contagious Barmaid*? Something like that. *The Girl Behind the Threshing Combine*? Probably not. Damn, it's something about a maid, I'm certain! He grinned. Beer was required to clear the brain.

Sweeney ducked under the green scalloped awning and turned into the door of the Bag of Nails. The bar was crowded. Over the cacophony of gossip and glasses and colliding billiard balls a tangle of tenor banjo, guitar and accordion scraped away happily at the back of the room.

He elbowed his way past the pool table and through bodies four deep, casually dodging the end of a cue aimed in passing at his navel. Stretching up on his toes he squinted out over the mass of talking and drinking and smiling heads bobbing in a sea of undifferentiated brown and gray. Faded and dogeared, portraits of James Connolly and Padraic Pearse, Markiewicz and

Wolfe Tone gazed down from the long wall facing the bar. Tired and worn, they seemed tonight to look perhaps more thirsty than heroic.

Vin Bowen, slouching on his elbows near the end of the bar, hailed Sweeney through the crowd.

"It's after nine. You're later than usual."

"Don't remind me. I've promised myself not to feel guilty."

Vin stopped for the briefest of quizzical looks. "It's just that considering the occasion I thought I'd see you bright and early." Vin looked up from his habitual stoop and scanned questioningly past Sweeney's shoulder. "Where's Rosie?"

"Things do seem to have gotten off to an early start." Sweeney glanced first toward the musicians who, through the haze, looked shabby enough to have been installed at the same time as the Fenian posters, then turned back to Vin.

"Rosie's grading papers tonight. She was about halfway through a bottle of zinfandel when I left. Better to leave her be when she's in that kind of mood—already gibbering about flat brain waves in the English Department when I got home from the office. I told her that at the rate she continued gibbering she might as well volunteer to host a seminar in 'angst' next quarter. She didn't think it was funny. What's the occasion, by the way?"

"You're kidding?" Vin looked genuinely surprised. "Well, that's what you get for working regular hours."

"Maybe. But chances are that my regular hours and I will outlive you." As far as Sweeney had ever been able to tell, his old friend had survived for years on shakily-acquired student loans and the occasional odd job. The precarious nature of this system never seemed to bother Vin much.

"Ah, but a drab and shallow existence, no doubt. Poor Niall. A married man. And so young. Shelved the passions of youth. Abandoned the chase." He sighed dramatically into his nearly empty glass. "It's so sad when an artist becomes respectable."

Sweeney rolled his eyes. "What is it about my damn bar-crawling friends lecturing me about my damn passions?" he asked himself, half smiling.

With a quick nod and a smile, Annie the barmaid reached a pint of Guinness to him past the potato-colored bar denizen to his right. He downed half of it without breathing and licked the foam off his upper lip as the first hint of a warming glow began to make its way up from the stomach toward the brain.

Joe Gilmore squeezed past Annie on his way toward the other end of the bar, exchanging a quick pat on her rear for an even quicker smile. The pat was the most demonstrative behavior Sweeney had ever witnessed between the gruff Ulsterman and his rather shy girlfriend-employee during business hours. Sweeney took another sip and began counting hats.

"A good fifty-percent night, this," he concluded to himself. Sweeney had hit upon a theory one boozy evening in Flannery's that the best sessions were those containing the highest ratio of hats to bare heads. He had not arrived at this theory through any scientific means, of course. He had just grown particularly partial to old caps in Flannery's, preferably those with greasy thumbprints on the brim. The shabbier the better. And the theory seemed to hold true even here in San Francisco. A good crop of shabby caps perched atop a crowd of middle aged Irish immigrants promised a Friday session of surpassing noise and ardor.

For those who didn't like hats, there was always the Blarney Castle a few blocks down Clement. Nobody in there wore hats. Sweeney was not sure that any of them had ever set foot in Ireland. They stood around capless, resplendent in white Aran sweaters or Guinness tee shirts, depending on the season, holding Irish coffees and looking like a herd of mute, alcoholic sheep, wondering where the music was. What a fun bunch. Sweeney marveled at the rich cultural diversity of the city. He turned to Vin and poked him in the sternum.

"So when do I meet her, eh, Vinnie?"

"Who?" piped the voice above the sternum.

"The new girlfriend, of course."

Vin raised one eyebrow. "Now, who said a thing about a new girlfriend?"

"It's written all over you. When was the last time you lectured me on the relative merits of married respectability versus the single life?"

"When I was going with Lydia."

"And that was?"

"Six months ago."

"Right. And how long is it since you told Lydia to stuff it and declared you would remain sober and chaste until you graduated and got a steady job?"

Vin looked sideways and raised the other eyebrow. When he pursed his lips his rust-colored moustache looked like it would take over his entire face. Stooping, he was several inches shorter than Sweeney and at twenty-nine, a year younger. He had been working on his degree in English Literature at San Francisco State for eleven years.

"Hell, Niall, I never said anything about sober."

Annie delivered another Anchor. Vin held up the pint and gazed through it as if he were testing the color of a glass of Château Latour. Then he turned and brightened as if someone had flipped a switch.

"Now, Christie's different, you know. You'll like Christie." Sweeney nodded attentively as the ever talkative Vinnie began to roll, accelerating to full speed.

"It's her first time here at the Bag. Wandering about the place now, as a matter of fact. I'll snag her when I see her. Met her at school. A junior. Been out together every night since Monday." Eyes rolled briefly heavenward. "She likes Irish music, of course. Couldn't imagine being interested if she didn't, certainly. She's pretty up on it, too, though she really hasn't been around much. And you know, she even has your CD!"

"No! Well, Jayzus!" Sweeney put on his most obnoxious stage Irish voice. "That is an occasion worth celebrating! Somebody bought my CD." He downed the rest of his pint with a flourish.

"She was quite impressed when I said I knew you; a real recording artist and all. She said your music was very visual, or something. Said it made you seem like you'd be a nice guy. Had to come down tonight and see you in person. Ain't that flattering?"

"I am deeply moved."

"I didn't tell her you really worked in a bank."

"Thanks, Vinnie, old boy. Sometimes it's better to leave untarnished the little fantasies of life."

"Tell you what . . . I'll go find her and introduce you. You gonna play a few tunes first or you want to sit here for a minute?" Without waiting for an answer he started prying his way back through the wall of bodies.

"Hey, wait!" yelled Sweeney. "So what's this occasion I'm supposed to know all about?"

Vin squeezed back to within arm's reach. "Oh, yeah, I forgot. Here, read this. Congratulations." He handed Sweeney a small newspaper which had been stuffed in his pants pocket and then disappeared.

Sweeney opened the paper. It was the *Irish-American Weekly*, a locally-published tabloid catering to what was left of the Irish community in San Francisco. Sweeney seldom read it. The paper skewed its coverage, its prose style, and its bias toward the older generation of the Irish in the City—the ones Sweeney had come to think of as the 'Irisher-than-thou' set. Nowadays, the casual observer would have a hard time finding many left in an increasingly Asian San Francisco. But there were still sufficient numbers of them tucked away in the old neighborhoods to fill the bars in the evenings.

Knowing the attitudes of the *Weekly*, he'd sent them one of the first promotional copies of *Among the Nightingales* anyway.

"Well, well, what do you know?" he mumbled as the realization dawned on him. "This'll be my very first review!"

He'd seen the *Weekly's* current music columnist, Michael Blayney, at the Bag of Nails from time to time, always at the opposite end of the bar from the music. He seemed a singularly unpleasant person from what Sweeney could observe, verbally aggressive when sober, and leaning toward the lecherous once drunk.

So many Irish drunks of Sweeney's acquaintance got pleasantly chummier and blurrier as each new round appeared. Not Blayney. In the six months since he had first appeared in San Francisco he had made it clear that he used drink to polish his nastiness to a fine luster. Sweeney sent him the CD knowing all this (after all, promo copies were free), hoping the guy would say something nice about it, if only to reflect favorably on his regular hangout and the only decent Irish session left in the city.

He skipped the bulk of the stories earnestly devoted to Irish politics and eagerly smoothed out the page with the baroque calligraphed headline 'Ceol Agus Rince.' Music and Dance. As always, a photo of two scrubbed, immaculately-attired, apparently terrified young step dancers dominated the page. At the bottom was Blayney's column. Sweeney winced at the title: *Celtic Charlatanism Exposed*. The review began:

> It has become necessary for me to comment on an increasingly frequent and highly unfortunate occurrence in Irish music. That is, the effects of non-Irish dilettantes who corrupt and mock our ancient musical forms in the name of 'cultural sharing.' This corruption can be seen to be fostered by Americans eager to make a fast buck and supported by an ignorant press . . .

"Oh, boy," said Sweeney to himself, "this is not going well." The column continued:

> So why is this so terrible? Surely it must be all right for pilfering hacks and talentless musical vagrants to make nonsense of Irish culture in the privacy of their own homes. But these same hacks are encouraged to perform in public and even record while the true Gaelic scholars and Celtic artists can't get work.

Sweeney gritted his teeth. Who was Blayney making out to be a Gaelic scholar? Himself? Surely not. Where did he get off spouting that stuff?

> So I come to easily the most flagrant example of the problem. My attention was drawn to a new CD recently. The package announced; *Niall Sweeney—Among the Nightingales*. On the back it proclaimed; 'Irish fiddle tunes with a San Francisco perspective.' What kind of conceit is this? Before even listening to the record I am alerted that here is another American who intends to alter Irish music into a parody of itself since he can't play or hasn't the dimmest understanding of the real thing.

"Jesus." He read on, his mood darkening.

> The 'musician' in question has not even a basic mastery of his instrument and no style at all. He fiddles with limping American phrasing that would make any true Irish musician ill. He is, in fact, a counterfeit Celt; an ingratiating Irish impostor. This CD fraudulently attempts to sell provincial Californian musical incompetence as ethnicity.
>
> Perhaps some serious students of Irish music will not view this CD as a deliberate cultural affront, assuming that since the 'performer' knows as little as he does about the real music of Ireland, he couldn't have produced such cultureless swill deliberately. But I find his release of a CD such as this to be both pushy and offensive. The fact that he is allowed to perform in public is doubly offensive.

Sweeney unconsciously made a fist.

> In short, every copy of this CD foisted off on the public represents one more nail in the coffin of Irish culture, hammered in by another petty bourgeois charlatan. When we can no longer enjoy beautiful music from Ireland, played by native Irishmen the way it was intended to be played, we can thank the likes of Niall Sweeney.

"So what do you think of the review?" shouted a cheery voice into Sweeney's ear. Sweeney nearly jumped off his stool.

"Don't do that, Vin!"

"Sorry. Remember? I wanted you to meet somebody. Christie, this is my friend Niall. Niall, Christie Reese."

Sweeney reached out automatically from his perch on the stool and shook a thin, pale hand. The hand belonged to a thin, pale girl, just old enough to be in the bar, rather pretty with blue eyes and a halo of short, curly brown hair. What made her especially striking in the crowd, though, was her height. She looked to be pushing six feet. Vin, making his very best and somewhat laughable attempt at standing up straight next to her, was a good three inches shorter.

"Delighted," she smiled.

"Pleased to meet you," said Sweeney, unable to keep the gruffness out of his voice. "Vin, did you actually read this before you congratulated me on getting reviewed?"

"Sure! It's really something, isn't it? What did you think?"

"Well, for one thing he spelled 'petit bourgeois' wrong. And he's a son of a bitch."

"No, I'm serious! I've never had a reviewer do a hatchet job on me."

"You've never done anything worth reviewing. Learn to play something and make a record. Maybe you'll get lucky."

"What's wrong? Is that the review Vincent told me about?" asked Christie. "Wasn't it any good?"

"Oh, some shithead who thinks he's God's gift to Irish music was let loose with a typewriter. I'd like to see him in here tonight. I'd give him a piece of my mind and maybe something to go with it."

"Let me see," said Christie.

"Here, I'll read you my favorite part," said Vin, deftly repossessing the paper from Sweeney and fussing it into a manageable bundle in the press of the crowd. "Here it is." He read the bit about hacks and vagrants while Christie looked at him and Sweeney nursed his Guinness.

"Oh, my," breathed Christie. "How awful for you, Niall. Don't worry, though. I wouldn't listen to people like that. Better to pretend they don't exist. Lots of people think you're a fine musician. Vincent and I think you're wonderful. In fact, I've been waiting all week to come in and hear you play."

Sweeney managed to find a smile under all the smarting pride. He eyed the tall girl more carefully, wondering if perhaps she really was different, as Vinnie claimed. Sweeney had never heard anyone but Vinnie's mother get away with calling him Vincent.

"So, Niall, tell me the truth. What did you do? Run over his dog or strangle his grandmother or something? I mean, it is sort of weird the way he got so personal. I didn't even know you knew each other."

"We don't. Just in the bar. I don't think I've said a dozen words to him directly. You know what he's like. More interested in the women at the sessions than the music. Of all the players around here, why should he hit on me? The man's crazy, that's all. I just can't figure it out."

"He just sounds hateful," said Christie. "Who is he, did you say? What could his problem be?"

"Beats the hell out of me," replied Sweeney. "But if you ask me, any man with as much hate in him as that ought to be hung up until it's all nicely drained out."

Sweeney hauled his fiddle case up from between his knees and got up from the bar stool. "Aw, to hell with him. Anything further he has to say to me he can say to my face. He will find me down the other end, producing cultureless swill. I'm just glad Brian Byrne isn't here tonight."

"Who?"

"Oh, nobody. A two-bit Irish philosopher I once knew who reads fiddlers' souls. I'm not sure I'd like him reading mine just now."

Chapter Two

The smoke hung thick at the far end of the Bag of Nails. There, between the dimly-lit juke box and a precarious sculpture of empty beer kegs stacked against the wall, Sweeney plopped himself heavily onto a folding wooden chair, his fiddle case across his knees. Still angry, he sniffed at the haze.

What a crock of vicious bullshit, he thought for the umpteenth time. Nail in the coffin of Irish culture! Christ! All I'm doing is playing tunes and enjoying myself. Who cares if I put out a goddam CD? Did I ever set myself up as some sort of fiddle guru? And who cares, anyway? Who reads that rag? Who listens to critics?

He paused, wondering if he really believed any of that himself. Absently, he pulled three or four hunks of decaying leather off the handle of the fiddle case. He flicked them across the table one by one with his thumb, aiming at the empty pint glass. He let out a breath and slumped his shoulders.

God, I wish Rosie were here. Just my luck to have her poop out tonight. She loves cramming bad writing back down her students' throats. Well, usually. I hope she's mellowed out by the time I get home. Yeah . . . I'll have her do a big, fat job on Blayney. She should enjoy that.

Around the familiar, stained wooden table littered with glassware, ashtrays and detritus difficult to identify in the low, yellowish light, five musicians labored to be heard over the prevailing din. Sweeney exchanged wordless nods with them one by one; Peter, Marjorie, Rod, Whatsisname the greasy-haired kid who never seemed to talk flailing on the bodhran with his double-ended stick, and John Kilbride.

At best, on crowded nights like this, whoever comprised the band might be able to toss jigs and reels about halfway down the bar, where the tunes would be beaten whimpering and exhausted to the floor. But accordion, guitar, banjo, bodhran and flute weren't working at projecting any farther than the other side of the table tonight. Peter and the rest looked content to work out the tensions of the week playing with each other, really only listening to themselves, ignored by all but the small, shifting gaggle of onlookers who loitered against the kegs or stood waiting for the john.

Sweeney sat listening, tapping his fingers, taking it all in. He felt more sociable now that he'd reminded himself that his literary wife would handle all the barbs from the press.

To his right around the table Peter Cole perched comfortably atop his home-made wooden accordion case tapping out *The Bucks of Oranmore*. Peter looked up and nodded across at Marjorie.

Bucks into Barley, thought Sweeney automatically.

The tune came around and Peter leaned into *Wind that Shakes the Barley*, an old groaner, but still somehow pleasant under the fingers after all this time. Across the table, Rod Hesse relaxed his grip on the guitar neck and reached out to suck on a smoldering cigarette. He watched Peter with his heavily-lidded blue eyes. Sitting next to Rod like a drop-shadow, little Marjorie fudged the first few bars, grimaced through black curls that cascaded down over the shoulders of her thin, black sweater, then dug a series of triplets out of the banjo and rolled along with Peter. The bodhran flopped along companionably like tennis shoes in a dryer. The kid had the drum pulled tightly in against his chest. With his neck craned forward and head down he was oblivious to all but the beat of the music. The room was too noisy for Sweeney to be sure Kilbride was playing the same tune as the rest of them. But it didn't seem to bother the quiet, ruddy Kerryman. The silver-chased end of his ebony flute described circle after circle beyond his right shoulder in time to the music. His eyes, never opened more than a slit, seemed focused off somewhere in the middle distance.

Sweeney looked down and cracked open his case. He tightened his bow a turn or two and traced a figure-eight in the air with the tip. The silver wire wrap had nearly all unraveled itself, battered for years by the same sweaty thumb and forefinger. The bow had molded itself to his own untutored grip to the point that he'd determined never to get it fixed.

He drew the bow down across the green lump of rosin in a slow caress, with an extra little scrub at the tip. He took out his fiddle, leaned back and tipped the empty case up against the juke box. He tried to check the tuning above all the noise, then decided it really didn't matter. Closing his eyes, he listened for where the reel they were now playing cycled back to grab its tail in its mouth. What's it called? Doesn't matter, either. Starts on the high D, and straight down from there. He began to play.

And a large weight lifted itself from Sweeney's heart. The phrases glided down across his strings and lapped against his bow like so many waves on a tethered curragh riding the tide in Dingle Bay. His wrist was at once loose and supple, the bow smoothly licking at the strings, coaxing languid ornaments and bow skips from his fingers as he let the reel carry him off, out of the pub, away from the crowd, far from the annoyances of his job or Michael Blayney. Here, disembodied, an extension of the concentric and overlapping circles and spirals of the music, Niall Sweeney was truly happy.

Tune blended into tune, modulated up, darkened to minor. Guitar, flute, banjo, bodhran and accordion were taken up and set down in an unchoreographed dance. Through it all Sweeney fiddled, feeling invincible and incredibly alive. Every reel seemed to grow from the last as easily and naturally as a wildflower pushing up between the stones of the Burren. Sweeney darted glances around at the other musicians, who were engaged in flying off in their own internal directions while the music proceeded under its own sweet, inexorable momentum.

Finally, in silent agreement that five times through *Pigeon on the Gate* was plenty, the group came to an unceremonious stop on three slightly different beats. There followed a smattering of applause from along the wall. Sweeney was breathing hard as he laid his fiddle and bow across his knees. Like a long-distance runner, he shook off the perspiration dripping down his temples. As he rolled up his sleeves he squinted through the grotty atmosphere to the clock at the end of the bar. They'd been playing without a pause for forty minutes.

"That is one fine tune," said Peter, turning with his lopsided smile, the sweat plastering his close-cropped mousy hair against his high forehead. He reached out and hit Sweeney a cuff on the shoulder. "Glad you came. I can never get these other guys to string a thousand tunes together without stopping when you're not here. I end up playing by myself, which ain't no fun."

He laughed as he extracted himself from his shoulder straps to stretch. Peter was probably forty but didn't look much over twenty-five, at least in this light. In fact, Sweeney could detect no major change in him since they'd first met here in the bar over ten years before. His plaid shirt and work pants hung loosely on a spidery frame. Everything about Peter looked a little too thin, or maybe a little too long, except for his hands. These were square and muscular and were everywhere at once on his accordion. And they knew more tunes than any pair of hands in California.

"Yeah, I think that set did the trick. I feel pretty good now!"

"Did the trick?"

"Yeah, I had to get some bad energy out of my system."

"Oh. Right. Gilmore showed me the review. Pretty intense. And for the *Irish-American* yet. They always used to be so candy-assed about reviewing Irish records. But then they used to just talk about records from Ireland. I haven't read it in ages. How long has . . . what's his name?"

"Blayney." *Just you wait, Michael Blayney. When Rosie gets finished with you you'll be fishing your teeth out of your typewriter.*

"Yeah, Blayney. How long has he been writing for them?"

"I don't know. Six months, maybe. He comes in here on the odd night. Somebody said he was a singer, though he never joined any sessions I've been in. You've seen the guy: thirtyish, pointy beard, always wears a tie, comes on like Casanova with the women when he's had a few." Sweeney couldn't imagine what women could see in the leering likes of Blayney. Well, no accounting for taste.

"Oh, him. Hah! I overheard Marjorie once at the bar up and tell him to stop staring at her tits."

"That'd be him."

"It wasn't really that bad, though, you know."

"What? The review?"

"No. Your CD."

"Gosh, thanks."

"No, you know what I mean. You're no Tommy Peoples or anything, but that doesn't mean you can't make a CD. By the way, how many have you sold?"

"Not counting the ten to my mother? About eighty, I think." *Well, seventy-eight, but you've got to think positive.*

"See? I wouldn't worry about what he said, then. You're sure as hell not getting rich or nothing. Didn't the review say something about you getting rich and all them traditional Irish musicians were losing jobs?"

"Well, not in so many words . . ."

Across the table Marjorie McAulliffe occupied her fidgety fingers in rolling a cigarette against the tarnished tone-ring of her banjo. Her deliciously pointed chin tossed seductively as she talked quietly with Rod Hesse. Lately they had been acting the consciously 'cute couple.' Sweeney was glad Marjorie and Rod's once volatile relationship had smoothed out the last few months. Next to Peter's accordion, her banjo was the only instrument you could be sure of hearing clearly enough to follow on nights when the bar was a can of bellowing sardines. The gang had missed her back when she'd decided that romance and the Bag of Nails wouldn't mix. Apparently that wasn't the case any more.

Rod and Marjorie gathered up the empties from a round of pints and Paddys and wandered off to join Peter on his way to the bar. The bodhran player . . . what was his name? . . . oh, yeah, Charlie . . . had retreated to the wall to chat with somebody. Sweeney hadn't noticed John Kilbride leave, but the chair was empty and his flute was resting carefully on its open case. And so the session rested while the chatter of the crowd rose in volume to fill the spaces the music had left, thickening like the smoky air.

Sweeney felt relieved that everybody had suddenly gotten up from the table. Conversation was sometimes too much in sessions, especially after a particularly long and energetic set. It was nice when you were all allowed to sit around quiet for a moment, panting and spent like drowsy lovers, 'til you each remembered where you were and began once again the ritualized tapping at cigarettes and poking at drinks. It was all so pleasant and soothing.

And it sure as hell beat working in engineering and electronics. Sweeney often wished that when he had graduated from college the technological revolution had been in some field other than micro-circuits. Blacksmithing, say. Or water divining. Marsupial husbandry. Anything. But this was the high-tech era and he liked to eat regularly. If he was going to be able to afford to stay in the town where he'd grown up and hang out at the Bag, he'd have to keep his straight job. Keep the job and play the game.

Peter was right. He wasn't going to make his wad on that silly CD. What a pipe-dream.

Sweeney looked up to see Vin and Christie yakking away happily and advancing with full pint glasses. The tall, curly-headed girl squeezed herself around the table, propped herself up against an empty keg next to Sweeney and deposited one glass in front of him.

"For you," she announced.

"Great. Thanks. And what are you having?"

"Oh, nothing for me, thanks. Vincent said you'd earned this so here you are."

"Well, thanks heaps. And Vinnie's right. I have earned it!" He raised the glass to toast Vinnie's health but his friend had already wandered off again. He poured half the glass down his throat and belched appreciatively.

"Excuse me."

She sat smiling expectantly. Sweeney smiled back. She wasn't as skinny as he'd first thought. Lithe, rather. Good-looking in a naïve sort of way.

"This is really wonderful," she said finally, her eyes sparkling with unabashed pleasure. "I mean, the music and all that. I bet there isn't anyplace else in San Francisco like this . . . is there?"

"You mean with music? Good music? I mean, Irish music? No. That is, there are several schools of thought. I'd say this is the most fun. I am biased, of course. And I prefer pubs to bars."

"I wouldn't ever come to a place like this on my own. But Vincent was so insistent. I wanted to meet you somewhere else but he said this place was best, even though it's too smoky."

"Oh, Vinnie is ever the master of ceremonies. How did you two meet, anyway? He never did tell me."

"At State. I was looking helpless in Existentialism in Modern English Lit. I need it for my major. Can you believe it?"

"I'll believe anything. My wife teaches in the English Department."

"Your . . . Rose Sweeney? Oh, how marvelous! Vincent must have told me but I spaced it out. I know her. My sister's in one of her classes. I think she's teaching something called Heroic Literature next semester, right? Where was I? Oh, yes, anyway, Vincent was in the class, too, and he offered to help me study."

"Really. And he straightened you out?"

"No, of course not. He was absolutely hopeless. More out to lunch than I was. But I thought he was cute. And he's terribly insistent."

"He is that," Sweeney agreed.

"So anyway, I let him talk me into coming here. Though, Niall, just between you and me, if my mother ever found out I'd been in a bar all evening, I'd catch holy hell! But don't tell Vincent. He'd just worry."

"Don't know why your mother should worry. Just take a look at some of the weirdballs walking around in the city these days. You've got nothing to worry about. And after all, these are the waning glory days of the twentieth century."

"Not in our house, they aren't." She grimaced, nibbling at a hangnail. "Tell me, why'd you call your album *Among the Nightingales*? It's not the name of any of the tunes."

"It was Rose's idea. A literary reference. I couldn't think of anything very clever so I passed the responsibility on to her poetic brain. I believe she said it was from T.S. Eliot. I meant to read up on it but I haven't gotten around to it yet. I probably would have ended up with *Sweeney's Greatest Hits* or something equally revolting without a reader like Rose in the house."

"I do like the album, but you really are much better in person."

Sweeney knew he was blushing. He cursed inwardly at his inability to take praise well. Maybe someday the praise would come often enough for him to get used to it.

"Jeez, how could you tell in all this noise? I can barely hear myself think tonight."

"I know. But I like the way you close your eyes when you play. Too bad you couldn't get that on the CD." She tossed her head appealingly, sending a delicate Celtic cross swinging on its silver chain. Sweeney could just see Vinnie falling all over himself in class at the first sight of her. He made a face.

"Well, I don't think MTV will be interested in a traditional Irish video anytime soon, if that's what you mean. But if they should change their minds, I'm sure they won't pick me. I'm not Frankie Gavin. But I did get lucky enough to get on an American label. A very small American label," he added, making a 'very small label' sign with thumb and forefinger.

"Oh, no. You may not be from over there, but you've got style. Why, you could be a real gold ring player, right enough!"

Sweeney burst out with a laugh. "Yeah, well, they don't call it that around here, but thanks just the same. Where'd you pick up 'gold ring player' anyway?"

"Oh, probably from my father. He was from Ireland. When we were growing up, my sister and I always thought Daddy had the most marvelous turn of phrase. Some of it snuck in over the years, I guess."

"You still live with your folks, then?"

"With my mother. Daddy died a couple of years ago."

Sweeney took a quiet swig of Guinness and changed the subject.

"So, how did you get interested in traditional music? Your folks took you out?"

"No, not really. I took a vacation to Ireland with a church group once. We toured some of the usual historical places. You know, Dublin, Glendalough, the Boyne Valley. We made it down as far as Kinsale to look up one of the girls' relatives. All in a couple weeks. We heard some good music there, but only in Dublin."

Sweeney nodded.

"Yeah, those group tours never do show you what you want to see, though. Too rushed. I really couldn't care less about all those buildings and monoliths and cairns and cliffs and things. They don't mean much unless you get a chance to get to know the people, too. And I always left the details of history and literature to my darling wife. That's why I took my fiddle with me over there. It's always been a great ice-breaker. Hear any good sessions when you were there?"

"Oh, no. We were never allowed to go to pubs. And I was too young, anyway."

Sweeney gave an expression of amazement. "Jesus, if you're tall enough to put money on the bar, you can get served in a lot of places I've been in. And kids come in to hang out regardless."

"Well, that's a problem I want nothing to do with. It's terrible, the way the Church turns a blind eye and allows the Irish to teach their children they're fated to become drunks. And so young." She suddenly looked quite serious.

Sweeney's eyes traveled from her stern gaze down to his drink and back. He was opening his mouth when Christie realized what she'd said.

"Oh, no, I'm sorry," she said quickly. "It's just that, well . . . I mean, it's just that pubs are no place for young girls to go, that's all." She looked around for Vin.

Sweeney thought to himself that he'd always done all right with his socializing in pubs.

"My friend Sylvia once wandered away from the group when Sister wasn't around and ended up in a pub all night."

"The church group, you mean?"

"Yes. This man who took her bought her drinks until she passed out. It was all we could do to keep Sister from finding out. Would she have been furious!"

"Yeah, I see what you mean. No place for young girls who can't hold their liquor, that's for sure."

Peter ambled over, adjusted his box and sat down. He strapped on his button accordion and made aimless noises for a few moments, staring at the floor and feeling around for a tune. Vinnie appeared and slouched down across from Sweeney in Marjorie's vacant chair, trying to identify what Peter was playing.

Peter turned to Sweeney.

"Hey, Niall, you know this one, don't you?" Pushing out his lower lip, he broke into a lightning-speed jig that skipped up the rows, danced at the top register and then blew all the way down to the bottom before circling around again. His fingers blurred as he swayed back on his wooden box, a look of near-religious ecstasy immediately lighting the angles of his bony face.

Vin sat up straight and hooted. Sweeney slapped his hand down on the table in recognition.

"Well I'll be! There's the tune!" He was already reaching for his fiddle. "I was humming it on the street just before I got here," he said to Christie as he pushed his pint glass out of danger. "I couldn't remember the damn name! Didn't know anybody around here plays it, though I should have known Peter does. He knows everything. It just came back to me. Learned it in a little town called Inagh in County Clare. Ever heard of Inagh?"

Christie's eyes were fixed on Peter's right hand.

"The proverbial wide spot in the road, just up from Ennis," he continued, more to himself, as he plunked at his E string.

"Yeah, you'd never know the place is even there. The tune was named after the pub. It was called, um . . . I played in a little competition there once . . . Glen Bolcain . . . *Maid of Glen Bolcain*! That's it. Weird name, isn't it? Means volcano, somebody told me. As a matter of fact, it's funny . . ."

"May I?" John Kilbride leaned between them, motioning politely toward his flute and folding chair.

Christie excused herself and skirted the table back to where Vin stood drinking. Kilbride dropped into the vacated spot and started warming up his silver-tipped flute.

Glen Bolcain . . . Glen Bolcain . . . funny the connections you make . . . I'd half-forgotten that little contest . . .

His foot was already tapping in time with Peter's lead as the tune came around again. Like a shot, Sweeney was in the thick of it, wrapping phrases around himself and spinning them off into the distance, oblivious to his surroundings.

Sweeney's attention was shattered by the sound of one of the folding chairs being kicked with a certain fervor against the juke box. Startled, he stopped and turned as a loud baritone voice demanded, "So, don't you know any *Irish* music?"

Michael Blayney stared down at Sweeney with his hands in his pockets and as strange an expression on his face as Sweeney had ever seen. It was as if Blayney was trying to determine just what sort of creature was seated before him at the table. His pupils, sharp as pinpoints, bored straight into Sweeney's eyes. His lips twisted into a curious, gloating rictus.

Okay, thought Sweeney. I admit it. I never really wanted to talk to Blayney. Please, Lord, make this brief.

"Well, now, don't stop on my account," sneered Blayney as he circled counter-clockwise around the musicians' table, glancing from Sweeney to Marjorie opposite him and back. He moved with a flat-footed, straight-kneed shuffle, strongly indicating that he'd been engaged in some serious drinking. One lock of brown hair trailed uncombed down over his right eyebrow. His white shirt was open at the neck, ever-present tie loosened to the third button under his brown corduroy jacket. From the other side of the table, Sweeney could see the jugular vein pumping furiously under the florid skin.

"I've come in special to hear the highly-touted Friday night Irish session. I've been listenin' for all of half an hour. I'm still waitin' for the Irish music."

His voice held almost palpable derision. The thought flashed through Sweeney's mind that he was right not to take this clown's review personally. It was plain that Blayney had a chip on his shoulder for the whole damn scene. Sweeney had just been an easy, momentary target.

Blayney stood opposite Sweeney and between Marjorie and Peter Cole. Always the nervous sort, Marjorie seemed at the moment ready to explode. As if he could sense her discomfort without even seeing her face, Blayney patted her on the shoulder with a condescending smirk.

"There, there, darlin'," he began.

Marjorie McAulliffe spun about with the speed of a striking rattlesnake and knocked his hand away. "Don't you dare touch me," she spat. The speed of her mood switch startled even Sweeney.

With narrowed eyes, Rod Hesse rose all at once, his guitar still gripped in one large fist, Germanic protectiveness written all over him. Marjorie grabbed his wrist.

"No, Rod, don't. He's not worth it."

At that moment Rod didn't appear to care whether Blayney was worth it or not. Marjorie halted his advance toward the disheveled troublemaker by grabbing him and hauling him, guitar and all, away from the table by his free arm.

Blayney didn't look surprised or even to care.

"Would you like to hear a song? I'll now sing *The Plains of Waterloo*." He cocked his head back and inhaled deeply.

"If you wanted to sing," Sweeney interrupted in a loud and angry tone, "you could have waited politely like the rest of us instead of being so damned offensive."

Blayney slammed both palms on the table and hunched forward.

"Listen, Mister Among-the-Bloody-Nightingales . . . I'm warnin' you. You think you're somethin' but I know better. I know who you are. Who you really are. You're bare-ass naked to me, as well you know! I know how you tried to fuck wit' me and you know that I know. So you're not gettin' away wit' it."

More than a little confused at this, Sweeney met his gaze and held it.

"Go home, Blayney. You're drunk. I don't feel up to arguing with a drunk."

"Drunk, am I? You'll never know just how fuckin' saintly inspired I am, drunk or sober! And since it's clear you were never one for takin' hints, I'm givin' it to you plain: Get out and stay out! I'd flap my little arms and fly away as far as possible if I were you! You have my curse if I ever catch sight of you again! I'll pluck those feathers and down you'll come! And you know I can do it!"

He leaned forward menacingly and flicked a back-hand gesture at Sweeney's fiddle. "Back up your fuckin' tree . . . And take that wormy prop wit' ye!"

Sweeney's brain spun as he tried to figure out what was going on. He looked around thinking, "Where's Gilmore, goddam it? It's his bar . . . he's supposed to deal with the drunks."

"What the hell are you talking about, Blayney?" said Sweeney, standing up slowly, a momentary flush of anger gaining an edge on his better judgment. "You make even less sense in person than you do in your lousy column. Who the hell are you to tell anybody anything, here or in print?"

Which was apparently the wrong thing to say.

Without a warning Blayney leapt out, tumbling over Peter Cole and toppling him backward off his seat. Peter kicked out helplessly like an overturned turtle as Blayney scrambled up again, his eyes still on Sweeney and glazed with hatred.

"Jesus Christ!" yelled Peter from the floor.

As he lunged toward Sweeney a lightning glint of metal slipped out of Blayney's coat and bounced with a sharp snap over the accordion onto the floor. With a disbelieving look of horror, Sweeney's eyes swept up from the black-handled switchblade to Blayney's face as he felt his attacker's fingers tighten on his throat. Without thinking, he let his fiddle drop as his hands jerked upwards in defense. He pitched back, his bow tossed clattering against the empty kegs.

His head caught a numbing blow on the corner of the juke box as Blayney's weight carried them both in a thrashing heap to the floor. Table and chairs overturned with a crash. Out of the corner of one eye he saw the polished blade just out of reach. Had Blayney seen it, too? With an explosive movement they both flailed in the direction of the knife. Sweeney found his hand gripping Blayney's right wrist as hard as it could, as he fought to get air. Blayney's mouth snarled wordlessly an inch from Sweeney's eye.

"Help!" he managed to shout, the confused commotion rising all around him. "For God's sake somebody get this lunatic off me!"

Faces and arms flashed around Sweeney, trying to find an opening. He tore at the hand clawing his throat as he desperately fought to roll over. The knife was closer. Blayney pressed down with inhuman strength, as Sweeney began to panic.

Out of the corner of his eye, Sweeney caught a quick movement. From the tumbling forest of legs, a hand snapped down with a beer bottle and delivered a sharp blow to the back of Blayney's head. His attacker's hand relaxed just long enough for Sweeney to squirm out from under him and get one knee on the other's abdomen. He had no idea what to do next.

It was done for him. A huge booted foot smashed down on Blayney's outstretched hand. A matching boot crunched almost simultaneously into Blayney's ribs. There was a yell of pain as the switchblade was knocked sliding away from the fight and across the floor.

Sweeney jumped up shaking uncontrollably. Hands began brushing him off and smoothing his jacket as he watched Joe Gilmore reach down and haul the wincing, mostly-limp Michael Blayney roughly to his feet.

"Where's my fiddle?" asked Sweeney. Marjorie McAulliffe pressed something cold to his temple.

"Ow! Christ!" he jerked around to see her with a look of real concern and a wet towel in her hand. It was stained red. Looking down, Sweeney saw that blood had spattered all down his jacket.

"Here. Let me," she said and placed the cloth back to Sweeney's throbbing head. "Are you all right? I don't think the cut's too bad."

"Yeah. Thanks." He took the cloth in his own hand and looked around. In the middle of the room Joe Gilmore, a large man with a mop of prematurely gray hair and a face that looked as if it had been carved from granite had Blayney by the collar and one arm. Curious strangers gathered close, trying to see.

"What happened?"

"What are they gonna do with him?"

"Wuzzy tryin' ta do?"

"I'll have whatever he wuz drinkin'!"

"What happened??"

"You say he had a gun?"

"Somebody call the cops!"

"Shut up!" Gilmore roared over the crowd, silencing those nearest to him while the excited buzz continued unabated back to the pool table. "Everybody just shut up and calm down! Everything's under control. Just sit down and mind your own business." He dragged Blayney, stumbling and inarticulate, out of sight along the bar and out toward the street.

"My fiddle," thought Sweeney and fumbled around the overturned chairs as somebody righted the table. There it was, lying somehow unscathed in the far corner. He picked it up gingerly, fearing the worst, but it was hardly out of tune. A nervous smile flitted across his face and disappeared as he noticed the irregular razors of glass jammed into one f-hole and a half-moon gouge below the instrument's waist.

"This yours, Niall?" said a voice. John Kilbride, crouching on the littered floor, handed Sweeney his bow. It had been splintered in half, a sad, useless tangle of horsehair and once-delicate wood. Behind Kilbride, Annie hurriedly swept shards of glass into a pile.

His adrenaline faded. Sweeney sat shakily to keep from falling over.

•

"That fix you up?" Joe Gilmore asked, placing another double whiskey on the bar. He gave a curt, dismissing wave as Sweeney fumbled for his wallet.

"Thanks, Joe," Sweeney murmured. The whiskey burned his throat. "Did they cart Blayney off?"

"He's outta here. Won't be botherin' you again. I can't fuckin' stand that kind. Should ha' barred him permanent when he first showed his face around here."

Squinting down another swallow of amber malt, Sweeney eyed Joe as he stood looking out the front door stiff and expressionless from behind the bar. The gray-haired man's large hand wrapped around the handle of the Guinness tap. The knuckles were white.

"So what did the police say?"

"The police? Shit! They're never around when they're wanted." He said it almost facetiously, Sweeney thought.

"I wonder what he can get for aggravated assault?"

"Who knows? Cops never charge the right man anyways."

Annie wiped glasses a little way down the bar. She glanced at the two men with an odd, worried look and continued with the washing up. It had been twenty minutes since the fight had ended and the session had broken up. No appreciable progress had been made in the cleanup of Friday's sloppy disorder.

Vin came up and sat down at the bar next to Sweeney.

"Some night, huh?" he said, attempting cheer.

"Whatever am I going to tell Rose? I get into a fight with a lunatic who attacks me for no apparent reason. He breaks my bow. He nearly breaks my head!" He gently touched his temple and grimaced.

"It all happened so fast," said Vin. "Oh my!" he noticed Sweeney's brown-speckled shoulder.

"Fast? Seemed like it took weeks. I thought nobody was gonna do anything till the maniac had me dead on the floor. Do I look like a fighter? And where were you anyway?"

"The whole thing was over in nothing flat. Really!"

"Shit, it seemed like Rod had time to down a three-course meal before he finally walloped him over the head with that bottle!"

"Was that Rod? Well, good for him. He was probably delighted to be given the opportunity. I was across the other side of the room when Blayney went for you," prattled Vin. "From where I stood it looked like a harmless drunk falling over and doing more damage to himself than anyone else. Couldn't hear everything he said. Then Christie came out of the bathroom, took one look at the fight, grabbed me and started yelling. She got pretty freaked out by it all. So I ran out the door behind her and walked her home. Poor kid was still a wreck when I got her to her house. Then I came back here to make sure you were okay."

"Yeah, yeah. Sure. Thanks." He couldn't think any more. He sighed and got up. "I've had it. Time to go home."

•

Clement Street passed unseen as a morose Sweeney plodded his way the several blocks back to the car. What the hell had happened tonight? He felt in his coat pocket for the copy of the review Vin had given him. It was still there. Rosie would want to know what started it all, as if he could explain even with audio-visual aids.

Sweeney fished through his pockets for his keys as he got to the car. He walked around to the passenger side to toss the fiddle case in with the CDs. He turned the key and grasped the handle. There was something wet and sticky on his hand. He looked at his palm. It seemed to be covered in chocolate syrup under the yellow-gray light of the street lamp. There was more on the door handle.

He stepped back to get a closer look and nearly lost his balance, slipping abruptly on the slick cement. He righted himself again and checked to see what he'd stepped in. A dark pool of liquid traversed the sidewalk in a foot-wide swath, over the kerb and into the gutter. Numbly, Sweeney's head turned to follow the liquid from the car and toward the row of Art Deco houses. The car was parked directly in front of a round-arched passageway, sheltering a round-arched door.

He looked down. There, half-hidden in shadow away from the street-lamp's cone was Michael Blayney. His eyes and mouth were open in a silent cry, his body sprawled down the three low steps leading up to the glass-linteled door. A gaping wound slashed across his abdomen. A coil of intestine emptied over his lap and hung to his knees. Blayney's coat was open to reveal shreds of once-white shirt now hanging red and glistening.

Sweeney looked from Blayney's stark white face to the viscous reddish-brown pool. He wondered why he didn't want to throw up. He looked away and closed his eyes, suddenly unable to keep his hands from shaking. He stepped back, turned, and took a few paces toward the corner. Breaking into a run, he stopped again and turned, absolutely at a loss.

Just down the street a middle-aged woman hurried out of the grayness holding her collar closed to the fog and walking a large German shepherd on a lead. Sweeney stood there watching as she drew nearer. Suddenly she stopped. With a muffled cry, her hand went to her mouth. Her dog sniffed at the blood. She looked up into Sweeney's face and screamed.

Chapter Three

"Now, let's go through this one more time, just to be sure I've got it straight," the balding police inspector said slowly. He heaved his large stomach up and straightened his back, trying to get more comfortably seated in the small, slat-backed wooden chair.

"You didn't know the deceased except to speak to casually at the bar. Yet you sent free CDs . . ."

"CD. Singular. Promotional CD."

" . . . a free pro-mo-shu-nal . . ." He sounded it out as he penciled the word into his notes, "CD to him at the newspaper where he worked. You know nothing whatever about his private life. He made no threats before tonight . . . against you. Right?"

Sweeney nodded patiently. *Christ, we've been all over this stuff already.* He looked around him, the back of his head a rhythmic, dull pounding. It was a little eerie to sit in the Bag of Nails with it so quiet. He surveyed the skeletal remains of the evening: scattered bottles and glasses, bar stacked high with dirties and empties, the half-extinguished lights of the juke box glowing dimly. Joe Gilmore had turned the sound off at the bar but the machine still hummed while the turntable continued to spin. The lively Friday crowd was now a memory less tangible than the smell of stale smoke.

God, this place is a dump when there's no music going on.

The dark and dirty bar was now deserted save for the inspector, two more cops and Joe Gilmore, who still leaned behind the bar on his elbows watching the proceedings with an expression of total and undisguised distaste. The cops, one in uniform, one in civvies, were both young Asians who were trying to look comfortable in this alien cultural context. They had questioned Joe and Annie briefly, squaring accounts of the fight and the ejection of the trouble-maker. A good number of regulars had volunteered to put their two cents in, claiming a drunken scrap of the evening's notoriety for themselves and occupying the police far longer than the collected information had warranted. All had been written down in the black leather notebooks. And now everyone else had gone home.

"The deceased entered the bar, verbally assaulted you, then without provocation physically assaulted you, subsequently producing a knife with which he attacked you."

"He didn't 'produce' the knife. It fell out of his pocket as near as I can remember. And he didn't try to stab me with it. He never got his hands on it. The bartender stopped the fight, like I told you, and out went Blayney."

"And what happened to the knife afterwards? You didn't pick it up?"

"No, I was looking for my fiddle, which at the moment was the only thing on my mind. I haven't the faintest clue who picked up the knife, but it wasn't me. Besides, if I'd picked it up, wouldn't I still have had it when you boys got here? I mean, you did search me after all."

The inspector ignored the question. "Why didn't you call the police immediately after the fight?"

"I didn't think of it. I guess I assumed that was the bar's responsibility. Why don't you ask Joe Gilmore?"

The policeman continued. "You then stayed in the bar for approximately twenty minutes and then walked straight back to your car, alone." The inspector took in Sweeney's eyes over the tops of his glasses frames.

Sweeney nodded again wearily. A bone in his neck made a slight crunching noise as he moved. He was stiff and sore, as well as dog-tired.

"And you had no idea that you had parked in front of the house occupied by the deceased."

That had certainly been a surprise. "Are you kidding? You know you park where you can around here. That's just a damn coincidence."

"Mr. Sweeney, I don't like coincidences." The inspector put his pencil down on the handwritten report and looked steadily at Sweeney, through his lenses this time.

"Fine. Fine. I understand your problem, but that's the way it happened, and that's the way I've told you it happened. I can't do anything else but tell you what happened the way it happened."

Sweeney allowed a note of exasperation to creep into his voice. It was past one-thirty, after all, and he'd originally thought he'd do his civic duty and then be done with it. Now he was nearly finished telling his story to the last of how many policemen and this one, round and fatherly as he might be, was agonizingly slow. Methodical, he was sure they'd say. He called it excruciating. A credit to the force, he was sure they'd say. The guy held his pencil like a third grader. The inspector read on from his notes.

"You never touched the body or anything else. How is it you left a bloody hand print on the door handle of your car?"

So that's it. A question they hadn't asked him before. "Look, Inspector, if there's something you're trying to get around to asking, why not get to it and be done with it. What are you driving at?"

The plainclothes cop standing a few paces away started moving vaguely in their direction. The inspector motioned him off. This ambiguous little dance-step was not lost on Sweeney. His thoughts were already racing back over the previous hour's conversation with the inspector and the others. Had he said something totally stupid without knowing it? Or did they think he was trying to be too helpful?

"Mr. Sweeney, I am merely trying to determine the facts in the case," the inspector said with a tonelessness which could only have been mastered after many years on the force.

"I'm sure this must have been a shock to you. But since you are one of two people who found the body, we are interested in everything you have to say. We are doubly interested in your information since you knew the deceased prior to his death. We have to know everything that led up to the discovery of the body in order to proceed from here. That is our job."

"Sure, sure. Just get on with it." Sweeney didn't believe a word of it. He sat tense and alert.

"All right. About the hand print on your car door handle . . ."

Sweeney interrupted, "Okay! One more time with feeling. The handle was already bloody when I touched it. I got the blood on my hand from grabbing the handle. Not the other way round. May I go now? My wife is certainly worried sick."

Right. More likely still grading those damn final essays and finishing off the bottle. She'll look at me all warm and comfy when I come staggering in and say, "Oh? Back so early?"

"Just another detail or two. You say you found the deceased at the scene at eleven-thirty-three."

"No, I didn't say that. I didn't look at my watch."

"Oh yes. That was in Mrs. Johnson's statement." He made a mark in the margin. "I think we're about through here, Mr. Sweeney," said the inspector. "When you discovered the body . . . You saw no one else on the street?"

"No one else. Except for that lady with the dog coming the other way."

The inspector got up laboriously, looking around for the most likely path to the bar through the random disorder of chairs and tables.

"That's all, Mr. Sweeney. Thank you for taking the time to help. We'll be in touch."

About time, thought Sweeney. Be in touch, hell. He sidled past the inspector and put on his jacket. "What about my car?"

"We'll call you when the lab is finished with it. Then you can come pick it up. Would you like an officer to take you home?"

Before he could mutter, "No, I'd rather walk," a bell-toned voice behind him said, "Taxi, mister?"

Sweeney did a little pirouette and came face to face with Rose. With a smile, Rose plumbed the depths of his eyes wordlessly just long enough to decide he looked all right. Her cheeks were ruddy from the cold night air and her wavy, auburn hair stood out behind her in an unconsciously fashionable confusion. Advancing and taking Sweeney's arm with an air of unconcerned ease, she distributed friendly little hello-looks among the policemen, who just stood where they were, attempting no pretense of politeness.

"Good evening, gentlemen," she said brightly. "I'm afraid you'll have to excuse us. It's past Niall's bedtime."

Sweeney almost laughed. Where'd she get this brazen act? Whizzing in like that with her petite figure wrapped up tightly in her new khaki, double-breasted overcoat, she stood every inch the hard-boiled Raymond Chandler female. Somehow, in the context of the rest of the evening's surreal events, Sweeney wasn't surprised in the least.

Rose took up the fiddle case in one hand, her husband's arm in the other. With the smile still dimpling her cheeks, she steered Sweeney through the open door. The two marched out of the bar and disappeared into the gray night.

•

Without a word Rose walked them briskly to the corner, where her sedan was illegally parked in the bus zone. She fished for her keys in the deep pocket of the overcoat, opened the door and tossed Sweeney's fiddle case onto the back seat. She turned her large gray-flecked brown eyes up into his face.

"So. If you'd told me it was going to be so exciting around here, I would have come along tonight after all. You think I enjoy reading subliterate drivel six hours at a stretch when I could be out witnessing murder and mayhem with the boys?" She gave her head a calculatedly carefree toss.

Her brown eyes held her husband's light blue ones for a long moment, sensing his hesitancy. Neither of them seemed to know just how to proceed.

"Um, do you want to know what happened?" Sweeney asked tentatively.

Rose opened her mouth but nothing came out. She'd only rehearsed her opening line. She bit her lip. Why hadn't she scripted it out farther? Well, as long as he didn't call her Rosie . . .

"Rosie," Sweeney began.

She burst into tears.

"Rosie, honey, are you all right?" he asked softly, caressing her hair and holding her close as she heaved great sobs into his shoulder.

She stopped suddenly and sniffed. Then she exploded.

"Am I all right? Oh, you oaf, I've been worried sick about you. I worked till one and turned on the news and heard about the murder and put two and two together . . . They mentioned the bar and . . . well, they didn't give any real facts, just those sensationalist crappy headlines . . . So I roused Vinnie and he told me about the fight and you hadn't come home . . . and I didn't know what to think, so I came down to find you."

"Are you through?"

"For now." She pushed her hair out of her face.

"Why, if I didn't know you better, I'd say you were really and truly worried about me!"

"Nonsense. What would give you an idea like that?" Tears still glistened on her cheeks as she made a concerted effort to put on a carefree, saucy expression.

"Mostly your shoes." He pointed at her feet. There she stood in the fog: a film-noir fashion-plate from head to ankles. But she had run out to the rescue of her darling boy wearing nothing on her feet but a pair of fuzzy brown koala-bear slippers.

She moved around to the driver's side and hopped into the car. He climbed stiffly in the opposite side. No sooner had he hit the seat than she slid across from behind the steering wheel and grabbed him, landing a hot and lingering kiss on his surprised lips. She could feel him relax as her arms pulled him tightly to her and one hand moved up, gently stroking the back of his neck and drifting up to tangle in his tousled . . .

"Ouch!" he cried. Rose reached up uncertainly and examined his scalp. "I hit my head."

"My poor, dear Niall," she said and sat up again, looking him quickly up and down. She turned the key in the ignition. The motor coughed and wheezed to life.

"Now," she continued evenly as they pulled away from the curb. "Tell me all about it. From the beginning."

●

Sunlight drifted in through the window like warm breath onto Sweeney's face. He stirred and opened one blue eye to inspect the new day. The backyards of Hartford Street were bright and cheerfully unkempt. A dozen cats were already sunning themselves on the stair landings in the spaces between the slowly migrating clouds. Pigeons came and went aimlessly among the gimcracks and gingerbread atop the wind-scrubbed Victorian eaves and spires. From the direction of the kitchen Sweeney could smell coffee and detect sounds of puttering and conversation.

He pulled on his robe and padded down the hall. The second, louder voice belonged to Vin Bowen. Vin stopped talking and smiled as Sweeney entered.

"Good morning. How do you want your eggs?" Rose inquired. She was already dressed in jeans and tee-shirt, most of her hair pulled back in a cockeyed barrette. She poked ominously at something in the skillet.

"Surprise me," Sweeney replied as he sat down. "What the hell are you doing here so early, Vinnie?"

"Vin has been telling me more of the juicy details of last night, Niall. I wish I could have seen it."

"No, you don't," mumbled Sweeney, scratching and trying to get his eyes to focus.

"Oh, but I do! You disproved a theory I had about you. I always thought that you'd fall flat on your face to keep your fiddle from getting smashed."

"Flat on my face, yes. Backwards into a juke box under a hundred and seventy-five pounds of homicidal Irishman, no."

"Oh, my poor little waterfront brawler," Rose leaned over from the stove and patted him on the cheek. "What was I saying? Oh yes. Why didn't you tell me what Blayney said to you before the fight?"

"Didn't I? Sure I did. I said that he claimed I had fucked with him but that I was really somebody else with feathers or something. Then he swore at me and went for my throat."

"No, Niall, remember?" interjected Vin. "Like I was telling Rose, he didn't just swear at you. He cursed you. The gang around the table heard that much plain enough. Peter was telling me. 'You have my curse,'" Vin made a failed attempt at an Irish accent. "Or something like that. It's funny, that doesn't exactly sound like the sort of thing a slobbering drunk would say under the circumstances."

"Yeah, I guess he might have, at that." Sweeney rubbed at his right eye, which still seemed intent on swimming about all day in last night's fog.

"You know, that makes it interesting," said Rose animatedly, turning from the stove. "I've been working on my reading list for Heroic Lit next term, you know. I've been trying to figure out how to glue it all together in more interesting ways. So I thought, one of the great arts in the good old days was the art of the curse. Now, if you cursed somebody a couple thousand years ago you damn well meant it and could expect immediate results. Some of those classic curses make great reading. The old tales are full of them. In fact, I'm thinking now about working up a special little running feature for the class. Might help keep the attention of those lunkheads. Ask 'em for a good curse nowadays and all you'd get would be Yo' mama, or Eat shit and die."

"Not much literary power in that," agreed Sweeney.

"Wasn't much literary power in Blayney's curse, now that you think about it," said Vin. "He just cursed you, like, and told you to go climb a tree."

The scene replayed in Sweeney's brain, his eyes suddenly clearing. "No, that's not what he said. He said, 'Back up your tree with you!' Well, 'Back up your fuckin' tree,' actually. I remember . . ."

"He said what?" Rose peered at Sweeney. "Back up your tree with you?"

Sweeney nodded.

She turned back to the stove and continued to poke at the hot skillet with an odd grin.

"I remember," he continued, "that was about the last thing he said before I told him he wasn't making any sense and he took off over the table."

"I see it all now," said Rose, addressing an imaginary lecture hall. "It's just like the old days. When you cursed you had to mean it. And you had to do it right or it would backfire on you." She paused. "That's obviously what killed him!"

The two friends glanced at each other, then stared patiently at Rose, expecting a punch line. She turned intently toward the table, brandishing her greasy spatula, back-lit by the late morning sun as it coursed through the tall panes of the kitchen window.

"So, this Blayney creature tries a classic curse form; claims outrage; calls upon the powers that be; and attempts to fling you off to the far trees where, presumably, you will be less of an annoyance to his musical tastes. He should have said, say:

> *My holy bell will banish thee to branches,*
> *It will put thee on a par with fowls.*

"But what does he blurt out instead? 'Back to your fuckin' tree?' Gack! No wonder Calliope sent some Under-Muse or other down to revoke Blayney's poetic license with the old Three-Fold Return. And justice is served."

The spatula twiddled triumphantly over her head. Random patterns of grease blobs now decorated the floor between Rose and the table.

"You amaze me sometimes," Sweeney muttered. "Why don't you just serve breakfast or sit down and let me do it? Please don't remind me any more about last night till I've at least had some coffee."

Vin was already reaching over and pouring the coffee.

Rose had turned around and scraped furiously at the now smoking mass in the skillet. "I like my explanation," she said as she flipped off the gas and brought the pan over to the table. "Do you think the police will thank me for making things easier for them?"

"No doubt," said Sweeney sarcastically. "It's certainly a load off my mind. What's this?" He pointed at the pan before him.

"Hashbrowns," she said.

"I thought you asked me how I liked my eggs."

"I did. Force of habit. Sorry about that. We're out of eggs." She smiled sweetly and rummaged for silverware.

"I think the police could definitely use your help," interjected Vin between swallows of coffee. "They've had all night and haven't got the faintest notion who killed Blayney or why."

"Haven't they? Is it in the paper already?" said Sweeney, wiping his moustache and looking over, interested. "That was quick, wasn't it? I've long believed they must hold the presses just hoping for a brutal murder when the bars let out."

Vin pushed the paper over to Sweeney. "I was waiting till you got up to read it to you both, Niall. Sounds like the usual clichés they put in a story when they don't get enough hard facts from the cops."

True to form, the *Chronicle* had included the murder in a box on the front page. Sweeney ran his gaze down the page.

> Police have thrown a mantle of secrecy over the grisly killing of an Irish journalist in the Richmond District late last night. The body of Michael Ronan Blayney, 35, was discovered in front of his residence near the corner of Clement Street and 10th Avenue just before midnight. Blayney had resided in San Francisco for only 7 months, since moving from his former home in Ireland. A spokesman for the Coroner's office would say only that Blayney had died from loss of blood after suffering one or more deep knife wounds to the upper body.

"Upper body!" Sweeney exclaimed. "No information is right! Nice investigative reporting job, boys. You're just guessing." Rose was now reading intently over Sweeney's shoulder as they continued down the column.

> Blayney, formerly a reporter with the Irish Press who had written articles sympathetic to the IRA, had not been tied to any IRA activities in the United States. He began working as arts writer for the *Irish-American Weekly* shortly after arriving in the Bay Area. Police refuse to speculate on whether the motive for the killing could have been political or whether the crime is connected with an increased number of violent sectarian acts reported across the country in recent weeks.

"God!" said Rose. "Sympathetic to the IRA, huh? Notice how they manage to stick the IRA into these stories? You're right, Vinnie. They obviously have nothing else to write about and they're upset because the police kept them from getting any good, gruesome pictures of the scene before they'd cleaned up the mess."
"Well, it could easily have been political," insisted Vin.
Rose didn't sound impressed. "Political, my Aunt Tillie! The Bag of Nails is probably the least political Irish bar in the city. It was just decorated in Early Easter Rising cause they couldn't afford ferns."
"Well, my dear, if it wasn't an IRA hit, who did it, then?"
"I don't believe they've ruled out robbery." She sat down and looked thoughtful. "Maybe he was smuggling peat out of Ireland . . ."
"Oh, be serious, will you?"
"Otherwise it has to be professional jealousy or the boy-friend of one of the women whose boobs he liked to ogle. But I still like my explanation best. I'd love to believe in divine retribution. But divine or not, there's something odd in this newspaper story I can't quite put my finger on."

"Why a boyfriend? Why not the wronged woman herself?" asked Vin.

"Jesus, after hearing Niall's description of the body, I wouldn't think a woman would have been able to do so much damage. Not too many men either, for that matter. Besides, a knife isn't the weapon of choice for a woman."

"How can you say that?" challenged Vin.

"Because I'm a woman. Well, okay, it's not my weapon of choice. Too messy."

Sweeney was going to ask Rose what her weapon of choice was just as Vin leaned forward eagerly. "Niall! What did it look like? They never did give any details except to say he lost a lot of blood."

Vin could be such a pain sometimes. "Look, Vinnie, I don't want to talk about it. But he didn't just lose a lot of blood. He lost all of it."

Vin leaned back in his chair again and whistled soundlessly. "Yeah. Sounds like a jealous boyfriend to me. And not somebody I'd like to meet in a dark alley."

Vin looked at his watch. He took a large mouthful of potatoes and got up from the table. "Oop. Gotta run. I told Christie I'd meet her at noon."

"Yeah, tell her I'm sorry about what happened. For a kid who doesn't hang around bars, she got her share of action last night. Bring her over one of these evenings and we can sit around like civilized people and chat over tea."

"By the way, Vinnie," smirked Rose. "You gallant fellow, you. Why aren't you sponging her youthful brow this morning instead of eating our hashbrowns?"

"She and her sister went to mid-morning Mass. I'll meet her back at her place afterwards."

"Mass, eh?" Rose's smirk grew wider, as if to say "Vinnie with a Catholic girlfriend? It is to laugh."

Sweeney prodded her in the side. "Let's not be nasty, my love. Not everyone can be as happily cynical as you." He reached out to poke her again but she forked up a mouthful of hashbrowns from his plate and jumped up to let Vin out the front door.

Rose led Vin down the long, straight hallway toward the front of the house. As she passed the front room her attention was caught through the white-curtained, glass-paned door by the figures of two large men mounting the stairs outside. Rose stopped inside the door as the men stepped up to the landing. As the closer figure reached for the bell, Rose opened the door. Vin stood right behind her, looking over her shoulder.

"Are you Mrs. Sweeney?" asked the dark-suited man in the doorway. He towered over both Rose and Vin by nearly a head. He held a black notebook in one hand. His coat, vest and tie all matched conservatively. Short-cropped brown hair framed an unmemorable middle-aged face that was doing its best not to show the years. Rose leaned to one side to check out the other man, a somewhat smaller, somewhat younger replica of the nearer one, who had evidently lost a protracted battle with acne during adolescence and had never learned to shave properly.

"If you're Jehovah's Witnesses, we aren't interested," she said, eyes sharp and voice all innocence.

The large man pulled out a badge. "My name is Elliot. I'm a homicide inspector with the San Francisco Police Department. This is Detective Leigh. We would like to talk with your husband. May we come in?"

"I guess so," Rose hesitated, looking back over her shoulder past Vin and down the hall. Vin suddenly realized that both policemen were looking at him.

"Are you Mr. Sweeney?" Elliot addressed Vin.

"Who, me? Oh, no. Just a neighbor. Um, thanks for the cup of sugar, Rose. I'll be seein' you." And he scuttled out between the two policemen and ran down the street.

"I take it you'd like to speak with my husband about last night," said Rose. "If you'll wait in the living room, I'll tell him you're here."

She backed up a pace and stood in the hall, motioning Inspector Elliot and Detective Leigh into the living room. Leigh walked around to inspect the bric-a-brac cluttering the mantel while Elliot chose an armchair and seated himself quietly.

Rose relaxed a little. Whew, she thought. In Nero Wolfe stories didn't the cops refuse to sit down when they came to arrest somebody? She watched Detective Leigh, who was distinctly uncomfortable-looking in his dark blue suit, sit down at the end of the sofa in front of yesterday's paper and immediately begin to peruse the funnies.

Oh well, so much for that idea. He doesn't look like he's ever read any Nero Wolfe.

Chapter Four

Elliot rose to his full six-feet-plus as Sweeney appeared in the doorway. Something about the policeman's demeanor gave Sweeney the uncomfortable feeling that he was about to be peeled like an orange. The tall man fairly reeked of self-confidence.

"Mr. Sweeney?"

"That's right." Sweeney considered offering a hand to the police Inspector. Elliot made no moves one way or the other. Sweeney decided against it.

"My name is Elliot. Inspector Elliot. I expect you know why we're here."

"To be honest, I do and I don't," said Sweeney, trying to clear away the last residual bit of sleepiness that clouded the edges of his mind. "I told everything I know to the other inspector last night. I doubt that I left out anything important. It took forever."

He sat down in the blue armchair opposite the policeman while Rose remained standing in the doorway, her arms folded. Elliot tucked up his trouser creases and resumed his seat, bringing his stern, gray eyes level with Sweeney's.

"So why isn't that other fellow here asking the questions?" asked Sweeney. "Sorry, but I can't recall his name."

"I was assigned to the case after the developments earlier this morning. Also, in reading the summary report from last night, we have met with some gaps and contradictions we want to clear up as quickly as possible."

"What do you mean 'contradictions'?"

"Just that. Important facts are still missing. I think it's probable that somebody is lying. I'm not going to be coy with you, Mr. Sweeney. We need all the facts. We are trying to determine why we're being lied to. We are investigating a particularly unpleasant murder. I would think you'd want those responsible locked up."

"As I said before, I think I've told you everything already, but . . . Somebody's lying about what? And what happened this morning?"

Elliot opened the briefcase and removed a clipboard full of papers. He leafed through a few and began reading.

"What are your politics, Mr. Sweeney?"

Sweeney's eyes widened a little. "I can't see how that could have any bearing at all on what happened to me last night," he replied, somewhat stiffly.

"Perhaps you should let us decide," said the Inspector. Sweeney felt the slap in his tone.

He continued, "Specifically, what is your opinion of the IRA?"

"For Chrissake, what do I care? I'm not Irish, except for a name borrowed from some immigrant ancestor. Why should I have any opinion of the IRA?"

"Blayney was pro-IRA. Everyone knew it. He wrote favorably about the Catholic cause in the Irish Press. You didn't like Blayney. Is it fair to assume that you also did not like his politics?"

"I never knew his politics. And even if I'd known them it wouldn't have changed my opinion of him, which was low to begin with. I thought he was basically a slimy barfly who was always cruising around looking to get laid, hitting up on any women who thought an Irish accent was sexy. It's a shame, since I like most of the people in the Irish music crowd. If I didn't, I'd spend a lot less time hanging out in a crummy place like the Bag of Nails."

"Did you know Blayney in Ireland?"

That was an odd question.

"Of course not. I never knew he existed until maybe six months ago. Why do you ask?"

Elliot simply continued in the same even tone of voice. "What do you suppose happened to the knife, Mr. Sweeney?"

"As I told the others last night, I haven't the foggiest idea. Somebody must have picked it up. It got kicked over to the wall and I'm sure somebody was standing there. Or Annie cleaned it up with the broken glass."

The Inspector nodded. "Somebody was there. When Joe Gilmore broke up the fight, three of your musician friends were standing off, away from the rest of the crowd."

Sweeney thought back for a moment. "That'd have been Marjorie and Rod and Kilbride, probably."

"Mm," said Elliot noncommittally. "The trouble is, they all agree that none of them touched the knife or anything else after the fight. And the barmaid, Annie Simpson, says she never picked it up either."

"If they said they didn't, then I guess they didn't. Oh, Kilbride did hand me my bow from somewhere over there, when I went to . . ."

"When you went to get your fiddle. That's right. The others all seem to agree that you were the only person besides the barmaid picking things up in the corner."

"Oh." From her vantage point in the doorway, Rose shifted her weight nervously. "So, you think I'm the most likely person to be lying about the knife, eh?"

Elliot maintained his unreadable expression. "Let us say that we are double-checking all accounts."

"What exactly did Annie say?"

"She says she swept up the glass and went back to the bar and stayed there."

"Well, I don't care what she said. If the two of us were the only ones who could have picked up the knife, it had to be her. 'Cause it wasn't me! Why don't you go check her out and let us finish breakfast in peace?"

"We already did. Her story has been corroborated. In fact, we know she didn't budge from behind the bar until after you left and . . . discovered the body. If somebody got the knife out the door after the bar owner threw Blayney out, it wasn't Miss Simpson. And no one saw her hand it to anyone else, either, to anticipate your next suggestion. So we're not concerned with her for the present. Tell us again about your activities after the fight."

"Your colleague wrote it all down last night. I sat at the bar for maybe twenty minutes. Joe Gilmore gave me a few drinks. I left and walked to my car. I saw Blayney and ran back to call the cops. Simple. Your men got there in about a minute. And I spent the rest of the night back in the Bag talking to your bunch till I was hoarse. You think I took the knife? I didn't have it last night. Why don't you search the house?" His voice had been acquiring a sharper edge of annoyance. He threw his right arm out to describe a rapid arc across the cluttered living room.

"That won't be necessary," replied Elliot in the same even, professional tone. "I might add, there was nothing found on the street, in the trash cans or down the sewers. I'm reasonably sure you didn't take the knife out of the Bag of Nails. But that still doesn't tell us who did. Have you any ideas?"

Yes, I have an idea. My idea is that you've been playing me for a sucker. If you already knew that I hadn't skipped with the goddam knife, what was all this cutesy hinting that I'm Suspect Number One?

He stared at Elliot, chewing on his upper lip and not feeling particularly friendly toward the cops and their even, professional tone. Under all the window-dressing, what did he really want to know?

Rose broke the silence. "You're being awfully chatty, Inspector, aren't you?" she asked with a slight sidelong glance from the doorway. An expression that might have been a smile flashed briefly across Elliot's face. "I thought detectives were just supposed to ask questions. Why are you giving us the complete blow-by-blow of your investigation? Or do you behave like this with all your suspects?"

Elliot licked his lips. "Mrs. Sweeney, at no time have I stated that your husband is suspected of anything." He glanced down at the papers on Leigh's clipboard which detailed half a night of phone calls and twelve hours of work following up leads in three countries.

Rose said something that sounded like "Hrumph." Sweeney tossed thoughts around quickly, concluding that the Inspector might be right, technically. It didn't make him any less nervous.

Elliot rubbed his temple and put the clipboard down on the low table in front of him.

"Look, Mr. Sweeney, I am in charge of this investigation by virtue of my training both with the FBI and with Interpol. I am directed to take care of this murder without asking for a lot of help from outside. If, as seems likely, this case carries international implications, the department can't afford to look lackadaisical. And," the barest hint of a sigh lingered in his voice, "it's an election year.

"From what we know so far, I am inclined to think that you are just an unlucky victim of circumstances with a lousy sense of timing. I'd leave it at that if it weren't for the international angles. We wouldn't even have bothered you at this stage if your name hadn't unexpectedly come up elsewhere. But what about the knife? Any ideas?"

"I have an idea," said Rose, moving quietly into the room in her stockinged feet and depositing herself on the near arm of Sweeney's blue chair.

"You weren't even there," growled Sweeney. "I doubt that Inspector Elliot is interested in a theory that . . ." Rose elbowed him just hard enough.

"It is certainly not the least charm of a theory that it is refutable." Before Sweeney could say anything, she added, "Look it up."

Turning back to the Inspector she said, "Anyway, what if the knife Blayney dropped wasn't the murder weapon at all."

Elliot sat quietly and blinked twice but said nothing.

Sweeney stopped in mid-thought. He tapped his fingers, replaying bits of last night in his mind, back and forth, back and forth. That notion hadn't occurred to him before.

"I mean," added Rose tentatively, "You really have no proof that that knife had anything to do with the murder, do you?"

"No, Mrs. Sweeney, we do not. However, a knife just vanishes into thin air after a barroom fight. One of those involved in the fight is stabbed to death a few minutes later down the street. No weapon is found at the scene. I must assume that the two incidents are somehow related until proven otherwise."

"Okay, okay," said Sweeney. "I don't know what happened to the damn knife and I don't care. The point is, you say I'm not a suspect. So, why jack us around when we'd just as soon forget the whole thing?"

"I simply said that I don't think you took the knife out of the bar last night."

Elliot eased himself up out of his seat and ambled over toward the fireplace, idly examining the assorted memorabilia competing for space along the narrow mantelpiece. He picked up a little silver-plated medal emblazoned with a fiddle and bow from its place atop a Smithwick's Red Ale coaster, turned it over, and put it back down. He turned to face the couple sharing the blue armchair.

"I have to attach human beings to these reports." He gestured toward the clipboard. "I can't know for certain till I speak to someone personally whether to believe them or not. And we're still interested in you as regards the other matter. The developments of earlier this morning. As I said, I wouldn't be here otherwise."

Rose spoke, "That's the second time you've mentioned 'developments,' Inspector. What developments?"

"That's right, I didn't explain," said Elliot, not quite smiling. "I thought I'd wait to see if it happened to pop up in conversation."

His not-quite-smile disappeared. "The bomb went off just after three this morning, as we were finishing up for the night."

"What?" squeaked Sweeney.

Elliot surveyed both faces for several seconds. "The bomb. At Blayney's house. At least three sticks of dynamite or a healthy handful of gelignite and a timer. Took out most of the second floor of the building and half the windows on the street."

Sweeney and Rose just looked at each other, stunned. Elliot continued in a matter-of-fact tone.

"It was placed in the bedroom, and a lucky thing for us. The last of our men was coming down the front stairs with a box of evidence when it blew. Five minutes earlier and four or five officers might have been killed. Leigh, here, could have been one of them." Sweeney and Rose each glanced at the younger detective, noticing for the first time the red abrasions on his hands and a small bandage behind his left ear.

"As it was," continued Elliot, "only Officer Ozumi took any of the blast and all he got was a broken tooth and glass in the back of his neck. You didn't hear about all this before, eh?"

Sweeney and Rose both fumbled around for words.

"No, of course not," Rose finally managed to get out. "How could we? It wasn't in the *Chronicle* this morning."

"The radio?"

"It's broken."

"I thought perhaps that neighbor . . ."

"No," asserted Rose. "Vinnie didn't know about it. He would have said plenty if he did."

Amen to that, thought Sweeney. Behind unblinking eyes, he wandered off in nervous thought. Twenty-four hours ago life was merely dull, he remarked to himself. I've been letting everything sort of cruise along without thinking about it. The job every day, and Rosie and her classes, and my little musical escape . . . I've been taking things for granted. And I thought I wanted more adventure! Ha! I'm sorry I ever thought about it. I take it all back. I never want to see another twenty-four hours like the last. Fight, murder, bomb . . . Jesus! Come Monday, I think I'll even be glad to see old Wendell P. Berenson at the office. What I . . .

Sweeney's eyes came back into focus with a snap and fixed on Elliot. "Wait a minute. What about the bomb?" he demanded. He felt Rose's hand resting on his shoulder.

"Pardon?"

"You said you wanted to see me about this bomb. But I didn't even know about it. You told us, remember?"

Elliot maneuvered back over to the chair he had previously occupied and, without sitting down, riffled through the papers on the clipboard.

"While you were in Ireland on business you worked with a man named Lynch. You remember him, don't you?"

"Lynch? You mean Sean Lynch? Yeah, I remember him. What about the bomb?"

"We'll get to that quick enough. What exactly was your relationship with Lynch?"

"He was one of the Anglo-Irish guys. They contracted with AdTech, you know, where I work, to design and program the ATMs that never got installed. He was one of their younger engineers. A pretty good one, as I recall. He enjoyed a drink of an evening and used to come out to Flannery's for the sessions from time to time. What about him?"

Detective Leigh jotted something in his notebook. Elliot stared at Sweeney for a full fifteen seconds in silence. He screwed his mouth up and exhaled with a low whoosh.

"You haven't been in contact since you were in Dublin?"

"I haven't thought about him since I was in Dublin. Why should I be thinking about him now? I thought we were talking about a bombing."

Elliot started pacing in front of the fireplace as he spoke.

"Lynch was arrested yesterday for his part in an IRA money scam between Dublin and San Francisco branches of the Anglo-Irish Bank. Interpol put the story out on the wires this morning. The whole thing was beautifully straight-forward, so straightforward, in fact, that nobody noticed anything wrong for almost two years. We know that Lynch used his position in the bank to gain access to international fund transferring. He used your company's teller machine project as a cover for setting things up. In fact, he may have helped to get AdTech the contract to go over there in the first place. And we know that of all the American engineers on the team that went to Dublin, he was chummy with exactly one if them. You."

Sweeney swallowed, looking around from Elliot to Rose and back again. Holy shit. The only way they could have collected this much information this fast is if they dragged Berenson out of bed and kept him up all night at the AdTech office. The only question now is whether he'll just fire me or if he'll want to kick me down eighteen flights of stairs first. He sank an inch farther down into the blue upholstery.

As if she shared this bleak realization, Rose ran her hand across Sweeney's shoulders. "Don't fret, Niall. It's only Saturday. By Monday all this will have blown over and Old Man Berenson will have forgotten all about it."

"Look, Inspector, I wouldn't say Lynch and I were chummy. A few drinks in a pub doesn't mean . . . Anyway, I never talked politics with anybody over there if I could help it, and certainly never with Lynch."

"Never?" challenged Elliot. "Isn't that a little strong, Mr. Sweeney, considering you were over there for eleven months, chatting away and drinking in the pubs?"

"Well, sure, people mentioned the troubles all the time in the pubs. That's not the same thing as talking about it. Hell, Inspector, you can't believe I had anything to do with that illegal money stuff. I never got near the banking end over there . . . just the incidentals, the electronics, and precious little of that as it turned out."

"And do they know where the money went?" asked Rose.

"Terrorists. Bombings. We're reasonably certain. Scotland Yard has connected the Anglo-Irish funds to several, including the Brighton Hotel bombing last month. It was aimed at a government conference as you may recall, and eight people, including one cabinet minister, were killed. As of this morning, the Anglo-Irish Bank has been shut down pending an Irish government investigation."

"I see. An Irishman is killed in San Francisco and his house is bombed. Then a bank turns out to be financing IRA bombings in Britain. And because my name comes up in both investigations, you think there's a link. Hell, you think I'm the link! That's just dandy! What do you want me to say?"

Elliot motioned to the stonily silent Detective Leigh, who began to collect his papers into his notebook. The Inspector steered himself back to his chair.

"Nothing, I guess, Mr. Sweeney. We seem to be finished here for the present. Thank you for your time. You can expect to hear from me again. And if you should recall anything else you think we should know . . . about anything . . . call me. Any time," he added. He slipped a card from one of his pockets and placed it on the coffee table.

From down the hall, the kitchen telephone rang. Sweeney jumped at the sound, mumbled "excuse me," and trotted out of the room.

Rose opened the front door and the two policemen passed into the warm sunlight and descended to the sidewalk.

"Inspector, something's still puzzling me."

Elliot turned and raised an eyebrow.

"You started out talking as if whoever killed Blayney did it because Blayney was pro-IRA. Then, when you told us about the Anglo-Irish scam, you as much as intimated that Niall might be working with a bunch of IRA bombers. So, if you're trying to say that Blayney was killed for his political beliefs, and that Niall's bank people had anything to do with it, then you need somebody who is both violently anti-IRA and violently pro-IRA. It won't work. You can't have it both ways."

Elliot smiled genuinely this time. "I like the way you think, Mrs. Sweeney," he said. "I assure you, if I knew all the answers I wouldn't be here bothering you."

"And in any case, Niall certainly isn't your man. He's not violently anything. He just had a really bad run of luck yesterday."

As Elliot turned again, Rose added hesitantly, "What do you honestly think, Inspector? I mean, about Niall?"

Elliot looked up with that same infuriatingly unreadable expression.

"What do I think? I think your husband had a really bad run of luck yesterday."

Chapter Five

Rose was still standing on the porch when Sweeney padded back down the hall to the front of the house.

"It's okay, Niall, they're gone," she said, her stare fixed on the pigeons battling for a cramped roost under the pointed eave of the opposite house. "Who was on the phone?"

Sweeney moved past her and deposited himself unceremoniously onto the top step. "It was Berenson," he said. The three words fairly dripped melancholy.

"The boss?"

"Wendell P. Berenson himself. I think I was just fired."

"Oh my," Rose found herself saying helplessly. She dropped down next to him and asked, "What did he say?"

"He said, 'Who do you think you are, dragging AdTech Financial into your sordid little intrigues?' I said something like, 'I didn't drag anybody into anything, Mr. Berenson. What seems to be the problem?' Then he said, 'You're through, Sweeney! I don't know exactly what you've been up to all this time, but until I find out, I don't want to see you near this office.'"

"Well, I didn't know what to do! I knew the old man had a temper but I've never heard him sound half that angry. And I never had it pointed at me. So I started to say, 'But Mr. Berenson, I haven't done anything!' He just started raving, "I've been in this business for twenty-seven years and I have never been awakened in the middle of the night by the police and informed that my company had been used by savages and criminals. Murderers! Terrorists! Embezzlers! By God, I'll see to it that every last one of you fries, but good!'

"I tried to explain when he stopped for breath. 'But listen! It's not me! The police only just told me about the Anglo-Irish Bank thing. By Monday they'll have found out who was responsible and everything will be fine.' 'Everything will not be fine, goddammit,' he yelled. 'You mean to tell me that all that money in your bank account didn't buy bombs?' I said, 'My account?' And he just got madder, 'Don't tell me you didn't know that they traced all that money through an account in your name at that damned bank?'"

Sweeney was gesticulating broadly by this time, emphasizing his tale with alternating skyward shrugs of disbelief and loud smacks with his palm against the old wooden handrail.

"He didn't give me a chance to tell him that I don't even have an account with the Anglo-Irish Bank. Anyway, he just kept yelling. 'And what about the secret authorization code numbering system?'"

Sweeney paused.

"Well," prompted Rose, "What about it?"

"They'd have to know how to break the code and avoid the built-in alerts in order to transfer any money internationally."

"And you know how to break the code?"

"I should. I wrote it."

"Oh." Rose's crestfallen expression now matched her husband's forlorn face as they sat together on the step. "Um, so what else did Berenson say?"

"I wouldn't know. Right about then I hung up on him."

Rose sat for a moment, staring off across the street. Then an unexpected thought dropped into her brain, rattled around and just kept rattling. She hoisted herself up and tugged on Sweeney's collar.

"Come on, Niall, let's go inside. I'm not sure what to do next but I think I've got an idea."

Sweeney turned and slowly paced down a hall that was a thousand miles long. Down the hall came the sound of music.

A pang of loneliness struck him and he winced as he searched for the source of the pang. The music came up in his ears and he was sitting in the smoky corner of Flannery's Bar, the general din of the crowd subdued for the moment to allow the voice of the single unaccompanied singer to be heard:

> *Does my love warm your heart through the long, cold night?*
> *Does it twine round your heart as the roses grown?*
> *Or has love burned away, leaving ashes as gray*
> *And cold as stone?*

It was too much to ask of him—to ask of anyone—to work day after day, sit night after night in a faraway dreamland without his love—his sweet, thorny Rose. He never should have taken the damn job knowing Rose couldn't be spared at the University. Sure, the music would distract him for an hour or two, but then what? The late night long-distance calls only made things worse. He and Rose had been sweethearts through college but had only been married for four years when he was sent to Ireland. Four years had not been long enough for either of them to get over that feeling of, well, newness. And yet, they'd never really talked about it, except in that fond, joking way.

Did he have any friends in Dublin? Was there anybody he really knew? Half the time in the pub he couldn't tell whether Brian Byrne was saying something profound or just having him on. He liked Byrne, but he never knew how or even whether the friendship was returned. As for the others in the bank office, that conniving bugger Sean Lynch, or Eamon O'Garagh the perpetual cadger, or Mike McKieran who bragged about his young daughter's wedding plans while everyone knew she was pregnant by a novice priest, and the rest who strutted about and stood rounds in the pub, what did he really know about them beyond their Irish bravado and comic-opera trappings?

He'd never thought about it in those terms before. He'd kept them at arm's length, too, he supposed, preferring the company of fiddlers and singers. He'd done it deliberately and, he had to admit, smugly. But what sorts of friendships had grown around the session gatherings he was so eager to keep to himself? Did they care what he thought about them any more than the rest did? Had he just made it all up?

A slow, sick feeling welled up in Sweeney's gut.

"They're practically strangers," he said. "Week after week I play my heart out for them and they're all practically strangers!"

"Who are practically strangers?" Rose's voice felt like a smack on the back of his head. Flannery's dissolved into its own smoke and Sweeney sat facing his wife across the kitchen table. He looked down to find that he was gripping her hand hard.

"God, I missed you when I was in Ireland!"

"I missed you, too, love," she replied, squeezing his hand. "But what brought that on?" She paused. "That's the past. We've got a problem to solve now." Her eyes still held the question.

"Rose," he began slowly, "I just had the horrible realization that any of the Friday night musicians at the Bag of Nails could have had a hundred good reasons to kill Blayney and I'd never know it. I've never bothered to learn a damn thing about most of them. They might have been waiting ages for an opportunity to throw suspicion on someone else and then calmly walked out with the knife and gutted him. It had to be the person who took the knife, and that person had to be one of the musicians!"

Rose thought in silence.

"I don't know, Niall," she said. "I'm not so sure about the knife. Besides, I told you I had an idea of my own." Rose deposited some of the dirty dishes into the sink with a splash and sat down again at the table.

"I think I know something about Blayney's murder that the police haven't thought of. If I can give them another theory to work on, they're bound to lighten up on you. And who knows? It might even lead to the real murderer."

Sweeney perked up somewhat, then shook his head.

"No, Rosie, why should we get involved in finding a murderer? I'm more interested in convincing somebody that the murder and the Anglo-Irish Bank bullshit had nothing to do with each other. Somehow I've got to prove to Berenson that I'm squeaky clean."

"But all you know about the AdTech thing is what Inspector Elliot and the boss told you. How do you expect to find out anything about money transfers if Berenson won't let you back in the office?"

"I'll think of something. I can't believe there's really any connection between the bank and Blayney. It's just too weird! The murder's got to have something to do with his old Irish connections. That's the only way it makes sense, although how that ties in with any of the local musicians is way beyond me! I wish I could wait for Elliot and his gang to come up with the answers, but I can't. And I'm damned if I believe they're even asking the right questions." He rubbed his eyes and squinted.

"I don't believe it," declared Rose. "The IRA thing, I mean. Blayney was no cold-blooded hoodlum. He was a jerk and nobody liked him, maybe, but he didn't seem the type to go bombing and kneecapping. No, if we're going to find out who killed him, it won't be by looking in the same places the police are looking."

Sweeney shook his head again. "I know I had nothing to do with it . . . with anything . . . but what business is it of ours who killed the guy? The police don't want amateurs jumping in with damn fool ideas. Anyway, they've got their scientific methods for figuring everything out."

"But what if the answer isn't scientific? What if the answer is in a damn fool idea?"

"Like what, for instance?"

Rose jumped up and ran down the hall. She returned a moment later with a small green, soft-bound book and plopped it down on the table. "Like what if the answer's in a thousand-year-old Irish mythic poem?"

Sweeney rotated the book to face him and read the cover. *Sweeney Astray, a version from the Irish*, translated by Seamus Heaney. He smirked and looked Rose in the eye. She looked absolutely serious.

"You've got heroic literature on the brain, Rose. What could this book possibly have to do with the murder?"

"Just listen," she replied and riffled through the pages. "Maybe it's a good thing I have this stuff on the brain. I got the idea from something in that newspaper article about the murder." She flattened the book with a slap.

"This is a modern rendition of the story of Mad Sweeney, a relation of yours." Her attempt at lightheartedness went unnoticed.

"The Mad Sweeney legend dates from as far back as the ninth century. It's not strictly heroic, of course, not like Tristan or Beowulf. It's a funny combination of Celtic legend of unknown antiquity and a post-Christian overlay designed to make an anti-pagan moral point out of the pagan story it's built upon. I'm only using the story in my Heroic Lit reading list as extra credit . . ."

Sweeney sat expectantly.

"I thought you read this after I named the album."

"No, it slipped my mind. This is where you got the title, eh? I thought you said it came from T.S. Eliot."

"It came from both, and Flann O'Brien, too. O'Brien used the legend in his novel *At Swim-Two-Birds* but this version will show you what I have in mind quicker. I'll get to nightingales later . . . they're just a passing part of the general air of melancholy. Here, just listen to the opening lines . . . first, we're introduced to old Sweeney, son of Colman Cuar and King of Dal-Arie, the subject of the tale, then it reads:

> *There was a certain Ronan Finn in Ireland,*
> *a holy and distinguished cleric.*

Ring a bell?"

"Well, I'll be," Sweeney looked back at the front page. "Ronan was Blayney's middle name. But that's silly. Even if it's not a common name, that surely can't have any significance. Blayney was no holy cleric. Anyway, it's just a middle name."

"Maybe it's his mother's family name. Back when they were cooking up the Sweeney legend plenty of mystical goodies were passed down through the matrilineal line, you know."

"Mystical . . . ? This makes no sense."

"Wait a minute. What was it again he said to you in the bar? Exactly. Think hard."

Sweeney thought hard. The curious conversation rewound and played back slowly.

"He said a couple of things that sounded strange. He said he could see through me—no, that I was naked to him! He said I'd done something to him and knew what it was, then he threatened to curse me and told me to get back up my tree."

"You mean he did curse you," prompted Rose.

"No, he said he would if I didn't get up my tree or something. Why are you so interested in what he said in the bar?"

"Check this out," Rose said, her finger moving rapidly down the page to another stanza. "First, about what you did to him:

> *Sweeney has trespassed on me*
> *and abused me grievously*
> *and laid violent hands on me*
> *to drag me with him from Killarney*

"You see, it seems that Ronan was preaching Christian stuff on Sweeney the Pagan's land. Sweeney heard about it, would have nothing to do with the Christians and went to toss Ronan out. Sweeney's wife tried to stop him and grabbed his cloak. He tore away, but she hung on to the cloak and he ran off stark naked. When he got to the church, in high Irish fury, he threw Ronan's psalter in the lake. An otter came out of the lake the next day and brought the psalter back to Ronan unharmed. Ronan figured he had God on his side with this obvious miracle so he up and cursed Sweeney, long and hard, including the line:

> *He shall roam Ireland, mad and bare*
> *He shall find death on the point of a spear*

"All right so far. Then Sweeney goes about his business killing his enemies. Ronan goes around like a referee, telling all sides they can only kill each other during certain hours of the day. This, he thinks, is Christian moral progress. But Sweeney pays no attention to the ref and keeps killing enemies before the starting bell and after hours, too. So, one day Ronan comes out onto the field of battle and starts blessing Sweeney's army with holy water. He sprinkles water on the army and then on Sweeney himself, who thinks Ronan is mocking him.

"Being a bold man of action, his immediate response is to chuck a spear through Ronan's assistant and chuck another spear at Ronan, which hits the bell around his neck, breaking the shaft off. This personal attack's too much for Ronan and he finishes up the big curse:

*My curse fall on Sweeney
for his great offense
His smooth spear profaned
my bell's holiness,*

*Cracked bell hoarding grace
since the first saint rang it—
it will curse you to the trees
bird-brain among branches.*

"That's the line that Flann O'Brien translated a little more literally as, 'My holy bell will banish thee to branches, it will put thee on a par with fowls.' And then Ronan gives the kicker:

*Just as the spear shaft broke
and sprang into the air
may the mad spasms strike
you, Sweeney, forever."*

The non-mad modern Sweeney looked up from the book into his wife's excited face. "And so what happened then?"

"Sweeney went bonkers, of course! He immediately went paranoid, thought he was a bird, had an uncontrollable fear of any place or person that was familiar to him, flapped his arms and flew away naked over the trees. He ended up roosting in various remote spots all over Ireland and living on spring water and watercress, while various people went looking for him. He spent the rest of his life composing mournful poems, which make up the last seventy pages of the book."

"And finally?"

"Finally he died. No happy ending. That happened a lot in the old legends. Remember that this is early Christian propaganda. So the tale had him killed by a swineherd and given last rites in spite of himself."

"Whew! And Ronan, I suppose, comes out the hero in the end."

"Well, he's not actually mentioned at the end, but elsewhere he's referred to as Saint Ronan, so I guess he might have been promoted in the church for successful cursing. But, you see now, it's possible that Blayney thought he was Ronan and you were Mad Sweeney! It could all fit!"

Sweeney leaned back in thought.

"Whether it fits or not, it doesn't really answer any questions, does it? I mean, who killed Blayney and why? I never chucked any spear at him, that's for sure! We can talk about his delusion toward me til we're blue in the face but that won't get the police off my case, will it? It's still a pretty far-fetched idea, you'll have to admit. And whether it contains a bit of sense or not, doesn't it connect me even more with the bugger?"

Rose's shoulders dropped.

"You're right. Elliot would just try to say you'd been feuding with him and this proved how nasty things had gotten. Unless . . . what could we find out about Blayney back in Ireland?"

"We could ask Elliot for Interpol printouts."

"Ha! No, what I'm thinking about are quirks that the police would miss. They'd have no reason to fix on them, nothing that would be noted in a charge sheet, but they could prove that Blayney was off balance before he came over."

Rose began using both hands to amplify her argument. "Suppose that before he started this weird Mad Sweeney thing with you he'd been known to have delusions before? Wouldn't that help prove that you were just an unlucky target?"

Sweeney found himself nodding. "You may be right. Why not call Brian Byrne at Flannery's? He knows everybody in Dublin. And he's always at Flannery's. For all I know he sleeps there. Still, the more immediate problem is to get my job back." He stood up and paced slowly to the kitchen window, looking out into the quiet, sun-drenched afternoon.

"I'll see if I can sneak into the office and look into the files. Maybe there's a clue there."

Rose joined him at the window. "What would you look for?"

Sweeney shrugged and laughed in spite of himself. "I haven't the remotest idea! But it's better than doing nothing." And he marched off to the bedroom.

Rose stood in the doorway as he pulled on his clothes, tapping the book in her hand. "You know, Niall, I think I'm going to follow up the Ronan-Mad Sweeney delusion. The more I think about it, the more I feel that somehow it's a key to the whole mystery."

"Suit yourself," said Sweeney evenly. "But, you know what I think? I think you're out of your mind. This is the real world, not some damn fairy tale!

Somebody out there killed Blayney and is perfectly content to let the police think I did it. I'd like to know who it is." And he marched out the front door, down the steps and up the street to where the car was parked.

•

Rose opened the book again and stared at the page, biting her lip.

I never did tell him about the nightingales, she thought, leafing farther along into the book in search of the passage. She skimmed for the story. Here Mad Sweeney had flapped around Ireland in terror for seven years and had returned to his first safe haven, the crags of Glen Bolcain. He was stalked to his hiding place by . . . she stopped and stared. Lynchseachan. Mad Sweeney's foster brother.

Lynchseachan. No, this is too weird, thought Rose. Lynchseachan . . . Sean Lynch . . .

She strode back in to her bookshelf and yanked down Flann O'Brien's *At Swim-Two-Birds*. Going right to the worn, dog-eared section in the middle, she scanned rapidly through the stanzas of poetry and connecting conversations between Finn MacCool and Furriskey and the Pooka.

Good, breathed Rose. It's just Heaney's choice of spelling. O'Brien makes it 'Linchehaun.' Hmm. Best to keep Lynch out of it. No need to go out of our way to manufacture coincidences. What else could there be in the legend to hint at Blayney—to hint at his killer? After Lynchseachan, Sweeney is pursued by the old hag who gets dashed to death on the rocks, then by the mad Briton, and by the mad-woman, and by Ronan again . . . This is getting me nowhere. It's Sweeney's tale, not Ronan's. It is starting to sound totally crazy. What am I looking for anyway?

She mused for a moment, then smiled. She picked up the phone and quickly dialed a number from memory.

"Sal? Rose. Sorry to call you on the weekend but I need a favor. No, it can't wait."

Hartford Street remained still. Across the street a few doors up, a young woman pruned at a rangy pair of rose bushes. The clattering sound of children playing echoed around the corner, disturbing one or two pigeons gawking along the gutter.

On the street corner below the house a man stood in the shade of the ornamental cherry tree which pushed its way up out of the old, buckled pavement. He lit a cigarette from a half-inch glowing butt. He tossed it to the sidewalk and scuffed it to death under his shoe, adding to the interesting pattern created by a dozen spent butts scattered beneath the tree. Then, in silence, he turned his dark gaze back up the street toward the front door of the Sweeney house.

Chapter Six

Inspector Elliot looked up from the reports and the scattered sheets on his desk, rubbed his eyes slowly and refocused them for a moment out the third-floor window and across the tarred rooftops of Market and Mission Streets. He punched at the intercom.

"Wayne, where's that sandwich?"

"You only just called, sir," a harried voice replied. "It'll still be a minute."

Elliot tried to get comfortable in the chair, failed, rose to stick his head out the pebbled-glass office door, and beckoned mutely toward the detective in the next room.

Detective Leigh, who seemed just about to sit down, reversed direction and entered the office carrying several manila files.

"Sir? Any breaks yet?"

"No, Bernie, there have been no blinding flashes on this side of the door," sighed Elliot with ill-concealed impatience as he sat back down. "I am waiting for information from you. And waiting for a goddam sandwich. What's taking so long on the passports?"

"You know the Irish," replied the tall young man. "Confirmation just came through on the wire. I thought I'd check them before bringing them in."

Elliot put out his hand. "Give. We'll check them together." Leigh pushed the manila files across the desk and perched one bony hip on the corner.

Elliot read quickly. Then he pushed the pile of papers back across the blotter to his assistant.

"According to that report we're no closer to nailing anybody at the bar with a lie than we were yesterday. Everything that Patrick Kilbride guy told us checks out. Bantry, of all places . . . that's about as far from the Troubles as you can get in Ireland without getting your feet wet . . . emigration

'71 . . . construction business . . . numbingly dull life . . . not so much as a parking ticket. We need more like him."

Detective Leigh appeared to relax slightly, without venturing a smile.

"Gilmore the barman is almost as bad. I thought we had a glimmer when the computer spit out his brother as a fugitive on the Belfast warrant, but nothing connects. Our boy is clean. Halfway around the world for 12 years when little brother got funky. Nothing from that hick town in south Australia except that he slung beers in the pub. Two years in San Francisco. Exactly the way he told it. No police record anywhere. You get anything else?"

"Just photostats of his Aussie passport. Only used it once; to come here. Never went back to Ireland. My guess is he didn't know Blayney or anybody else from back there after all those years."

Elliot nodded. "Yeah. He's just been out of the picture too long. And his girlfriend is a local . . . nothing political there."

"So we're back to Marjorie McAulliffe, her boyfriend Hesse, Charlie Levinson and Peter Cole to round out the musicians who were near the knife. Besides our dear, obvious friend Sweeney, of course."

"I thought we'd eliminated Levinson and Cole," put in the young man seated on the desk.

"For now, for now," answered Elliot. "Levinson's a snot-nosed kid who doesn't strike me as being particularly bright and Cole doesn't . . . No, nobody's eliminated until I find that knife." He poked at his stack of papers with a pencil.

"The girl was the only one who exhibited any animosity toward Blayney, and according to her, it was because he was just a general jerk towards women in the bar. That much we got from half a dozen others. Anything else on her?" He looked up with brows raised.

"No sir," replied Leigh. "She was pretty tightlipped about her private life, though."

"Any more than any woman we've questioned lately?" commented Elliot.

"Well, sir," suggested Leigh after a moment, "What about that Baker woman in the see-through kimono who ran the phone sex business upstairs from the Scientology Center and . . ."

"Okay, okay! Forget it! See what you can come up with." A uniformed cop appeared at the door with a brown paper bag.

"We're still missing it then." He sent a daggered look down at the list of names and notations staring up at him and stabbed it with the pencil again.

"There they are. All neat and tidy and innocent. Why don't I believe it?"

"Believe what, sir?"

"All right, Bernie, out!" snapped Elliot irritably as he reached for his lunch. "Bring me the latest lab reports on the bombing, the complete list of names from Dublin, and let's have another look at those newspaper clippings." Detective Leigh scooted out.

"And find that knife, will you?"

•

If Friday had been one of the all-time bad days in Sweeney's life, Saturday wasn't much of an improvement. It took him fifteen minutes to navigate his way through the bustle and the tourists to the financial district but all of perhaps ninety seconds to get thrown out of the AdTech office.

"I'm sorry, Niall," Al Karamardian had said. Ha! Karamardian! Nothing but a junior engineer and not nearly sorry enough. "I got specific orders. Berenson will never rotate me off weekend shift if I so much as let you set foot in here."

Then he'd got a cagey look and said, "Hey, what are you doing here, really? Rumor in the office had you in jail for murder. How come you're out on the street? Cops gettin' soft or what?"

Sweeney hadn't bothered continuing the conversation. With that sort of moral support from his work mates he'd better start looking for another job pronto. Speechless, he roared back across town, scattering jaywalkers and trying to realign his thoughts into some useful direction. Stewing at a traffic signal, he remembered his modem and began to relax a little. It was still in the original box, but he could dig his home computer out from under the piles of books and detritus and hook it up. God knows he hadn't used that old machine in ages, but maybe he could hack into the office electronically. He wasn't sure what he'd look for, but anything was better than just sitting back and taking that crap from Karamardian. Considering this new possible course of action, he pulled in near a small coffee joint on Haight Street, got out of the car and ran headlong into Vin Bowen.

"Niall!" greeted his surprised friend with a look of honest relief. "I was trying to get up the nerve to come and ask how it went with the cops! C'mon, sit down and tell all. God, you were grumpy this morning! Lemme buy you coffee!" And he dragged him into the cafe.

They elbowed their way into the only available table, sandwiched tightly between gabby young artists all in black leather and a knot of tie-dyed street freaks. Vin rapidly conjured two strong coffees.

"I would have come around sooner, really, Niall, but I told Christie I'd take her out for tennis this afternoon. Perfect day for it, only she didn't feel like playing. If she wants to sit around and mope inside with her sister, that's fine, but I'm getting some fresh air. Ah, maybe it's all for the best, she'd have beat my socks off again with that backhand of hers. So, tell me what happened!"

Sweeney delivered a short summation of the meeting with Elliot and of his abortive sortie against AdTech. He sipped his coffee as the population of Haight Street wandered back and forth aimlessly outside the cafe window and Vinnie wriggled his moustache in thought.

"Rosie thinks Blayney was murdered as part of some thousand-year-old Irish legend about a thoroughly unlikeable bird-man named Sweeney."

"You're kidding? You're not kidding. Is she serious?"

"I can't always tell, you know. But at least if she busies herself with that ridiculous idea, she won't brood on the fact that I'm out of a job and she'll have to come up with the rent."

"But look, Niall, as soon as the cops find the killer, Berenson'll have to let you back. He'd have no reason not to."

"And I'd have every reason to tell him to shove the goddam job! I've had it! I'm not sure why I put up with those creeps for so long, but I'm out of there now! The only thing left for me to do is to clear my name since the cops aren't doing it. Clear my name and start playing music for a living."

"And how do you propose to clear your name if the cops can't do it? Got any better ideas than Rosie?"

"Damn it, I'm sure somebody in the bar did it! Somebody must have seen something. It had to have been while I was getting beaten on. What do you say we go back and ask Gilmore and Annie what they saw?"

"Okay, Sherlock, if you're going to start playing detective, get real and think suspects! That includes Gilmore, Annie, and everybody else. Like, how do you know Gilmore didn't bump him off, anyway?"

Sweeney looked surprised. "He never left the bar. Or did he? The police let him be, even though . . . wait a minute! Why didn't he call the police after the fight? I remember asking him what the police said when they took Blayney away and he didn't answer straight. He said the police were never there when they were needed. But he never even called 'em! That fight was no joke, either! He could have lodged a complaint and had Blayney locked up and out of the Bag permanently. But he just let him go."

"Wow!" ejaculated Vinnie. "See what I mean? You suppose Gilmore and Blayney were mixed up in that IRA stuff?"

"I never heard Gilmore utter a single political word, let alone start wrapping himself in any flag."

"Well, maybe they knew each other in Ireland or . . ."

"No, Vinnie, can't be," said Sweeney. "Gilmore took over the Bag two years ago and before that he'd lived in Australia for years. I remember him talking a while back to some fishing nut at the bar about the town he'd lived in. Claimed that Laver's Bay was the best fishing spot in the world and how he'd hauled in the biggest marlin on record about fifteen years ago. You've seen the picture; it's hanging behind the bar."

"Where's Laver's Bay?"

"He said it was on the south coast—west of Melbourne. I remember thinking that if I ever did embezzle a million bucks, that would be the ideal place to disappear to."

"Why'd he go down there, do you suppose? What was he doing for a living?"

"Same as here, working in a pub. I think he said that there was nothing there but a couple of pubs and the fishing boats."

Vinnie straightened and raised a finger. "You know, if you were going to be thorough, you'd check out his story before eliminating Gilmore from your list of suspects."

Sweeney grimaced. "And how would you propose that I do that, Watson? All our police have to do is have the Aussie authorities wire name, rank and serial number. Not quite so easy for us, is it?"

"It just so happens that a friend of mine is flying to Australia tomorrow for the university Aussie bike trek from Melbourne to Adelaide. I'm almost certain she said they were going to cycle down the coast. Maybe it wouldn't be out of her way to hunt up the pub and find out if Gilmore really did serve beer and pull in that marlin or if he's part of some insidious international plot!"

"You don't say! And just who is your friend, Vin?"

"Lydia, of course," he replied. "I don't know anybody else who's crazy enough to do such a thing."

"I was not aware that you were still speaking to the old flame."

"Well, we reached sort of an amicable truce since I was replaced in her affections. She's going on the trek with her current heart-throb Ramon or Omar or whatever his name is, who's enough of an outdoorsy jock to keep her diverted for a while. I'll just explain to her that it could help get you out of hot water with the cops. I'm sure she'd be happy to do it. And it'd be quicker than calling or writing, even if we knew who to write to."

"But why would Gilmore lie about his past, or about the knife if he didn't pick it up or leave the bar last night?"

Vinnie shrugged. "So maybe that's for Lydia to find out."

"Oh, shut up and let me think," said Sweeney, reaching for his cup and staring out the window. A very young thing all in fashionable black shreds and a haircut like a jet-black tennis ball met his eyes through the window for an instant, then turned her unconvincing, world-weary pout away down the block.

Sweeney turned back to Vin. "Well, let's go."

"Go? Go where?"

"To do the only sensible thing when confronted with a mysterious murder: cherchez la femme."

"Any particular femme you have in mind?" queried Vin as he got up and unwedged himself from the chair.

"How's about Marjorie McAulliffe? We've got to start somewhere. And I'm remembering the way she nearly bit Blayney's nose off at the session." The two men hustled back toward the car.

"Do you know where she lives?"

"Haven't the faintest, but Gilmore or Annie'll know. We'll ask them."

•

It had been a great relief to Rose to know that she had done something constructive toward proving that there was something to her Mad Sweeney theory. After hanging up the phone, she gathered her uncorrected class papers and moved out to the front steps to sit in the sun. In two hours she was able to rocket through the last ten papers, though her sense of satisfaction had not dulled her eye for slovenly syntax or lessened the number of red-inked scribbles and margin commentaries that decorated most of the papers like the Saint Valentine's Day Massacre.

She stretched, yawned, and massaged the scalp behind both ears, wishing either that she were a dog or that Niall was there to scratch her head for her. As she moved back indoors a figure at the end of the block caught the corner of her eye. With only a momentary pause, she went back inside trying not to turn her head.

That man was still there! She'd seen him that morning when the policemen had left, but hadn't thought anything of it. He'd been there again in the shadow of the tree when she'd started correcting papers but had moved away around the corner when she'd looked in his direction. Was she getting paranoid or was somebody actually watching their house?

She peeked out through the curtain at the row of reflections in the front windows across the street. And there was the silent figure, his body in shadow, his head silhouetted against the neighbors' white-washed iron grille, lighting a cigarette and watching. Watching! A rush of adrenaline speared her in the back of the throat and she involuntarily lunged to throw the deadbolt.

The police know more than they're telling! she thought. Is there something really damning about Niall that they don't want us to know? But why are they watching the house? Where's Niall? Why is he taking so long?

•

Although the sun beat down warmly from a cloudless sky over Clement Street, Sweeney shivered as he opened the half-open door of the Bag of Nails. Inside, it was as if no time had elapsed since the previous night. The tables and chairs were still frozen in disarray and from the back of the room issued Mary Black's *Song For Ireland*, the old juke box making it sound sibilant and distant. But the bottles and glasses were all cleared away, except for those placed before the five or six daytime regulars hunched in conversation at the near end of the bar.

From behind the bar, Annie Simpson looked up at Sweeney and Vinnie, turned quickly and hurried through the door to the storeroom without a word. As the two reached the other end of the bar, Annie re-emerged with Joe Gilmore immediately behind her, nodded a silent greeting and scuttled off toward the regulars.

Gilmore leaned on the bar and wiped a lock of grey hair out of his eyes with the back of one hand.

"Afternoon, lads," he said pleasantly. "Pretty rough last night, eh, Niall? Bad business. Bad business all around. Okay, are you? I didn't expect to see you back here for a while."

"No?" replied Sweeney. "Why not?"

"Would you like a drink, lads?" he asked quietly.

"Thank you, no," said Sweeney. "About it being bad business . . . it didn't get any better today. I've been canned from my job and the cops have been all over me as a prime suspect in croaking that miserable Blayney!"

"You don't say," said Gilmore, sounding more interested. "Well, they can't be too serious about you if they've let you go traipsing around the city unescorted, now, can they?"

Sweeney glanced to the right and caught Annie staring at him, her hand on the Guinness tap. She immediately looked down. Turning back to Gilmore, he continued, "We just came in to ask if you knew Marjorie McAulliffe's address."

Gilmore looked surprised. He coughed quietly. "Marjorie? Well, no, I don't know. I had a phone number somewhere." He looked vaguely toward the back room. "I could hunt around and let you know if I can find it . . ."

Vinnie piped up, "Annie knows, certainly! She and Marjorie used to pal around. Hey, Annie!" He beckoned. "Where can we find Marjorie McAulliffe?"

With a general air of reluctance Annie rejoined the three men.

"Marjorie? Why are you looking for her?"

Vin started to say, "We thought she . . ." An unseen kick in the shin stopped him as Sweeney smiled at Annie.

"I wanted to thank her for helping out last night, that's all. She was real sweet and this morning it occurred to me that I didn't even know where she lived."

Annie seemed to relax and returned a rather wan smile.

"Oh sure. Yeah, that was a nasty crack on the head you got. She's a sweet kid. Fourteen-fifteen Parnassus is the address. Upstairs. What are you goin' to do, send her flowers?"

"Maybe. Not a bad idea. About that crack on the head, Joe, where were you when Blayney jumped me, anyway?"

"Hooking up a fresh keg to the tapper," said Gilmore through unsmiling lips. "I was under the bar or I'd 'a been there sooner and scotched the crazy bastard." He looked distinctly uncomfortable, as if his manhood had been questioned.

"Of course, of course . . ."

Still smiling, Sweeney looked around at the musician's corner; juke box, kegs, Pat Kilbride handing him his shattered bow. Who had picked up the knife? An idea popped up in his head. He looked Gilmore in the eye.

"Joe, who did Blayney know when he first got to San Francisco?"

Gilmore stiffened. "How do you mean, know?"

"I mean, how do you suppose a guy as unsavory as Blayney got a job so fast after hitting a town full of total strangers. By all accounts, nobody knew the guy before he showed up. No references, no nothing: instant employment. Doesn't that strike you as odd?"

"Odd, all right," answered Gilmore in slow, measured syllables. "Couldn't tell you. But this is the land of opportunity, they tell me." His hands didn't move from where he'd placed them on the bar, but the knuckles again were white.

"You know, Niall, if I were you I'd leave the snooping to the cops. It's bad business to poke your nose in where it's not wanted." He motioned his companion away curtly. "Annie, get old Mulreavy another pint before he has a stroke."

As she scuttled off, Annie looked nothing short of terrified. Sweeney just watched. These two were scared stiff of something. He and Vinnie stood again in the suddenly chilly bar.

"Yep, Joe, we'll be off to pay our respects to Marjorie. And you're right. It's bad business all around, just like you said. Thanks, Annie. Be seein' you."

And out the door they strode, conscious of two pairs of eyes boring holes through the backs of their heads.

•

"Bernie, when did this come in?" demanded Inspector Elliot.

"Just a minute ago, sir. Along with the cross-check reports on Lynch and the other Anglo-Irish employees. Would you like to have a look at them?"

"Oh, no, Bernie, this is just fine. Just fine." He read the wire report through again and whistled. "Goddam peculiar, though! I think I'm going visiting again. Assuming all the others are clean." The other detective gave a tired nod.

"Don't wait up." Elliot pulled his jacket back on, shook the crumbs off his pants and marched out of the office.

Just after five o'clock Rose opened the door to admit Inspector Elliot. Locking the door behind him, she glanced through the curtain at the shadowy form still reflected in the neighbors' Victorian glass. She bit her lip nervously as she ushered the policeman into the front room. Elliot mentally noted that this was a substantial change from her demeanor of earlier that day.

Without preamble, he began, "Mrs. Sweeney, does your husband have family in Ireland?"

Rose looked nonplused. "Why don't you ask him?" she responded, sitting stiffly in the blue chair.

"I'd be delighted to. Is he here?"

Rose stopped in mid-breath, stared briefly at Elliot, let the air out and sat back in the chair.

"You haven't arrested Niall then?" she asked, her voice barely above a whisper.

"Of course not. What makes you think we had?"

Rose passed her hand over her face and motioned "never mind."

"I'm sorry. I've been worried, that's all. What do you want to know about Niall's family anyway?"

"Simply if he has family in Ireland. Other Sweeneys, that is. Anyone at all."

"That's easy. If he does, they're such distant relations they might as well be a different species. Niall's great-great-grandfather Sweeney came over to seek his fortune back when Texas was a sovereign country all to itself and was advertising for hardy homesteaders. Old Gramps wasn't as hardy as he thought and got starved out in a couple of years and moved back up north somewhere. His son built railroads and ended up in California. Niall is a third-generation California Irishman. He never even thought to look up family when he went back to work in Dublin. No point. Why do you want to know?"

"We just received this wire from Dublin answering some questions about Blayney and, well, your husband, among others. What would you say if I told you that Blayney mentioned the name Sweeney in one unpublished article and some notes found in Ireland, dating back to before your husband admitted knowing the man."

Rose's face betrayed utter surprise. She thought for a moment in silence, suddenly feeling very satisfied indeed. It fit.

"In Ireland, eh? I'd say you've found out that Blayney knew another Sweeney in Ireland, that they didn't like each other or worse, and that you've dismissed Blayney's notes as either meaningless ranting or bad poetry."

Elliot just stared at her. "I'm not here to bring you updates, Mrs. Sweeney," he said shortly. "But, in a word, yes, that's about the size of it. Now tell me what you know about all this."

"Oh, I don't know anything. Just ask my husband. He thinks my literary ideas prove I'm a crackpot. Still, in my field you stumble on things that other people miss."

"I don't like the idea of people in any field stumbling around, playing cops and robbers. And unless you can convince me that you're just making lucky guesses, we'll have to ride downtown for a few more questions!"

Rose laughed nervously. "No lucky guess, Inspector! Just chalk it up as the curse of overliteracy and the desire to get Niall out of this awful mess. It started with a book I'm using for a class and what Blayney said in the bar last night. A connection you wouldn't have seen in a million years." Deciding that it was best not to anger the Inspector unnecessarily on the subject of meddling, she made no mention of the phone call she had made earlier.

She reached for the two paper-bound books on the small table and, reading passages from each in turn, sketched out the tale of Mad Sweeney and Ronan the vengeful priest to the somber-looking Elliot. Elliot finally scratched his nose and started pacing back and forth as he had done earlier.

"This is fantastic! You can't expect us to believe that this . . . this fairy tale is a clue to Blayney's murder?"

"Maybe not to his murder, Inspector," replied Rose, "but it does tell you what sort of a nut case Blayney was. It was all in his head, don't you see? There was never any bad blood between Blayney and Niall. Blayney didn't even know Niall. In fact he didn't have to, to go insane the way he did. Something way back when started him off thinking that he was the reincarnation of the great Ronan. For all I know it was his mother. Anyway, it should be plain even to you that the delusion was entirely Blayney's and that my husband was an innocent target, wrongly attacked and wrongly accused! He had no motive! Why not ask that other Sweeney?"

"Oh, we'd like that. We'd like that very much. Only he's unavailable for a chat. There are a great many things besides Blayney that the authorities would like to chat with that other Sweeney about."

"Still," he said as he made for the hallway, "You've been more helpful than you realize. I'll be checking some of that fairy tale stuff of yours. And just lay off playing detective and leave that to us."

"Wait a minute, Inspector!" piped Rose. "Does that mean you're not planning to arrest Niall?"

"As of this moment, no, Mrs. Sweeney."

"Then you'll be taking your watchdog off the corner and leaving us alone?"

"Watchdog?"

"The man watching the house from the corner."

"I have no one watching your house."

Rose jumped up, threw open the front door, and ran down the steps to the sidewalk. The shadows had lengthened all down the street and the westerly breeze carried the heavy scent of fog, gently ruffling the leaves of the cherry tree at the corner. The man with the cigarette was gone.

Chapter Seven

"Well, that's done," smiled Vin as he scampered from the phone booth and stuffed himself back into the car. Sweeney turned up the hill toward the Park.

"Lydia was a little confused but then she's generally a little confused. Said she'd be happy to find out what she could when she gets down to Australia. It's not a race, you know, so they can pick their stops. I wish I could have told her just what to ask about, though."

"If we knew that I'd be a lot less nervous," replied Sweeney, deep in thought. "But remember we're just shotgunning. We don't know anything about Gilmore or anybody else. Frankly, I'd rather believe that none of them had anything to do with the murder at all. Let's hope it's all a stupid wild goose chase."

Vin nodded. "So what are we going to ask Marjorie, then?"

"About Blayney, I guess. That's the key. It's got to be. And I keep thinking about how she snapped at him last night. I'd never seen her do that before, had you?"

"Nope."

"Somehow maybe we can find out something about that dead asshole from her to point to his killer and to clear me."

"Sure. Easiest thing in the world," said Vin disconsolately as they pulled up in front of the tall, dark blue house where Marjorie McAulliffe lived. Light shone dimly through the pebbled glass of the front door.

Marjorie answered the bell dressed in what looked like the same black outfit she'd had on the previous night at the Bag. She didn't look surprised to see them but shot her eyes down the steps as if expecting someone else as well.

"Oh, hi, Niall. Vin. C'mon in. How's the head?" She turned and walked back down the hall toward the kitchen. They let themselves in, shut the door and walked in toward the light. The air in the hallway was lightly scented with roses and stale cigarette smoke. Picking up a half-empty tobacco pouch, then tossing it next to the sink, Marjorie lit a hand-rolled cigarette and leaned against the counter, motioning to the available chairs.

"Never been here before, have you, Niall?"

Sweeney smiled and shook his head. Glancing around, he took in the kitchen and the dining room beyond, neat and uncluttered and decorated with a profusion of flowers arranged in thrift shop vases and bowls of all shapes and sizes. He leaned over and sniffed at the generous clump of purple gladiolas peeking out of a shorter ring of multi-colored carnations, tulips, lilies, and pretty blooms he couldn't identify in a ceramic bowl on the kitchen table.

"Nice, eh?" said Marjorie off-hand, noticing his interest.

"Sure are. Flowers are expensive, though, aren't they?"

"Nah. Not for me. I work down at Cameron's Flower Shop and get all I can eat of the old unsold ones. Usually I bring them home on their very last legs. These are nicer than most."

Sweeney smiled remembering friend Annie's suggestion that he bring Marjorie flowers. Some joke.

"I didn't know you were a florist."

"You never asked. The sessions are weird that way, aren't they? You can sit and play with somebody every week for ages and never know what they do during the day."

"Rosie and I were just talking about that this morning."

Marjorie moved over casually to poke at two gladiolas whose long stems were beginning to sag toward the wall.

"Damn zombie flowers," she said. She poked again without effect and propped herself back against the kitchen counter.

"Huh? That's not what you tell your customers they're buying, is it?"

"But that's what they are, isn't it? They're just dead, pretending to be alive. They just sit around for a few days and finally can't keep up the pretense. Boom. Dead. Really dead. It's sad."

Sweeney fingered the nearest zombie gladiola. "I thought flowers were supposed to be cheery."

"So did I, for the longest time. Now, I'd just as soon they left them in the gardens. People ought to get out more, anyway. Maybe I've just been working there too long. Being stuck inside all the time can't be any better for people than it is for dead flowers."

She looked at the cigarette she'd been gesturing with and chuckled quietly. "I'm the one to talk about what's good for people, aren't I?" She stared at Sweeney as she inhaled, exhaled and tapped the ash into the sink.

"Still, I somehow expected to see you. Been quite a weekend, hasn't it?" She took another drag and blew it toward the ceiling.

"So far, yeah, I guess. I just dropped by to thank you for helping out last night, really."

"Really. Well, that's okay. Can't let fiddlers get killed at sessions, you know. Still . . ." She shook her head and stubbed out the half-smoked cigarette in a coffee cup. There was an awkward silence.

"Uh, speaking of . . ." began Sweeney haltingly, "You know, I never could figure that guy Blayney."

"Let's leave that, shall we?" she responded in a low, firm tone. "I've had to talk plenty about him to the cops last night. Rod and me both. And me going over everything with them again this morning. I'd rather not think about him anymore. He's dead, isn't he? That's finished." She paced back and forth in front of the sink.

"Unfortunately not for me, Marjorie. The police think I had something to do with it, you know."

"They as much as said the same about me this morning!" she flared, spinning around and brushing her hair out of her face. She leaned forward as if she'd waited all day for an opportunity to tell somebody about it. "Jesus! Rod and I split right after the fight. What do they think? That just because Rod hit him with a bottle we lurked outside waiting for the dude to finish the job? Christ! Why the hell would either of us . . . ? Give me a break!"

"You have nothing to worry about, though. You didn't even know him."

"You didn't know him either, right? I'm sure they believe that." She pulled out the third kitchen chair and sat down across the table from Sweeney, playing with one of the scattered books of matches.

"Look, Niall, since you're here, I don't know what other people have been saying about me, but there's nothing . . . there was nothing . . . you know." Sweeney didn't know, though her expression flashed a plea for understanding, then clouded again.

Vin listened, leaning on one elbow, his moustache sticking out between his fingers. "But Rod thinks different, does he?" he asked quietly.

Marjorie shifted in her seat, staring down at the match book. "You know Rod, you guys." She looked up and half-smiled. "Yeah, okay, maybe you don't know him. But we've worked things out. Really. Everything's really nice."

"I know," said Vin. "We all have our ups and downs. I sure as hell do, anyway." He saw the half-smile flicker across Marjorie's face again. "But an excitable guy like Rod, he had no business being jealous of just a guy in the bar."

"There was nothing like that! Annie wasn't there. She should have kept her big mouth shut."

"Annie was the soul of discretion, Marjorie, I assure you. She didn't tell us anything except your address."

"She talked to the damn police, didn't she? Don't tell me she didn't . . . It was so obvious . . ."

"Not to us, she didn't, I swear. But what did Annie tell the police?"

"Honestly, I'll never tell that woman another thing as long as I live!" She quickly rolled another cigarette and lit it with enthusiasm.

Sweeney leaned closer. "Listen, Marjorie. That could help, you know. What did Annie say to the police?" Marjorie seemed not to hear the question.

"The cops talked to you and Rod separately, did they?" asked Vin.

Marjorie snorted. "Yes, thank God!" She unknotted a little and gazed into the bowl of flowers.

"You know," she added, "it's just that some women go for that smooth Irish turn of phrase. If the guy's not bad looking he can fool a certain kind of woman for quite some time before she realizes that he's no poet and no gentleman. There's nothing behind the sweet talk but a perpetual lump in his pants."

Both Sweeney and Vin squirmed uncomfortably.

She looked up angrily. "I told the shit to leave me alone when he pulled it on me and that's the truth, whatever Annie says. Just like a vulture. He thought he could pick me up like . . . well, I don't know what when Rod and I . . . you know. In town exactly three days and he's trying to split me and Rod up! Thought he was a real pro. You can bet he's played that game often enough to get goddam good at it! And then all that fancy-dancy hinting to Rod. Sure I'd have liked to have seen him dead then myself. But that was then. Everything's been fine. Just fine."

The three sat in silence. Sweeney looked from Marjorie to the again sagging gladiolas and back. The pretty, dark-haired girl did not look like everything was fine at all. It was getting dark. All the delicate floral scents seemed to have backed away and disappeared from the smoky kitchen.

Yep. Definitely zombie flowers.

•

Sweeney was frustrated. Why couldn't life be like a Perry Mason episode, with some clown jumping up when all seemed lost and screaming, "Yes, I did it and it was the best thing I ever did in my life! He deserved to die, the swine!"

"So we don't know much more about Blayney than we did an hour ago," he muttered as he navigated the car back toward Hartford Street.

"Not much, but we confirmed that he put the old eye on Marjorie and that Rod wasn't crazy about it."

"True. That all must have happened when Marjorie stopped coming to the Bag for sessions. And that was right when Blayney first hit town. But did she stop coming because she was having a hot time, or to avoid Rod, or to avoid Blayney after the hot time cooled off, or for some other reason?"

They both rode in silence as the traffic crawled along.

"And how hot was it really? Did she sleep with him, do you think?"

"Aw, c'mon, Niall, what do you think?"

"How do you know?"

"It was something about the vehemence of her denial. I'd bet money that they had some sort of fling. And how casual was it if she remembers it was exactly his third day in town? He must really have been a foul son of a bitch, though, for her to snarl at him like that in the bar. I'd hate to think what he acted like after the lights were out." He shuddered theatrically.

"Oh, and she lied to the police about the affair, too."

Sweeney felt like he was about one synapse behind his friend. "How do you figure that?"

"Cause the police came and questioned her twice. Why would they have done that unless she lied to them and they called her on it? And the first time they questioned her she was with Rod and the second time she wasn't. Which means the cops got two conflicting stories about Blayney and Marjorie, the clean and innocent one from Marjorie first, no doubt, for the benefit of the darling boyfriend. Which means maybe we learned something about Annie, too."

"What's that?" queried Sweeney, trying to piece together his memory of the conversation.

"We thought Marjorie and Annie were great chums, right? And we've just seen how tight-lipped Annie can be when she's pressed. So, I'd have guessed that she'd have clammed up completely when the police asked her about her friends and all, but it seems she gave them all sorts of info or at least something suspicious about Marjorie having a romantic entanglement with Blayney. I ask you, whether the story was true or not, would a true friend have done a thing like that?"

"That is weird," conceded Sweeney. "That either means that Annie was pissed off at Marjorie for something or that Annie was so scared that she was willing to sacrifice even her friends to the police to get them to go away and leave her alone. Which do you think it is?"

The car lurched forward and Vin tugged at his seat belt with a grunt.

"From the way she acted in the bar today, she's certainly scared of something. But scared enough to toss friends to the lions? I couldn't say."

•

Elliot pulled into the curb on Castro and casually walked two blocks down to Eighteenth, then over toward Hartford Street. Castro Street was the usual frenetic tumble of dance music and yammering knots of people hurrying this way and that, all consciously on display. Elliot smiled as if to acknowledge that in his sensible gray suit he was hardly likely to blend in with the crowd in this neighborhood.

But as soon as he'd walked twenty paces off the bustling main street, the neighborhood seemed to quiet down to a murmur. It always seemed calm here. So close to the hubbub and yet so far. A leather-clad man walked a meticulously groomed poodle over on the other side back toward Castro, giving him no more than a cursory glance. Two children ran giggling down a flight of stairs and disappeared around the corner, leaving the street even quieter than before.

Elliot continued to walk, rounding the corner into Hartford Street, his eyes on the sidewalk, looking. For what?

He turned up toward the Sweeney house and stopped. He leaned against the cherry tree in thought, eyes flickering up and down the street, searching, taking in each male figure, noting build, dress, attitude. His eyes drifted down. There were eleven cigarette butts scattered in a small arc on the pavement. Dumped carelessly out the window by a passing motorist? No, each had been carefully ground out beneath a leather-soled shoe. Ground out on a corner where no one was likely to hang around long enough to smoke eleven cigarettes.

Elliot checked the street. He was standing in a shadow, yet was in a position to see anyone entering or leaving the Sweeney's front door. And he could clearly see the front window reflected in the large window of the ornate house across the street. Yes, someone had stood here watching for some time and had then moved on. But who? And why?

•

Vin pushed open the door and slouched out of the seat as the car rolled to a stop in the driveway. He waved up to the face that smiled briefly through the white lace curtains before vanishing.

"It'll be easy to find that bodhran player Levinson's address. He's going to State, so Christie'll have him in her student directory. Pete Cole's up in Santa Rosa someplace, Pat Kilbride's somewhere in town and Rod's at Marjorie's place. So do you want me to talk to any of them or just find out phone numbers and addresses?"

Sweeney bit his lip. "Better let me do the asking, Vinnie. I appreciate the help, but I'd better go home and try to come up with some idea of just what to ask."

Christie bounded down the steps and planted her hands on Vinnie's shoulders. "What a surprise! Would you two like to come in for tea or something?"

"Sorry, I'm just dropping Vin off to borrow your phone. I've got to go collect what's left of my wits." He smiled at the eager young face and drove off, having just decided what his next move would be.

•

Sweeney was so lost in thought that he didn't notice how relieved Rose was to see him as he walked in the door. Her relief quickly turned to curiosity as Sweeney wandered briefly into the living room, then turned and took a few paces down the hall.

"So what happened at the office? And what have you been doing for hours and hours?"

"I'll tell you in a minute. I've got an idea how I can get into the office another way."

"You didn't get into the office?"

"I said I'll tell you in a minute," and he disappeared into the bedroom.

It took Sweeney fifteen minutes to unearth his computer from the pile of books and laundry in the corner of the bedroom and slide it across the floor close enough to the telephone extension to connect the modem. Another ten minutes and he'd assured himself that he'd hooked the up modem correctly and the whole dusty mess was up and running. Rose peeked through the doorway once or twice, then decided to leave him to it, retreating quietly down the hall.

He hadn't touched the PC in ages for two equally compelling reasons. First, AdTech had upgraded to such a powerful office mainframe that anything slower made him feel as if he were wading through jello. Second, he was damned if he was going to let his work eat up his life like it was eating the lives of ever more of his AdTech colleagues. The zeal with which the big companies were wiring up their workers for 24-hour access triggered Sweeney's Luddite instincts. He could see it coming but he was determined to go down swinging.

Hence, the shrink-wrapped modem had been tossed in the corner and neither Old Man Berenson nor any needy code-jockey could invade his blissfully low-tech off-hours existence. But things were different now. His two worlds had collided with a vengeance.

He sat cross-legged on the floor, tapping out the access codes and general office IDs at the keyboard until the screen prompt blinked, telling him that he'd gained access to the AdTech mainframe. The prompt asked him for his secured access code. He scratched his knee and pondered what to do.

I wonder if they've locked me out of the whole system? he thought. Probably didn't bother, since the real barriers are set up around the individual applications and works in progress. Everybody knew I never logged in from outside. They probably forgot I even had a machine at home. He quickly tapped in his secured code and grinned. Hah! There was the menu listing all the access options, including the job he was writing on Friday and twenty assorted open projects the rest of the engineers were working on.

He chose his current job and tapped in his secondary access code. It came up invalid. Damn! He grimaced silently and tried another job and code. Again the system refused to respond. Busted.

He fidgeted with the mouse, clicking a series of menus listing more corners of the mainframe now barricaded behind a very solid, if electronic, brick wall. What exactly am I looking for? he asked himself finally. Even if I could find an archived copy of the Anglo-Irish code, I know what it said because I wrote the damn thing. However the launderers bypassed it, they didn't get in and alter it . . . or did they? He stared blankly at the computer screen for a moment, then rolled his eyes and muttered, "You idiot. Use the trap door."

Sweeney exited the menus and tapped out a dozen lines of assembly code, clicked once, and the screen was filled with baffling and user-hostile lines of gibberish. But this was gibberish that Sweeney knew well.

Sweeney's trap door wasn't fancy or foolproof. Just a few lines of assembly language code. But they were buried so deep in the AdTech operating system that someone would have to know exactly what they were looking for to find them. Sweeney had never planned to hack surreptitiously into AdTech from outside. He'd squirrelled away his trapdoor as a safety valve so he could get in clean without having to admit he'd forgotten his PIN numbers. So now he was in. Within ten seconds he was scanning down the code he'd written for Anglo-Irish Bank.

He scanned quickly. Hundreds of lines were exactly as he'd remembered them. He'd been scrolling through for over five minutes before the first anomaly appeared.

"Jesus," he whispered as he realized what the added lines would do. These were "Black Ops" commands, bypassing the cascading menus and creating nearly limitless connectivity within the Anglo-Irish system, which meant between damn near any bank and any other bank. The kicker was that they were "white rabbits." After the command had done its thing, the keystroke wasn't recorded. It was as if the transaction had never happened. "Jesus," he repeated. A phonied-up bank account in his name could be the least of his worries.

But what about me? he thought. Berenson froze me out of the job stuff, but did he bother to disconnect my phone? Sweeney typed in his extension number and the word GUINNESS. His phone messages appeared. He smiled.

Sweeney's momentary glow of victory dimmed quickly as he read through the mundane and unhelpful messages. A company softball game. A reminder to attend a Tuesday meeting that he would now surely miss. A stupid question from Karamardian. All left before the end of Friday and never erased. Nothing about the scandal.

Of course there would be nothing about the scandal on his phone. But what about Berenson's? Sweeney quickly logged off and typed in Berenson's extension. Again the screen answered with a polite request for a PIN number. So what was his number? It'd be somewhere in the system's assembly code, but it might take hours to find it. Sweeney shifted his weight and tried to think how imaginative Wendell P. Berenson would be about a PIN number. Not imaginative at all, he decided, typing in his boss' initials.

"Bingo!" he cried. Several messages dated Saturday and signed by Crane, the VP of Operations, a couple of programmers and a secretary in payroll rolled blithely across the screen. It seemed likely that the whole staff was working through the weekend, from the look of the message activity.

The first few messages dealt with the initial Anglo-Irish panic. But there was nothing beyond the information Sweeney had received from Inspector Elliot already. The last two messages, however, were decidedly different.

The first of the two read: "WPB—After analysts' meeting, please contact Insp. Elliot. He returned your call to say that no charge is pending against Niall Sweeney. Seems to think entire fraud run from other end. Thanks you for your cooperation. Wishes to talk further.—Crane/Sat/4:35 pm"

It was followed by: "WPB—N. Sweeney final paycheck prepared with termination paperwork. Do we mail it to listed address or will he pick it up here?—C.W., Payroll/Sat/8:10 pm."

Well, that's what I call good news and bad news, nodded Sweeney. He wasn't going to be thrown in the slammer . . . at least not for laundering Irish money . . . but his boss was going to fire him anyway. That hotheaded old coot never would listen to reason.

He could find no more messages worth reading and logged off, disconnecting the machines in disgust. He shoved them back into the corner and sprinkled the laundry back over them until they'd again disappeared from view. Then he walked slowly down the hall in search of human companionship.

•

"And from that Vinnie deduced that Marjorie had had more than a casual fling with Blayney?" asked Rose, as Sweeney stacked and restacked the music books on the corner of the coffee table.

"That's what he said. And that's the whole report of the conversation. Make any sense to you?"

"As a matter of fact, it's a long shot but I reluctantly admit it might make sense. Vinnie has more savvy about women than you credit him with, Niall."

"Then why does he waste his time with women like Lydia? I know, I know, he's grown out of that phase and is now enamored of wholesome Catholic girls. But getting back to Marjorie, what the hell am I supposed to do now?"

Rose perched on the arm of the blue chair. "Your personal interviews and telephone espionage haven't turned up anything earthshaking. How about doing nothing for now. Just wait and see what happens next."

"And you know what's likely to happen next? Guilty or innocent, Berenson's thrown me out in the cold rain and snow."

"Well, I made a call to Dublin."

"What?"

"Don't worry, we can afford it. I remembered my friend Harry from the English Lit Department was on sabbatical and doing some research on Joyce at Trinity. I checked at the office and Sal had a number for him so I called for help." She straightened proudly.

"You just called him? Just like that?"

"Sure. It's easy. You pick up the phone and take your finger and push the little buttons until . . ."

"You know that's not what I mean. I mean, what could this Harry fellow possibly tell us that will help get me out of this mess?"

"That's what I'm trying to tell you. I asked Harry to fax me everything he can find that Blayney ever had published or anything else he can find about him. My guess is that Blayney's been on this Saint Ronan kick since before he came to the U.S. I expect to find evidence to prove that he was harboring a long-standing fixation and that by sending him that CD to review all you did was make yourself the last in a string of Sweeneys that he felt obliged to destroy as the avenging, if addled, Saint Ronan. I'll bet I'll find lots of Sweeneys if Harry comes through with the goods."

"Hm. I suppose there's no harm done, so long as Inspector Elliot doesn't hear about this."

Rose jumped up in alarm. "Hell no! We have to let him believe that we're letting the wheels of justice roll along by themselves. But besides pissing off a few cops, what do we have to lose?"

"What indeed. And you've given me an idea. What if I call Brian Byrne and see what he can find out about Blayney."

"Brian Byrne? But you don't even know where he lives. Knowing him, he probably doesn't have a phone."

"I'll call him at Flannery's. He's always there. And I still have the number in my old address book. What's the time difference . . . eight hours? I'll set the alarm for two and call him at 10 a.m. Dublin time. If anybody can find out something about Blayney that the cops missed, it'll be Brian. And he'd do that much for me, no questions asked. Ten a.m. He should be there by then."

"But it's Sunday tomorrow. Aren't the pubs closed for Holy Hour or something on Sundays?"

Sweeney had never once set foot in a church during his stay in Dublin. He racked his brain but could only remember Sunday morning as his morning to sleep late.

"I honestly don't recall when the damn antediluvian laws let them open on Sundays. But if my theory is correct, Brian Byrne will be at Flannery's, open or closed, if only by special arrangement with the management."

•

The reel was running so fast it sent explosions of adrenaline down the spines of the musicians, as they feverishly sawed, plucked, fingered and banged away. Sweeney sat in the middle of them all, his shirt open to the waist, a glazed expression on his face, his head tilted back, letting out occasional inarticulate whoops as the melody swung back around and began again faster than before.

He looked down at his fellow musicians and his eyes swung from face to face. They all were staring hard at Sweeney: Marjorie, Peter, Rod, Levinson, even Kilbride, their faces strangely expressionless and intense. Not missing a note, they played faster and faster, all with the same curiously hard looks in their eyes.

The room began to spin. Just behind him Sweeney heard someone step into the circle. Then a screeching roar filled his ears and he spun around to find himself staring into the end of a floating, disembodied bagpipe chanter, playing as furiously as all the rest of the musicians, but in the wrong key.

•

"Niall, get up! It's two a.m.!" Rose's muffled voice came from under the pillow. Sweeney snapped the key down on the annoying drony electronic alarm clock and fumbled for his robe and slippers.

He wandered to the kitchen, poured a glass of orange juice, scuffed back to the cluttered guest room, scratched his head and sat down, staring at the phone.

The line crackled and bleeped, there was a funny echo and then the familiar double pips of the Irish telephone system rang distantly through the wire. Paddy Flannery's gruff, clipped voice answered, "Flannery's."

I'll be on the phone all night if I start talking with Flannery. "Is Brian Byrne there?"

The few tinkling sounds in the background weren't enough to tell Sweeney whether the bar was open or whether it was merely occupied by friends of the family at this time of day. In a few moments a familiar voice said, "Hello, this is Byrne. Who's talkin' please?"

Sweeney greeted his old drinking companion as casually as if they'd been together the night before.

"Sure, this is an unexpected pleasure, Niall, boy! Did I ever thank ye for the card at Christmas? And how's the wife? Any children yet?"

"No, fine, and no in that order, Brian," Sweeney laughed. Of course Byrne had never thanked him for the card. No one in Ireland ever wrote or called you back. "But Brian, I have a problem, a very big problem that perhaps you can help me out of. It has to do with the murder of a fellow named Blayney. There are some police types here who think I killed him." And Sweeney gave the rough facts of the murder as briefly as he knew how.

"He's quite the subject of conversation hereabouts too, is Blayney. Quite a notorious class of a fellow, he is. Got himself eviscerated, say the papers. You saw it, did ye? This'll be great crack for later on."

"I'd rather you kept this to yourself for now, Brian."

"Ah, well, every Garda patrolman in Dublin knows who done it. Of course, no two are agreein' on the culprit or the reason for it at all. Never heard such gold-plated opinion bein' bandied about and none of it makin' a penny's worth of sense. It's been a source of great amusement for me to sit and listen to all this talk and decide if your man the Garda with a pint or two in him is just blatherin' or if he's the right Sherlock he claims to be. And whether it turns out to be a jealous husband on the one hand or a notorious international crime syndicate on the other, there's no Sherlocks standin' at this bar. Not in my considered judgment."

"I wish I could say I'm as amused by it all as you are, Brian."

"Oh, of course, of course, boyo. Dreadful business. But you say it was in an Irish pub? How is it possible to maintain a real Irish pub as far away as San Francisco, now?"

"Well, I admit the Guinness isn't nearly as fresh, but it's not bad as far as it goes. Gilmore, the owner, is Irish himself, after all, and manages to impart enough realism to the place."

"Gilmore? He wouldn't be a Dalkey lad, now, would he? I thought young Declan Gilmore bought a pub out west there someplace. San Francisco, or maybe San Antonio."

"It's not Declan, anyway, it's Joe, and he's from Belfast via Australia. You wouldn't know him. But that's not all of it. I've been cashiered from my job because the cops have let my boss believe I might be mixed up with the Anglo-Irish Bank scam as well."

The voice on the other end of the wire said nothing for a moment, though Sweeney heard the continuing clink of glasses in the background.

"Now that's something new, me boy. There's been nothin' in the papers here to connect the killin' with that, now!"

"That's what I'm telling you. I'm in deep shit!"

"An evocatively American and entirely unpleasant metaphor, me friend, but one singularly applicable. Right enough. I'll keep this bit to meself for now, I think. So it seems there are political facets, rather than romantic ones, eh? I'll find out what I can. How am I to be reportin' me findings to ye, though? If Paddy Flannery thought I was after usin' the bar phone to ring America he'd have me filletted and hung to cure as sure as you're born!"

"I'll call you back same time tomorrow, Brian, there at the bar. And thanks for whatever you can come up with. Only do try to keep the police from knowing you're asking around at my request."

"Now why would I be tellin' the Gardai anything, lad? They know less than nothin' about this boy and he'll be happy to see it stay that way. But, don't call me this early, lad. Give me till evenin' sometime. I might have somethin' for ye by then. What time is it there in San Francisco, anyway?"

"Two in the morning."

"Jesus! You sound all in. Run along to bed and I'll do what I can. God bless."

Chapter Eight

A gray light from a gray sky woke Sweeney. He reached over sleepily toward Rose's pillow to find she had already gotten up. The pillow was cold. He lay staring at the ceiling for a moment, scenes from the last two days parading through his mind. No, they weren't parading. They were just staring back, all jumbled up, disordered and disconnected in time and space. A deep longing washed over him. A longing simply to fall asleep again and let the dreams sort themselves out without him.

A trash can lid in a neighboring backyard clattered noisily, triggering a half-hearted bark from a dog down the block. Even the dogs sounded reluctant to wake up today.

Wrapped in the comfortable familiarity of his bathrobe, Sweeney ambled down the darkened hall to the kitchen, where a warm, yellow light illuminated the steam from the softly boiling kettle. Rose sat at the table, holding the phone, scribbling rapidly on a legal pad, the tip of her tongue stuck out in concentration. The scribbling stopped and the tongue retreated.

"That's great, Harry," she almost shouted, stopping Sweeney dead in the doorway where he attempted unsuccessfully to sort all his hair into the same direction. Rose flashed a distracted smile in his direction. "But did you read any of . . . mm hm . . . no, you're right, I'll know what I'm looking for. So you don't know when . . . Right. It'll get here when it gets here. Thanks a ton, Harry! I owe you one."

Rose cradled the receiver, slapped the pen down on the pad and turned to Sweeney with an expression of satisfaction.

"Sorry about yelling like that. Bad connection. Did I wake you?" Tipping her chair back, she turned off the kettle and beckoned. He leaned down, tolerated a kiss, then rubbed his unshaven chin, wondering why this woman he'd married was always so damned alert.

"I feel like I could sleep for a week," he said as he rummaged for the coffee.

"That's not surprising, when you get up in the middle of the night to make phone calls and lie staring at the ceiling for hours."

"You know that's not what I mean."

"Yeah," she said quietly as Sweeney assembled and poured the coffee.

She took a breath and continued. "But don't you think you've had enough coffee? Why not just go back to bed and let everything work itself out. What do you think you're going to accomplish wandering around in a foul, caffeinated humor?"

"Jesus Christ, Rose! What do you expect me to do? Sit and grin? All that running around yesterday, getting all excited, looking for God knows what . . . what good did it do? And what the hell is the point of calling up old pub crawling buddies in Ireland? He probably forgot all about me two minutes after I hung up."

"That's not what you thought last night."

"I don't know. I don't know what matters anymore. I don't know what's real anymore." He rattled open the window, then closed it again.

"I'm real."

He just stared out through the dusty glass, gesturing helplessly. "No, I didn't mean . . . It's just that this other bullshit is more real than I'd like it to be." He turned and looked into her eyes in silence.

"The real world doesn't just disappear when you want it to, does it? We've been pretty good at pretending, though, these last few years. You always had your fiddling and I just dove into the old books. Instant Never-Never Land. Good-bye modern world both ways. But sometimes pretending doesn't do any good."

"Like now, for instance."

"Like now. No sense in feeling like the universe has it out for you personally, though. Stuff like this happens to everyone, one way or another. Well, maybe not just like this. But you have to deal with it, Niall. Nobody can do it for you. Snap out of it."

Sweeney rubbed his eye and essayed a smile. "I'm sorry, Rose. This isn't like me." He took a large swallow of coffee and smacked his lips theatrically. "Right," he said with slightly forced optimism, "I'll soon be ready to face the real world."

Rose glanced at him again, then tapped her pencil on her assembled notes and redirected her attention. "Speaking of the real world, I've just had a call that might help us out."

"Oh, right, that was Harry, wasn't it." Sweeney sat down clumsily, splashing coffee onto the legal pad.

Rose leaned over her notes with a controlled eagerness. "Harry's being a huge help. Of course, nothing was open on Sunday, but he's in tight with the head librarian." What a lucky bastard Harry was. The thought of unlimited access to the Trinity Library made her smile in spite of the otherwise somber mood currently occupying the kitchen.

A wry look tweaked one corner of her mouth. "I said two years ago that the wrong person in this house got sent to Dublin. In six months I could have laid the groundwork for two PhDs! All you did was learn 642 fiddle tunes and try not to fricassee yourself on the high-voltage sockets."

"And drink a carload of very good beer," added Sweeney, suddenly thirsty for a Smithwick's Red Ale out of the tap, an indescribable nutty brown joy he'd almost forgotten. "And that's all the more reason I should have gone instead of you. All you drink is California wine. Imagine what that would have cost over there if you could find it at all! You would have scurried home in a month, bankrupt and starving."

Rose brightened inwardly at the realization that at least for a moment she'd coaxed some humor out of her husband. She felt her wariness recede a little as she returned to her scribbled notes.

"Anyway, Harry apparently got into the research stacks after hours in exchange for the promise of some fabulous restaurant feed."

"A fabulous restaurant feed in Dublin? Wasn't Harry a vegetarian?"

"Don't be mean. There must be good vegetarian restaurants in Dublin."

"Sure, if you like your salad fried."

"Anyway, he's faxing a bunch of articles to me at school as soon as he can sneak in and use the department fax machine at his end. He found some very interesting things."

"Like what?"

"Well, he's sending over all the articles Blayney had printed in the *Irish Press* and in some smaller papers around Belfast and Dublin. He even found some of his poetry printed in a small literary journal published out in County Clare. He didn't know what to tell me about it all, since I didn't tell him exactly what we were looking for. But it sounds like a good start."

"But a start toward what?" Sweeney got up and stared out at the still-gray haze obscuring all but the closest rooftops.

"I told you. The key to Blayney's murder is his Ronan-Sweeney fixation. We find out all we can about Blayney and his weird delusions and then we work backwards and figure out who had enough of a reason to kill him. And in the process we clear you."

"Ha. You make it sound so simple. So when do we run over to the office and examine the documents in the case?"

"I don't know. When they show up. We'll have to give Harry a chance to be devious. Shouldn't be too long, though. Maybe he can sneak the pages in when the department shuts down for the day."

"And what do we do in the meantime?"

"Well, you might take a nap."

"I might." He reached over and gently and deliberately unfastened Rose's hair clip.

•

The low fog still hanging lightly over Hartford Street felt a little colder and lay a little thicker along the waterfront and up Mission Street to the angular gray edifice of police headquarters. Inspector Elliot sat with his back to his desk and perused the contents of the manila file in his lap by the chill gray morning light. He ignored the bustle beyond the glass partition. His third reading of the file was not revealing any glimmer missed in the first two readings.

"People should demand more information on tenants before renting out their damned apartments," he muttered to himself, as Detective Leigh entered and glanced over a little warily. Elliot closed the file and tossed it across the desk.

"Blayney's landlady had nothing useful to tell us. She's an elderly absentee landlady living in Nevada City with her even more elderly sister and had checks deposited directly into her savings account. She never thought much about the apartment, except when the local real estate agent listed for a new renter. She doesn't have a clue whether she's insured for explosions and her insurance company is not being particularly helpful. She doesn't know a thing about Blayney, either. Never even met him."

"Never met him? How'd she agree to rent to him, then?"

"Through a rental agent. So she did know one thing. She recalled that the agent had said he was a writer. She'd agreed to rent to him because that seemed to her to be a safe and quiet career for a young man."

"She must have stopped reading books before Henry Miller was published to think anything like that," mused Leigh. Elliot merely grimaced.

"Anything to report?"

"I came to tell you they've finished with Mr. Sweeney's car in the lab. It checks out clean. No fingerprints or anything else unusual beyond the obvious bloodstains on the door."

"No fingerprints, you say?"

"No sir, somebody touched the car door that one time, but must have been so wet that the blood just globbed. Nothing we can use, I'm afraid."

Elliot dropped the papers on his desk and looked up. "Bernie, how did Blayney pay for that damn apartment?"

"By money order, sir. It should be right there in the report."

"No, I mean how did he pay for it? Rent was $900 a month. He couldn't have made more than what?—two hundred a week writing part time for that dinky little paper? Where'd the rest come from?"

"We couldn't find out a thing from Immigration. Blayney was still over on an extended tourist visa, so he hadn't had to prove income or savings balances to get in. He bought the money orders for cash at the post office, so there's no tracing it."

"Right." Elliot gazed down at the file while Leigh fidgeted. "Oh, go ahead and sit down, Bernie. There's something still eating at me about all this—something I can't add up no matter how many directions I come at it."

"I think I know what you mean, sir. I've got a few nagging questions myself."

Elliot stood up and cranked open one of the windows. He turned and leaned heavily against the sash, letting the coolness pour down his open shirt collar and past his ears.

"The bombing was done by a professional. That much we can be sure of. And the knifing was done with a professional thoroughness as well. The problem is, why the knifing at all? Why knife the guy in the doorway if you were going to blow him up in his bed four hours later?"

Leigh nodded. "The bombing was probably meant to destroy some evidence of IRA connections or something. You know, wipe out any papers or anything. I thought you suggested that yourself, sir."

"Did I? Then I was hasty. Look, there's an obvious flaw to that theory. What is it?" He stared immobile at Leigh, fixing him with an expression that said his chances of promotion might depend on his answer.

Carefully, the younger man replied, "The bomb was meticulously prepared and placed under the bed. We know Blayney did all his work at the desk in the other room. That means that the bomber wasn't trying to destroy the desk and papers and stuff. If he'd wanted to do that he'd have blown the thing off in the other room. He must have expected Blayney to be asleep in bed at 3 a.m. Therefore . . ."

"Therefore the bomb was a murder attempt on a man who had already been murdered! Right." Elliot smiled as Leigh exhaled in relief.

"But does that mean that there were two professionals going after the same victim? What is this, some sort of bizarre contest? A bet? What?"

"Well, that touches on what was bothering me earlier," said Leigh, leaning forward with his hands on his knees. "I've been wondering why a professional killer would have cut Blayney up on his doorstep where anybody could find the body at any time, rather than picking the lock and doing it in the apartment, where there'd be so much less danger of discovery."

Elliot tapped the desk with his pen for a moment. "You mean that a real pro would have picked the lock and laid in wait inside?"

"Something like that. It's just that there's so much random foot traffic out in the Avenues that somebody might wander by at any moment and witness an attack. I know if I were a pro, I'd have done it behind closed doors if I had a choice."

"Good point. So would I. But that gives us a choice of two questions to answer. Was the murderer really a pro? Or was it that the murderer had no other choice?"

The two men sat in silence for a minute. Elliot said, almost to himself, "The door was closed and locked. The key was in his pocket. Was he just going in or had he come down to answer the door?"

"Um, sir, about Mr. Sweeney's car. Do you want me to call him and tell him he can pick it up?"

"No, I'll tell him in person on my way home. He ought to be happy about the news from Dublin."

"And do we continue with the surveillance team?"

Elliot looked irritated. "Have they learned anything yet?"

"No sir, not yet. They're not sure yet that there's anyone to watch."

"Bah!"

Leigh took the comment as a dismissal and left Elliot tapping the desk again with his pen.

•

Sweeney was just getting out of the shower when the phone rang. Rose ran to the kitchen and trotted back a minute later and stuck her head excitedly around the bathroom door.

"That was school. Somebody in the office noticed a huge pile of papers addressed to me littering the floor around the fax machine, so they asked me to come down and clean up my mess. I don't know why they get so upset. I'm not the one who monopolizes the stupid machine. Anyway, I'll be back soon!" Sweeney reached for a towel as she turned and jogged down the hall.

Flying out the door she plowed into Vin on the porch. "Whoa! Where's the fire?" Behind him Christie giggled as both Rose and Vin grabbed at opposite banisters to keep from falling over. Rose righted herself and smiled.

"I'm running over to the office to get some new information. Sorry I can't stop and talk. Oh, if you go in to chat with Niall, give him a minute to get decent. He's just getting out of the shower."

"Well, we really just came by to see if there was any news. We were on our way out to the campus to drop off term papers. Mind if we hitch a ride? It would save us both driving. We can see Niall later. I hate rousting a man out of the shower."

They all maneuvered themselves into the parts of Rose's unkempt old Dodge not stacked with boxes, magazines, journals, and papers and drove off.

"Term papers? At least I know they're not from my class."

"No, I had one due in Poetry. Did it on Blake's *Marriage of Heaven and Hell*. Pretty good, if I do say so myself."

"The Perilous Path, indeed," nodded Rose in approval. "One of my favorite Blake works. Are you taking poetry, too, Christie?"

"No, not this term," answered the silhouette of brown curls in the back seat. "Mine's just for the History survey course. On Thomas Aquinas and the changes he brought about by giving a religious support to reason and realism." She managed to get it all out in one breath.

"That's a mouthful! Sounds like more of an undertaking than Blake."

"Not really. It was easier than the other suggested topics the professor gave us. You see, Daddy was always studying religious history, even though he wasn't always completely reasonable and realistic about it. So he had plenty of unusual books in the house I could use."

Rose was impressed. "It must be great to have a father like that to help you with your papers. Do you let him . . ."

Vin tapped Rose on the knee and coughed. "Christie's dad died of a heart attack a couple of years ago, Rose."

Rose darted a glance into the rearview but couldn't make out Christie's expression in the shadows of the back seat. "I'm sorry. I didn't know."

She drove on in silence for a block or two. God, she thought, it must be awful to lose your father at that age.

"So, Rose," prompted Vin, "what's all this new information you mentioned? I thought the police told you to leave things alone."

Rose glanced at Vin as Christie leaned forward intently. "I don't know, Vinnie. I could get into trouble with the police for this, and maybe it's better you didn't know about it."

"Not know about it? Rose, I swear I'll burst if you don't tell me what's going on! I mean, I've been helping Niall up til now, haven't I? I've got some ideas about all this. That is, Christie and I have been talking and . . ."

"Okay, Vinnie! Enough! I'll talk, but keep your lip buttoned if you know how." Vinnie uttered a snort of protest.

"And Christie, you are sworn to secrecy. Whatever Vinnie has told you up to now—it's to go no further, understand?"

"My lips are sealed, Rose. We just want to help."

Rose gave them a brief outline of her Ronan versus Sweeney theory and how she intended to prove the literary crime connection. Both Vin and Christie listened with interest but with expressions betraying skepticism. Vin chewed for a while on his moustache before commenting.

"I don't know. There was something distinctly fishy going on with Marjorie when Niall and I talked to her. And pardon me for saying so, but it does sound a lot more likely."

Rose thought about the meaning of the word 'likely.' Her idea may not be 'likely' but—she couldn't explain just why—it felt 'right.'

Vin continued, "Why don't we go back and make her tell the truth about her and Blayney?"

"What truth, Vinnie?" Rose asked, shaken from her train of thought. "And how would you force her to tell if she didn't want to? You've been watching too many bad detective movies. Anyway, I don't think she had anything to do with it, no matter whether she had a fling with Blayney or not. It might be more useful to talk with Rod about it. Just because she went out of her way to lie about Blayney to the police to keep Rod from hearing about it doesn't mean he didn't know all about it already."

Vin whistled, then opened his mouth to say something, but was interrupted as Rose pulled up to a stop light. "I think Rose is right, Vincent," put in Christie. "After all, you can't blame a girl for falling for another guy if she's broken up with her boyfriend, can you? I understand how some girls can fall for that stuff."

"What stuff?"

"You know, that Irishman stuff. All glib and convincing. My friend Sylvia, you know, she ran off with that Irish guy on the church trip. Boy, was he smooth! Like a regular poet. Sylvia'd never had that kind of attention from the dumb boys back home. She didn't come back til the next morning! If I hadn't lied to Sister, Sylvia might have gotten sent home, or worse."

"That was true and blue of you. But still, you can't say all poetic men are assholes. Mostly guys with poetic souls are utter gentlemen."

"Oh no. But I'd never want a guy like that."

Vin spun around. "Huh? A guy like what?"

"No, Vincent, I like you because you always say the wrong thing and then apologize so sweetly."

Rose's gales of laughter echoed down the street as Vin sat next to her, unable to think of a thing to say.

•

One cigarette lay smoldering in the ashtray cluttered with the corpses of a dozen more. Alone in the far corner of the darkened bar, the man downed the last drop of whiskey in his glass and quietly pulled a small black notebook from the inside pocket of his jacket. Page after page was covered in erratic, angular script. The man leafed impatiently through the notebook as he had done countless times, stopping at familiar references, poring over passages whose sense remained elusive.

A spark of frustration flared in his eyes for a moment. Then just as quickly his expression snapped back to one of reptilian cold as he turned back a few pages to one that did make sense, that did show him his next step. There was no reason to get angry. With a ball-point pen he crossed out one name on the page, then circled another, writing carefully: "not what he seems?"

The man replaced the notebook in his pocket. He left the forgotten cigarette burning in the ashtray as he emerged from the bar into the subdued brightness of the San Francisco midday and turned to walk unnoticed up Clement Street.

•

Sweeney took no nap. He made another pot of coffee and looked ahead nervously to his next call to Brian Byrne. At least tonight he had a fighting chance of sleeping until morning.

This has all got to blow over soon, he thought. Brian will come up with something I can tell the police to end this nightmare. Then I can get some rest again. He ran some water in the sink and half-heartedly washed a few of the accumulated coffee cups.

The ocean breeze wafted among the Victorian eaves and through the kitchen window, carrying with it the tinkling echoes of music collected from the windows down the block—bits of bottom-heavy rap mixed with Brahms,

Sinatra and who knows what. These were the simple city scraps of melody that Sweeney and Rose enjoyed so much in the quiet afternoons of Hartford Street. But today, rather than soothing him, the sounds just made him more aware that the simple quiet days of the past were probably gone for good.

He wandered into the living room and picked up his fiddle case absentmindedly, perching on the end of the coffee table. He opened the case and gazed disconsolately at the instrument, his dear old friend, now scarred and scuffed and forever changed.

"Dammit!" he exclaimed. "I'm not going to let this shit bleed all the music out of my life." He went to rosin his bow and stopped suddenly. What was left of the bow was still tucked into the top of the case, but it would never make another note sing. He lifted it out gingerly and ran his fingers up and down, as he would try to soothe a broken limb. But the smooth, carved wood could never heal itself.

Sweeney placed it on the table, unable to bring himself to toss it in the trash or in the fireplace. He went around to the hall closet. Digging in the back end, filled with complex smells and unidentifiable gloomy shapes, he came up with another fiddle case even dustier and shabbier than the other. This was just a flea-market special, the home of a cheap cracker-box fiddle that he'd picked up for $25 and saved for a rainy day. The strings were slack and the soundpost rattled uselessly around inside the instrument, but the old student bow clipped in the top still had some hair on it, so he retrieved the bow and reinterred the old fiddle and case back in the forgotten recesses of the closet.

It would take more than a few swipes of rosin to make this bow work well, Sweeney knew, but he would have to be satisfied with any port in the storm.

I suppose one has to be realistic at a time like this, he thought to himself. I'm going to have to get used to a new one sooner or later.

He began playing a slow air while he paced in rhythm in his accustomed figure-eight route around the middle of the room. The recent days' events began to blur a little in his mind as the melody came and went, repeating and echoing in a natural reminder of the basic circles and loops the universe was supposed to be woven from.

One air became another. The melancholy strains interwove with new melody, changing keys, changing voicings. Occasional scraps of lyrics would wander into Sweeney's mind along with an appropriate tune. More often, though, the melody was its own lyrics. The emotion carried by the tune was too ancient to be sung in English, perhaps too ancient to be understood in any human tongue.

Sweeney lost track of time, pacing there with his slow airs. Eventually, pulling his mind back to Hartford Street with a conscious effort he noticed that he had been playing a particularly haunting air, one that he hadn't played in ages.

The image of the rocky, barren hillsides of West Clare flooded his mind with a multi-sensory clarity and force that stopped him in mid-stride and left him standing, fiddle in hand, staring unseeing into the cold fireplace.

The Fiddler's Gold Ring, it had been called. It was just a plain gold-plated Claddagh ring. But it was given to the winner of the slow air contest. I played my heart out for that contest. I really did. Funny little place, the Glen Bolcain Pub. Inagh was a spot where the Clare fiddlers were proud to collect once a year for a ceili and contest and conversation. I was lucky even to hear about it, it was so small and local. Some of the players as close as Galway had no knowledge of it. Still, it wasn't so local that they didn't welcome any outsider who loved the slow airs as much as they did.

And I came in second. The ring went to a red-cheeked kid from Kilfenora, but that's hardly surprising. He'd grown up listening to Tommy Peoples and had even led the old master home to his red-painted door when the last jar had gotten the better of him. Yes, I came in second. And I never played that air better before or since.

Sweeney began playing again, letting the melody linger even longer on the bow than before. He closed his eyes and was sitting again on a worn wooden bench before a peat fire, a fresh pint of Guinness placed on the table before him. The murmur of conversations just too low to catch rounded out the warm brown corners of the oak-beamed room. But this was no true memory of the past. This was a wish for the perfect past—or was it the perfect future—because Rose sat there by his side, basking in the warmth of the hearth, her strong presence beside him.

The past was never perfect. Rose had not been there to hear his entry in the Glen Bolcain contest. Perhaps it was her absence that had allowed him to feel the poignancy of the air deeply enough to play it so well, just that once. He sighed and then shook his head, silently cursing.

Enough of the maudlin crap. What I've got to do is to knock this fluff out of my brain. I've got to think! And with that, he launched into the fastest reel he could think of, squeaking a little with the funky old bow, but sending tiny powdery tufts of rosin floating toward the carpet at each emphatic downbeat.

•

When Rose strode expectantly around the corner toward both her office and the department fax machine at the end of the hall, a knot of students lounging in the hall greeted her outside her door.

Oh, Christ! she thought, picking up her pace and rummaging in her purse for her office key. I forgot—today—office hours! She aimed a quietly apologetic smile toward the waiting students, unlocked the office and flicked on the light. With her mind locked on Niall's predicament and her hopes that Harry's articles would solve it all, she couldn't remember at first what she'd been teaching in class.

She spent the next hour dealing with the real and imagined panics and horrors of her undergraduate students. For all her complaining, she did have a few talented writers in her survey course this term and was looking forward to what they might accomplish in Heroic Literature next term. She found she was really only giving half an ear to the students, though, wishing that this continuing parade of academics would evaporate and allow her time to sprint down the hall and retrieve Harry's Irish treasures. Finally she imparted some kind suggestions to an earnest pre-law student who couldn't write a sentence without at least one subordinate clause, firmly refused to change the grade on his last paper, and grabbed her purse to leave.

A head popped in the doorway, followed by the rest of a pretty, red-headed girl in a yellow parka. Rose started to groan, then recognized her. A good student. Not a complainer.

"Oh, hello, Violet," she said warmly, standing at the desk holding her bag. "What's up?"

"Were you just leaving? Sorry to hold you up. I was looking for Christie and thought she came in with you."

"She and Vinnie hitched a lift to campus with me but I haven't seen them in an hour or so. She probably went home. Do you have her address?"

The girl giggled. "I should have it! We're sisters!" Rose rolled her eyes to signify "Aw-shucks-I-should-have-known." Of course they were sisters. Violet Reese was a little shorter and fairer but had the same delicate curls dancing on her forehead and a little silver Celtic cross of her own hanging above her collar on a thin silver chain. Rose had been so caught up in the whirlwind of the last few days that she'd never connected up first-name-only Christie with Violet Reese.

"So, Violet, what sort of disaster are you trying to avert this afternoon?" Rose felt immensely relieved when Violet pulled out her most recent paper and made it clear that the most important thing in the world was her grade point average.

Chapter Nine

Rose carefully inserted the sheaf of slippery pages into a large manila envelope, which, in turn, she popped into her oversized shoulder bag and headed for the door and fresh air. She was dying to dig into all the stuff Harry had sent through the wires, but had to admit reluctantly that it was only fair to do it together with Niall.

It seems I can only last in that building about an hour, she thought, before oxygen deprivation kicks in and my brain begins to turn into an oversized raisin. Oh, for an office with a window!

The soft breeze and the warmth of the afternoon brought immediate color back to her cheeks as she descended the wide cement stairs and began to cut a diagonal path across the campus.

San Francisco State bustled at its usual level. Students in pairs and knots of three or four sauntered this way and that, engaged in animated discussions. A few earnest readers lay propped on one elbow or sat hunched cross-legged on the grass, absorbed by their studies. The ever-present roaring rush of the boulevard in the distance kept the place from ever being a quiet study spot. But most of the young urban students seemed able to tune out the background noise as if it were just so much tape hiss.

Rose broke step suddenly as she realized she'd almost trodden on the heel of the boy walking down the path in front of her. He was a lanky-haired student, dressed in a culturally acceptable uniform of faded blue jeans, lightweight red windbreaker, worn sneakers and backpack and sauntering along with the same youthful abstraction as most of the other students on the quad. But the boy she'd almost tripped over piqued Rose's interest in that he was pacing along with a bodhran under his right arm.

Well I'll be, she thought. I've seen him before. And jogging a couple of steps to catch up, she tapped him on the shoulder.

"Excuse me, but haven't I seen you playing at the Bag of Nails?" The young man turned his thin face to her, wearing an expression of slightly vacant interest. It seemed to dawn on him that Rose was not a fellow student as he flicked his eyes up and down and began to fidget. He ventured a slight smile which didn't light up his face as much as it accentuated the unfortunate way his features were arranged. Under the sprigs of dirty brownish hair his eyes were small and deeply set over unnecessarily prominent cheekbones. The cheekbones made his weak chin look weaker. The smile just made it worse, but he responded pleasantly enough after the moment's hesitation, "Oh yes. The Friday night sessions. Are you a musician? I don't remember you playing."

"No, I go in sometimes with my husband, though. He plays the fiddle. He played last Friday, in fact. Niall Sweeney?"

"Oh yes." The young man looked down for a moment at the drum in his hand. "That was a very unfortunate evening, wasn't it, um . . ."

"Rose. Rose Sweeney."

"Charlie Levinson. Pleased to meet you," replied the student, his words muscled out with an effort through a hint of a stutter. He offered a limp handshake. He looked uncomfortable but didn't offer anything else.

"I was wondering if you might be able to tell me something about what happened the other night. My husband was hurt, you know, and I've naturally been a little concerned."

"Yes, and that other guy who was killed," Charlie Levinson intoned haltingly, as if he were considering every word with utmost care. "That was a very negative thing. I've been processing that evening pretty constantly but it's all still kinda unclear. I don't . . . don't know. You teach around here, don't you?" He slung his backpack off his shoulder and plopped it down on the pavement. From where Rose was standing, she could see it held a few messy notebooks and a bright red trade paperback emblazoned 'Janov.'

"That's right. English Lit, mostly. You said you were processing?"

"Oh yeah. Well, um, you see, that's really why I was there in the first place. I've been studying psych for three years and finally found some good ways to process my negative energies. You know, the deep-seated resentments and blocks that keep you—keep me, that is—from growing into a whole man. You know?" The subject was apparently a difficult one for him. The stutter had become more pronounced.

Rose nodded, less in agreement than simply to keep Charlie talking. Yes, ever since her undergraduate days, it was her experience that it was always the painfully shy, the self-absorbed and the unhappy kids who were most likely to major in psychology. Whether Charlie Levinson was one of the above or a combination of all three, she couldn't say.

"So, a while back I went on this men's sensitivity retreat up on the Russian River," he continued, pulling his hair out of his face, displaying a certain flash of weak-chinned earnestness. "We were all given drums. That was the first time I ever played one. It was great! I'd never heard of a bodhran before, but it felt wonderful to meditate with it. It's a perfect channeling device for unburying all sorts of negative energy and dispersing it, you know. Of course, it's hard to play around here without pissing people off." He glanced around the quad.

"Yes, but about last Friday . . ."

"That's what I'm telling you. I was working on a family problem that night with the drum. My mother, you see, has been dying for a year and a half." Rose had only begun a gesture of compassionate understanding when Charlie shook his head. "No, it's not that she's really dying, but every few months she calls my brothers and me home for one last bedside farewell, propped up on the pillow, live-in nurse wringing her hands and all. She always pulls through, though, you know, once she's made everyone in the family utterly miserable and guilty. So, anyway, I had almost drummed away my mother on Friday when that guy started the fight."

Rose eyed the psychology student with as neutral an expression as she could muster. Drummed away his mother. Oh boy. "Yes, I see, but did you notice anything or talk with any of the others?"

Charlie shook his head. "I don't know anybody at the bar. I've never spoken with . . . you said your husband's name is Niall? . . . and the others leave me alone. I think it's better that way. Too much social involvement would make the processing more difficult, you know."

Rose cracked a smile and couldn't resist just one barb, "So, Charlie, do you find that it's the jigs or the reels that most efficiently process your negative energy?"

He seemed not to notice the sarcasm as he considered the question. "It doesn't matter," he finally decided. "Actually, I can't really tell them apart. The tunes, I mean. That is, I'm sort of tone-deaf. I play at the sessions because it lets me process all evening without bothering anybody. I don't really talk to the others much in the bar."

Probably the best thing for all concerned, thought Rose emphatically. But she felt she hadn't gotten particularly far in her questioning about the night of the murder. "Do you mean you don't learn the music? You just play along with the beat?"

"Well, yeah, I guess. I don't listen to music much. I'm just doing the drumming until I can finish beating out my mother and then start work on my father."

"Oh, so your father's a problem, too?"

"Well, he's a colonel in the Marines . . ." The stringy-haired youth's halting preamble and pained tone spoke volumes. Rose stopped him with an upraised palm. She could just picture what sort of relationship this 'sensitive boy' had had with his father. No amount of bodhran-beating was likely to square that upbringing, of that she was certain. Maybe six months of bashing on a J. Arthur Rank gong would do the trick for him, but she wondered if even the Russian River retreat was remote enough to handle that sort of industrial strength New Age processing. In any event, she didn't want to hear about it.

"So you didn't see the fight?" she pressed again half-heartedly, beginning to stroll slowly in the direction of the parking lot.

"No, I was over at the bar when it all started. When the fight was over, the energy was so negative I just left. Took the bus home and listened to my tape for a while to get centered."

"Tape? I thought you said you were tone-deaf."

"It's a tape of the waves breaking on the rocks at Big Sur. It's very soothing. I just put the tape deck on auto reverse and leave it running. Sometimes I fall asleep and the waves are still going in the morning."

"Really? And your roommates don't mind that?"

"Oh, I live alone."

"Really! What a surprise."

•

A little while later, as Rose pulled into the curb in front of the house, Inspector Elliot parked across the street and walked over to join her at the steps.

"So, Inspector, have they busted you to beat patrolman or is this just a social call?" As the words came out, she felt immediately and thoroughly foolish. Who was she trying to kid, putting up such a front for this policeman? She tucked her large, paper-stuffed handbag further under her arm, trying to make it look smaller.

"Neither, actually, Mrs. Sweeney. I hoped to catch your husband at home." They both glanced toward the house as the faint sound of a fiddle filtered through the closed windows.

"From the sound of it, he seems to be in better spirits than the last time you came by. First time he's touched his fiddle since . . . um . . . yeah." She led the Inspector up the steps and into the house. She watched from the corner of her eye for any perceptible change in the Inspector's demeanor, but could detect nothing, at least nothing new to worry about.

Inside, Sweeney propped the fiddle and bow upright in the blue chair as Rose and Elliot entered. "I'm sorry to interrupt your practicing, Mr. Sweeney, but I just dropped by to say that you can pick up your car at the yard any time. Here's the address." The Inspector handed him a plain white business card.

Sweeney stared at the card for a moment without rising, then passed it to Rose who stood between the two men. "So, you didn't find anything on the car?"

"Not on it or in it. Nothing at variance with your account, sir, no. I am sorry for the inconvenience, but we have to be thorough. And it's still rather a mess, I'm afraid. I'm sure you understand."

"Oh, I understand, all right," Sweeney replied, firing a hardened look at the Inspector. "I understand I'm thoroughly out of a job and thoroughly under suspicion in a swindle I never knew was happening and a murder I was luckless enough to report." There you are, Inspector. Now are you going to tell me what you told Berenson?

"I wouldn't say that, Mr. Sweeney."

"What would you say, then?"

"Mr. Sweeney, you know that the Anglo-Irish Bank reported an account in your name with considerable activity through the San Francisco branch involving questionable money transfers over a period of two years. You claimed to have no knowledge of any of this."

"We've been all over this from every possible . . ."

Elliot held up his palm. "I know. And though I have no departmental reason for telling you this, it happens that nowhere on either side of the Atlantic can anyone find either a single fingerprint or written signature to connect you in any way with the money laundering activity. In fact, two experts in our department assure me that the signature on file with the bank at this end and the one signing for the cash, are not in your handwriting at all."

Sweeney blinked and waited for the other shoe to fall. "Is that all?" he said finally. Looking up at Elliot's face, he judged the Inspector's expression to be more guarded than reassuring.

"Not all, no. Not as far as the death of Michael Blayney goes."

"But what about my job at AdTech, then?" Sweeney got up and began picking absently at lint on the top of the chair. "Are you prepared to call my boss and tell him officially that I am pure as the driven snow?"

Inspector Elliot's expression did not change. So, thought Sweeney, one story to the boss and another to me. Is this all just to keep me nervous and off balance about the murder?

"There still remain, of course, the unanswered questions pertaining to your relationship with the deceased and your possible connection with the murder weapon. You will forgive me if my good news is tempered by the reality of the situation."

"Reality," repeated Sweeney. He swung around to face the window overlooking the quiet stretch of street. "What could be more unreal than the last two days?" He turned again to face the Inspector, trying again for a straight answer. "But do I get my job back or not?"

"I'm sure I couldn't say. You'll have to remember that AdTech is still under close scrutiny internationally. The fact that your name seems to have been used without your knowledge in no way changes the state of affairs between AdTech and Anglo-Irish. Two million dollars have been ferreted out of Ireland and have apparently vanished without a trace into the San Francisco fog."

Rose squeezed her husband's arm, partly because the ludicrous rhyming phrase "out of the bog and into the fog . . . out of the bog and into the fog . . ." began to cycle in her head until she banished it with a conscious effort.

"He's trying to tell you, Niall, that win or lose, you're out on your ear. You've become far too embarrassing to have in the office." The unpleasant scenario didn't seem to surprise her. Sweeney found he'd already pretty much accepted the fact.

Elliot seemed to soften a little as he added, "From what I observed in my last meeting with Mr. Berenson, he doesn't seem in too receptive a mood right now. The fact is, I personally told him all this earlier today over the phone. His reaction was . . . well, maybe you can let him cool off for a day or two. You may find him a little more reasonable later."

Reasonable, hell, thought Sweeney. My good riddance check's in the mail.

Rose saw Elliot to the door. He watched her as she glanced nervously down toward the corner before he descended the steps and crossed to his car. He shook his head as he started the engine and rolled down the hill.

He slowed at the corner and took in the quiet block to the left. The leaves of the young tree riffled in the light breeze that had pushed the fog back toward the farthest ranks of houses to the west. At the other end of the street, the afternoon bustle that would become the daily rush-hour crush of eager pedestrians had begun to clog Castro Street. If a strange man had been standing there, watching the Sweeney house, he wasn't there now. Elliot turned back toward the Mission.

Chapter Ten

Rose checked to see that the front curtains were well drawn after satisfying herself that Inspector Elliot had driven off and had not left any obvious lingering helpers to keep an eye on the house. For his part, Sweeney had had enough of fighting out tunes with the sorry old bow and lounged back in the blue chair, one foot on the coffee table.

"I had a strange little chat with Charlie Levinson just now at school," said Rose.

"Levinson? You mean the kid with the bodhran? I'd be surprised if he noticed anything Friday night. He's always got his head buried in the drum and his eyes screwed shut."

"Yeah, that was the impression I got, too."

"So, could he tell you anything? About who left the bar, for instance?"

"Niall, he doesn't even know anybody's name. He comes into the bar once a week for a kind of Celtic primal therapy and I'm not sure he really thinks about anyone but himself. He's so busy learning to be sensitive that he's completely oblivious to his surroundings."

"Wonderful. Any good news, though?"

Rose plowed into her bag and spread out sheet after sheet of shiny, curling fax paper, bumping her husband's foot off the table with her shin as she moved around next to him and surveyed the information.

"So this is what Harry sent you from Dublin?" the fiddler inquired, perking up instantly and trying to make out if it was in any particular order.

"Yep. These are all the articles he could find in a hurry. The dates and names of the papers are flagged up in the corner, see?"

Sweeney glanced at the top sheet, a year-old feature story about how a down-at-the-heels Dublin neighborhood had to go all the way to the Prime Minister to have their street and footpaths repaired. It was a reasonably well-written denunciation of Irish politicians in general. Nothing here, at least, to point to a radical revolutionary political temperament on Blayney's part.

Rose began rearranging all the sheets purposefully. "Let's get them in chronological order so we can try to get a progression of thought from them."

Agreeing that it was as good a place to start as any, Sweeney let Rose finish placing all the articles from top left to bottom right, covering the entire table. The earliest piece was from a Belfast daily, almost ten years old, entitled "Men of Stature." Rose fairly squeaked with excitement as she got about two paragraphs into it.

"Niall! Listen to this! He's ranting about how today's politicians are tiny men in comparison with the great leaders of the past. I'm afraid the local politicians' names he mentions here don't ring any bells, but here he makes clear that every one of them is wretchedly bad, regardless of party. And check this out: '. . . and a certain Sweeney would be well-advised to reconsider a career in politics. Far grander Sweeneys than he have been driven mad from Ireland for their misdeeds and stupidity . . .' That proves it! At least ten years ago he was up on his Mad Sweeney legend and made reference to it while laying in to some politician. This is probably what Elliot was talking about when he asked you about knowing Blayney in Ireland. He must have seen this article!"

"But that thing's ten years old. I was only over there a couple of years ago."

"Don't forget the vacation trips. The first one was ten years ago, wasn't it?"

"But they were just for fiddling in the pubs and only for a few weeks, anyway. There must be a more recent Sweeney article. Keep reading."

They kept reading. For the next hour, they read through the articles, over a dozen in number, Rose kneeling on the carpet and passing the sheets to Sweeney as she finished them, making few comments. An unspecified Sweeney was mentioned in passing in a piece dated two years after the first, but only as one of several people Blayney had considered unworthy of a local accolade. But aside from that, no further article, political or otherwise, made another mention of any Sweeney. She had gotten halfway into the last hard-to-read page when she heeled over to give her knees a rest.

"I'm afraid this is pointless," she sighed. "All we can tell from this stuff is that Blayney didn't like anybody very much and had little pleasant to say about any politician who lived more recently than the Easter Rebellion. He's not even particularly pro-IRA, despite what the local papers seem to think, unless there are other writings Harry missed. But knowing Harry, these are mostly the same bits and pieces that Elliot could get hold of."

She handed the page to Sweeney without finishing it. His eyes were getting tired as he reached over to switch on the lamp. Determined to finish what he had started he began reading the mild, pastoral piece on South Clare Blayney had written for a small travel magazine. It was the third item from the same publication and Blayney was listed as their regular Clare columnist.

The article could add nothing about the hidden character of the author, but Sweeney sat up as he glanced down at the credit box toward the bottom of the page.

"Of all the . . . I was just thinking about that place when you came home," he shook his head and nodded.

Rose looked up. "What place?"

"The Glen Bolcain Pub in Inagh. There was this little contest there, I'm sure I told you about it. Slow airs were the local favorites and this little pub put on an annual Gold Ring fiddle contest that I entered when I was working in Dublin."

"But what about it?" asked Rose with sudden interest.

"Look here, down at the bottom, they give an address where readers can get in contact with the columnists. Blayney's address is listed as in care of the Glen Bolcain Pub in Inagh."

Rose peered at the page intently. "The date is almost exactly two years ago. If Blayney was collecting his mail there, this puts the two of you in the same pub at the same time, two years before you met."

Sweeney whistled and rose slowly to begin pacing in front of the fireplace. Surely the police couldn't know about this strange development. Or could they?

Rose let him pace a few times before getting up and putting her arms around him, the paper still in her hand. "Not to worry, darlin'," she said brightly. "The secret's safe with us for now." Sweeney wrapped his hands around her slim waist and kissed her on the forehead.

"Doesn't make much sense, though, does it?" he said, looking back at the paper-covered table.

"No, I can't say that it does. But did you happen to notice another small point of interest here in this last article?" She pointed back at the address box. Sweeney shook his head.

"Glen Bolcain, silly. You remember about Mad Sweeney?"

"What about him?"

"Glen Bolcain was the name of the place where Mad Sweeney was banished by Ronan in the ancient legend!"

Sweeney felt as if he'd been slapped. "That is too weird!" was all he could think to say. But he shook his head and sat back down on the arm of the chair.

"It's just the name of a pub, Rosie. I'll bet it's a common-enough name. I remember it means valley of the volcano or something. Just a simple place name referring to local geological features."

"Niall," said Rose patiently, "there are no volcanoes in Ireland."

"I need a drink," was Sweeney's response. Rose made no objection as she followed him down the hall in search of two glasses.

•

An hour later, Rose was no closer either to a connection between Glen Bolcain and Blayney or to convincing her husband that the whole direction of inquiry wasn't ridiculous. She finally threw up her hands and piled up the various Sweeney texts she had been riffling through, ready to relax.

The two of them sat together in silence for a while. Sweeney began to hum a melody softly to himself.

"That's a nice tune," remarked Rose, eager to change the subject for a while.

Sweeney smiled at her wistfully. "That's the slow air I played in the Gold Ring fiddle contest in that stupid pub we've been arguing about."

Rose wrinkled her nose. Then a thought struck her. "What was it you said about you thinking about Glen Bolcain before I got home? I mean, it couldn't have had any special significance, could it?"

"Not really, no. It was just one thing leading to another. You see, there's a peculiar fiddle tune, a jig called *Maid of Glen Bolcain* that was stuck in my head the other day when I was going out to the session. Pete Cole the accordion player started it at the session and all of a sudden I remembered the name." He stopped for a second.

"Somebody said something earlier in the evening to remind me about the fiddle contest in Inagh and the names came together. It was Christie, I think, was mentioning me being a Gold Ring player and I hadn't heard that phrase in a long time."

"How do you suppose Christie heard about Gold Ring players?"

"Oh, probably from her Irish daddy. Or some young friend on that church tour she took who was a little more inquisitive than she was."

Right, thought Rose to herself. Some little Catholic hell-raiser like that friend Sylvia whom she'd mentioned. That one was probably no stranger to the pubs on that trip, knowing that her well-behaved and loyal girlfriends would cover for her.

Thinking of covers, Rose suddenly wanted to be under them. She tugged at Sweeney's elbow, pointed wordlessly at the mantel clock, and marched him off to bed.

•

Sweeney lay in Rose's arms, staring at the ceiling. The slow air that had threaded itself through his thoughts had faded eventually off into the distance, leaving only a low, aching melancholy that banished sleep. Though the dimly-lit clock on the side table claimed that it wasn't much past eleven, Sweeney felt as if the night had crept along for an eternity.

He extricated himself from Rose's embrace gently enough not to wake her and got out of bed. Unanswered questions nagged at him. He'd come up empty in his attempts to get answers at AdTech. Well, maybe not entirely empty, but he still had no real answers to the questions that most needed answering. Rose had run into that strange bodhran kid and had come away satisfied that he was well out of the picture. That sounded like progress, he supposed. Maybe now was a good time to try to check off the rest of the musicians. He'd meant to collar all of them to collect their accounts of the violent evening, but so far had only spoken with Marjorie. That left boyfriend Rod, Peter Cole, and John Kilbride.

Peter's living on some holdover hippie commune up in Santa Rosa, thought Sweeney as he pulled his pants on and quietly moved down the hall. I'll figure out some way of finding him in the morning. Maybe Kilbride's in a chatty mood. It's not too late for him . . . hell, the nights he shows up at the Bag, he's there till closing. Typical Irish biorhythms. If I'm lucky, he'll be in the book.

He pulled the well-thumbed directory from under the phone and scanned the listings. There were three John Kilbrides in the city, but only one within an easy walk of the Bag of Nails.

Arguello Street. That'll be the one, Sweeney thought. He hesitated for a moment, considering the hour, then shrugged and dialed the number. The phone was picked up in two rings. The voice on the line was Irish but unfamiliar.

"Hello," said Sweeney, feeling momentarily unsure about handling his questions over the phone, no matter what time it was. "Can I speak to John Kilbride?"

"Eh, ehm, well, John's here, but . . . ehm . . . he can't quite make it to this side of the room. Ye callin' about the session?" Sweeney could now clearly pushing its way past the voice, indicating that a fairly ... was in full swing.

... unconsciously. "Yes, that's right. Just checking the address."

"... at all," said the voice. "Good for another hour or two, I'll wager. It's 1488 Arguello, first floor front. Panel truck's in the drive. Can't miss it."

Feeling that he had just been granted some sort of lucky break, Sweeney swept out into the breezy night armed with his fiddle case and his questions.

Three long blocks south of Clement Sweeney pulled into the curb across the street from the Arguello address. This part of the Inner Richmond District was made up of block after block of redwood-beamed Victorians, two- and three-story, shoulder-to-shoulder with alternating straight, wide staircases and rounded bay windows. The house fronts on the east side of the street showed the wear of eighty to a hundred years of buffeting from the salty, cold wind off the Pacific. At this time of night, the neighborhood was quiet, with only a few windows still lit from within.

Sweeney crossed to a chalky white three-story house, the only house on the block completely ablaze with light. From an open window, an accordion sprinkled notes down to the pavement. In the driveway, a large, beaten-up white panel truck stood, the lettering on the side reading "Kilbride Construction Company-General Contractors."

Sweeney was halfway up the stairs when the front door opened and three happily chattering women poured out onto the porch, buttoning their coats. Sweeney recognized them as regulars at the Bag, Irish girls who had been over here long enough to have almost . . . but not quite . . . lost their hometown accents. They grinned at him as they skipped past him down the stairs.

"Fresh blood," giggled one, gesturing toward the fiddle case in Sweeney's hand and winking recognition. "It's a good one tonight! Cheers!" She waved prettily as she and her companions descended to the sidewalk and disappeared down the street.

Sweeney pushed open the unlatched door and found himself bathed in a pleasant, sweaty warmth and the familiar, pulsing melody of a Willy Clancy reel, being exuberantly played on flute, accordion, concertina, and perhaps something else as well, with the hypnotic bass notes provided by the drones of an uilleann bagpipe. He proceeded into the hallway past a dozen coat hooks occupied by a dozen coats, a couple of serious-looking tool boxes against the wall, and two closed doors. In the kitchen at the end of the hall he could see several people digging for refreshment in the refrigerator. He stopped where the high-ceilinged hallway opened up into the living room and surveyed the session.

The room was utterly packed. There were people perched two and three at a time on the stuffed chairs, with other straight-backed chairs wedged between them and any remaining available room occupied by beer bottles and instrument cases. John Kilbride was stuck at the far end of the group, on the bay window seat in t-shirt and jeans, playing his flute with his eyes shut and his elbows tucked in close. A fine young piper from Palo Alto sat next to him, granted enough room to extend his drones safely. Sweeney hadn't seen him at the Bag of Nails in quite some time. He hunched over his instrument in standard piper fashion, his chin down against his right shoulder, his sleeves rolled up, his mind turned inward as his arm tirelessly worked the bellows and the chanter sang the melody, chirping ornaments at the cadence points.

Sweeney brightened considerably to note Peter Cole playing along merrily, seated off to the right on his usual wooden accordion case. This was indeed a happy stroke of luck. He caught Peter's eye with a smile and nod of greeting, but the gangly musician seemed not to notice and kept on playing. The concertina player with his back to Sweeney was a heavily-bearded guy named Solomon, who turned up occasionally at sessions when he wasn't teaching Arabic at a college in the Central Valley. A couple of girls Sweeney didn't recognize were joining in on whistles on either side of Solomon. The rest of the crowd was soaking in the music, tossing out tune requests or general encouragement at intervals, and passing a never-ending conveyer belt of beer bottles around the circle of musicians. It was a truly glorious sight.

The whole scene reminded Sweeney of O'Donoghue's Pub off Saint Stephen's Green in Dublin—the site of possibly the most miserably crowded sessions he'd ever experienced. The press of the crowd had been so inhuman at times in O'Donoghue's that money and pints had to be passed from hand to hand over the heads of at least a dozen intermediaries before thirst could be quenched. Making for the door had been out of the question. And the musicians were stuck just inside the painted-over front window, without a hope in hell of getting out until closing time emptied the place. God help the poor fiddler without an iron-lined bladder in O'Donoghue's!

Sweeney stood for a moment and just listened. The music was being shaped and directed by the rounded bay window, reverberating then through the rest of the house from wall to sparsely decorated wall. It was an all-too-rare treat to hear the pipes in a session that wasn't drowned out by bar noise. Although he'd brought the fiddle mainly as a prop, he felt his fingers twitching, his eyes scanning around the room for signs of a spot big enough for a fiddler to squeeze into.

"Didn't know you were comin', Niall," said a sunburned and chiseled bar regular who had bought rounds for Sweeney in the past, but whose name he couldn't quite recall. He landed a tap on Sweeney's shoulder with his beer.

"Yeah, I didn't hear about it until late," replied Sweeney truthfully. "How do I shoehorn myself in there? It looks like the stateroom scene from 'Night At the Opera.'"

"Ah, well, they're about due for a breather. They been at it nonstop more'n an hour. Somebody gets up to stretch their legs, grab their chair!" He grinned and moved off toward the kitchen.

The jigs and reels wound down and degenerated into tuning and drone adjustment. A few sweaty participants wandered off in the direction of the bathroom or kitchen or sat continuing individual pools of conversation. Kilbride glanced over at Sweeney, got up slowly and made his way to the kitchen. Sweeney followed him to the refrigerator where Kilbride retrieved another beer and turned to face him.

"I don't remember askin' you to come tonight, Niall," he said in a voice flattened and uninflected.

"I phoned a little while ago to talk to you and whoever it was answered the phone said the session was going on. I didn't really come to play, to be honest about it. Just wanted to ask a few questions."

"And what makes you think I'm eager to answer any more questions? I arranged this little hoolie to forget about what's happened these last few days. I distinctly avoided inviting you. I also didn't invite the police. They had the decency to stay away."

Sweeney flushed. "Well, if you feel that way about it, I'll be going. I'm sorry."

Kilbride shook his head sadly. "What the hell. You're here already. Only forget it with the questions. I'm up to here with 'em." He drank deeply without offering a bottle to Sweeney. Then after a moment he seemed to change his mind about the subject of the night of the fight and the murder.

"It's a shame you had to provoke him. A man that drunk. Why not take him outside and cool him off?" Something in the quiet man's tone suggested that any number of people in his experience might have handled maniacs like Blayney with more even-handed common sense than Sweeney had.

"Provoke him?" blurted Sweeney. "He came in looking for blood. What did I say to provoke such a crazy fucking attack?"

"I didn't hear what you said," Kilbride replied dismissively. "But as for lookin' for blood . . . he found it, didn't he? Him gettin' killed and all . . . it's made life very unpleasant. For a lot of people. Now, I'm not sayin' you knifed the bugger, but somebody sure as hell did, and it's played holy hell with my business."

"Business? What do you mean?"

"What do you think I mean? An Irishman killed in a city full of Irishmen. What are the police gonna do but start questioning Irishmen about it? So I've got my business and I hire construction workers—good Irish lads, all of 'em, and hard workers." He pounded his palm against the refrigerator door with emphasis.

"So some haven't done all the paperwork to make the Immigration people happy. So some of 'em might be a tiny bit late gettin' a visa renewed. So fuckin' what? I don't ask 'em questions as long as they do a right proper job. But the police start comin' around askin' to see everybody's papers and what-have-you, and my bloody crew evaporates into thin air. Where I come from, even your most honest man learns to steer clear of the cops. And then some eager bastard in the contractors licensing office starts askin' me for employee records. Jesus, I'd be surprised if my crew don't stop runnin' 'til they get to Chicago."

"But what do the police suspect? Surely they don't think your company was even remotely connected with the murder."

Kilbride just laughed flatly. "No. I don't think they suspect anybody and I don't think they have a single bloody lead. That's why the bureaucrats are making as much noise as possible. Justify their existence and prove that they're earning their salaries, the clueless bastards. And now I've got a job half finished on Judah Street and not one of my regulars is gonna dare show his face to finish the damn thing. If I'm still in business in a month it'll be a miracle." The tension showed plainly in the Kerryman's jawline as he fixed his eyes steadily and coldly on Sweeney's.

"I'm sorry. But it had nothing to do with me, and that's the truth." Sweeney couldn't tell if the shake of the head he received in response was a signal of disagreement or merely of dismissal. Kilbride turned and elbowed his way through the kitchen door and back to his seat in the living room to rejoin the other musicians.

Sweeney fought off a desire to get out of the house as fast as he could. I'm here, he said to himself. I might as well get something to show for it. If Kilbride won't talk, I'm sure Pete will. He's always been the friendliest of them all. And maybe I can get in a decent tune or two in the bargain.

Slightly strengthened by that final thought, he noticed that the overstuffed chair arm to Peter Cole's right was now vacant. He sidled in through the middle of the room and settled himself next to Peter's accordion case. Peter was sitting with his back to Sweeney and his elbows resting on his accordion, talking quietly and earnestly with the piper.

As the rest of the room filled with the pleasant murmur of a dozen quiet conversations, one of the whistle players began to play *The Gooseberry Bush*. Sweeney looked around at the other musicians, but no one else seemed ready to join in yet. What the hell, he thought. I'll talk to Pete in a minute. The lilting melody caught hold of his mind and he felt his spirits beginning to lift. But as he pulled back the lid of the case his heart sank in horror. He could scarcely believe it.

He had left his bow at home.

He sat there, crestfallen, feeling cruelly exiled from the one activity he turned to to make everything else seem all right. It had never happened before. He had never forgotten his bow. Ever. Of course, the only bow he had to play with now was that annoying old thing he'd dragged out of the closet. Sure, he hadn't put it in the case where the broken one used to be. It was leaning up against the wall next to the fireplace. Silly, really, but . . .

Jesus, he thought. I should have turned and walked out the minute Kilbride had told me I wasn't welcome. What the hell am I to do now?

Peter Cole straightened and turned toward Sweeney. Sweeney smiled, but Pete was not smiling back. Sweeney knew Pete had his moods and was deadly serious about his music, but the expression of hostility and distrust now aimed at him was one he'd never seen on Pete's face. His lips tight together, Pete's jaw was working in silence, as if he were trying to swallow words before they escaped into the room. His eyes were burning—anything but friendly.

"Look, Pete, I don't know what's going on, but . . ."

"Just beat it, Niall," spat the thin accordion player. "Don't fuck it up here, too!" His voice was low but several of those seated nearby stopped their conversations and turned to follow the exchange.

"Pete! You can't mean . . . What did I . . . ?"

"The one thing I truly enjoyed in San Francisco has been totally fucked up! The only really beautiful reason to come down every week. If you had a problem with that asshole, why'd you have to air it out at the session?"

"Me? But, I didn't have a problem with the guy. You were there. You must have seen what happened! That's why I'm here. I'm trying to find out something . . . anything . . . that'll help me get my life back to normal again."

"Ha! Give it a rest, Niall! I mean, a fight! At the session table, yet! You've caused enough grief. Now the whole thing's screwed. The Bag sessions have been my second home since Keegan first played there. Twenty years! Probably never be the same now—thanks to you."

"Thanks to me? It was just a stupid fight. It could have happened to anybody!"

"You know what I'm talking about!"

"Jeez, Peter, you're acting like I killed the guy!"

"Well, how do I know you didn't?"

The expression on his face combined with his words to turn Sweeney's guts to ice. There were shutters behind Peter Cole's eyes. There was no point in discussing it further. Without replying or turning around, Sweeney picked up his fiddle case and made his way to the door.

Rose stirred and opened her eyes as Sweeney sat down on the bed and began to remove his shoes. She glanced at the clock, sat up and shifted over to rub her husband's back gently.

"Where have you been at this hour?" she asked muzzily.

"I couldn't sleep," Sweeney replied, kicking his shoes into the corner and lying back on the pillow. "I got this idea about calling John Kilbride and finding out what he knew about the other night. Turned out there was a session going late at Kilbride's place and I ran over to talk."

"And?" prompted Rose, a little more awake now.

"And, nothing. I talked to Kilbride. And Pete Cole was there, too. They didn't tell me anything new, really, but I'm left with the feeling that neither of them were involved with Blayney. I suppose that's something."

"I'll say that's something," agreed Rose eagerly, now propped up on one elbow. "But what did they say to knock them out of the running?"

"Well, Kilbride, for one, stands to lose a bundle. After the murder, the police came crawling all over his construction contracting business and scared away all the dubiously-documented Irish laborers he depended on. He's now hung up on an important job with no one to finish the work. According to him, there's a good chance he'll lose his business. No, he wouldn't have set himself up for that sort of grief. I'm certain of that. I can't imagine him having anything to do with it."

"What about his movements after the fight? And what about the others? Did he see anything?"

"You know, I didn't even ask. He was pretty goddam angry with me for just being in the fight. After he had his say about his business he cut off the conversation and that was that."

"And what about Pete?"

"He seems to think I killed Blayney." He repeated the rest of the conversation he'd had with the accordion player. Rose nodded.

"Well, that doesn't prove anything. Pointing the finger of blame doesn't make him innocent, does it?"

"No . . . but the way he said it . . . it's hard to put into words. It was as if he blamed me for screwing up something so precious it was more like a godly tradition than a bar full of drunks and folk musicians . . . like the session was some kind of sacrament for him, and I'd spit in the holy water."

Rose couldn't think of anything bright to say. They lay there silently, lost in the separateness of their thoughts until each drifted off into a troubled sleep.

Chapter Eleven

By the time Sweeney was out of bed Rose was almost ready to run out the door to school.

"I've got to run," she said as she finished her coffee. "If I can think of anything else brilliant, I'll call you. You should try to go back to bed and get some sleep. You look terrible."

"I don't feel that bad, really. Not sleepy anyway. I just wish that Peter hadn't . . . hell, I don't know what I wish."

"Well, there's nothing more you can do in that direction right now. Are you going to call that fellow Byrne again in Dublin?"

"I thought I'd wait until later. I had an idea I'd go around to the *Irish-American* office this morning. Nobody else I can think of to talk to is likely to be up before noon, so at least I have something to occupy my time until I can track them down."

Rose kissed him on the cheek on her way out the door. Sweeney gazed at his reflection in the hall mirror, decided that his hair wasn't dirty enough to need washing, and wandered off in search of clean clothes.

•

One would never know to look at it that the ramshackle and long-neglected Mission District Victorian house boasted the office of *The Irish-American Weekly*. It evidently hadn't been painted since the Hoover administration. Like the old buildings to either side, the façade and long flight of steps leading up to the double front door leaned slightly toward the south.

Sweeney climbed the stairs with some trepidation, relieved to find that the landing was more solid than it appeared. The name of the paper was stenciled on the glass in the door and a young woman with wavy hair and a businesslike manner could be seen working at a desk just inside. Entering the hall, he was greeted with a pleasant smile. The rhythmic whirring of a copy machine could be heard from somewhere in the back, mixed with muffled conversation.

"I wonder if I could ask a few questions," he began, addressing the receptionist. "I need some information on Michael Blayney."

"Oh, you with the papers, too?" inquired the girl brightly. "I don't know what else we can tell you that your mates didn't get before. You're alone? No photographer? Well, they said there'd be a followup bit on the Six O'Clock News tonight and I think I'll be in that and . . . who did you say you were with?"

Sweeney was breathless just listening to her. "Well, um, I didn't . . . that is, I just need to check a fact or two to finish the story." He quickly pulled a fold of paper and a pen from his pocket, trying to look instantly journalistic.

"We know that Mr. Blayney worked here right after he arrived in town. Could you tell us again how he got the job?"

"It was just a coincidence, I think. Like I told them before, there was a vacancy on the staff and he showed up, that's all."

"So he wasn't recommended for the job?"

"Recommended? Sure, he must have been recommended. No idea by who, though. You know, we get guys in here all the time looking for work. You know the sort. Mr. Burke, he always has me tell them that nobody gets hired by the paper without a personal reference." Sweeney looked interested and pretended to write something down.

He glanced through to the next room and down the hall of the converted flat, wondering how to proceed when the closed door behind the receptionist opened to frame a stout man in his shirt-sleeves standing in the doorway.

"Maggie, have you finished the proofs yet?" he barked at the girl behind the desk before fixing upon Sweeney. "What can we do for you?"

"I need some information on Michael Blayney, if you don't mind, Mister . . ."

"Editor. Burke. Mind, hell. We've been doing nothing but talking to the damn police and news hounds all weekend. We have nothing further to say. I'm sick of this kind of publicity and just want to be left alone. What paper is he with, Maggie?"

"I didn't say I was a reporter. I just want some information. My name's Sweeney, Niall Sweeney, and I have no more interest in publicity than you do."

The receptionist reddened, grabbed a manila file and darted into the next room. Burke stepped around the desk and stared. "You're the fiddler? The one who was in the fight? I think you'd better leave, man. What the hell are you doing nosing around asking questions anyway?"

Sweeney hardened in response to the confrontational tone suddenly taken by the editor. If this line of inquiry was going to get him into another fight, that was just too damn bad.

"Maybe I don't like being questioned by the cops for a murder I had nothing to do with. I'm out of a job and there are people out there who seem to think I not only killed a man but helped fund an IRA bombing."

Rather than making any move toward Sweeney, Burke stood there as if he'd been turned to stone. Carefully, he lowered to seat himself on the corner of the desk. "So what are you doin' here? What's this about a bombing? And what's that got to do with Michael Blayney?"

"With any luck, nothing," said Sweeney, deciding that this was not a time for half measures. "As for what I'm doing here, I've been set up, Mr. Burke, and I'm getting precious little help proving it. I'm suddenly the link connecting a murder of one of your employees with a nasty little IRA bombing at a Brighton hotel and I don't like it one bit."

Burke's expression remained stony. "I've told the police everything they wanted to know about the man. They didn't say anything about any bombing."

"Must have slipped their minds. Listen, I'm damned if I'll die for something I didn't do. Now I can be as quiet as the next guy when it comes to keeping the lives of my friends private. But the way things are going, I'm not sure who my friends are any more. And if they haul me off to trial I'm letting loose the greasiest bastard lawyers you ever heard of to dig up dirt on everybody who's so much as looked cross-eyed at me until they find out the truth. Personally, I'd much rather avoid the whole nasty mess." He stared straight into the editor's eyes.

Burke turned away without blinking and walked back into his office. Sweeney followed him through the door as he sat down at his cluttered oak desk. "So what can I possibly tell you that I haven't already told the police?"

"I don't know. There must be something they missed. For starters, why did you hire him?"

"He was a capable enough writer. Happened to show up when a vacancy appeared."

"You say no one recommended him for the job?"

"No. He showed me a good stack of articles he'd written in Ireland. Not bad stuff. So I gave him the job."

He's a cool one, thought Sweeney. He let it pass for the moment. "So he did a good job for you?"

"Fairish. He did all right."

"Does a writer like Blayney need much editing, or do you just print whatever he submits?"

"Ha! You've never worked for a newspaper, have you?" scoffed the editor. "There's always more copy than column inches no matter who's doing the writing. I usually had to carve up Blayney's columns. Like I do everyone else's," he added.

A thought occurred to Sweeney. "What sort of stuff exactly did Blayney write that needed regular editing? Ignoring for the moment the lovely bit of verbal violence you let see print in the last issue."

Burke bristled but responded evenly. "He did tend to get a bit more poetic than was good for him sometimes," he admitted. "Not that the readers of *The Irish-American Weekly* are less than literate, mind. But sometimes the references were a tiny bit beyond the credible."

"Did the police ask to see what you edited out of Blayney's columns?"

"No interest at all. They didn't seem to care about anything in the poetic line. They asked about political material, but I showed them plainly that Blayney never wrote one word of political commentary for this paper at any time. Full stop. Wasn't his job."

Sweeney had run out of questions as his eyes scanned around the cluttered room that more closely resembled a newspaper recycling center than an editor's office. "So, did he work in his own office or what?"

Burke snorted a laugh. "His own office? On our budget? Not likely. He worked at home and brought the typed articles in for each issue. Of course, when he first started he knocked out some stuff at the desk in the back room on the communal machine. He got his own gear after that and didn't need to come in any more to work."

"He typed his articles? I thought modern technology had come to the publishing trade."

"We have exactly one Macintosh we use for a word processor," replied Burke, sarcastic but plainly proud. "Locked up back there. Maggie does the input when we get all the copy from our various poverty-stricken contributors. We do accept hand-written articles as well. It's a tradition I grew up with and I'd rather not see it die."

Sweeney raised an eyebrow in interest. "The typewriter—mind if I have a look?"

The editor shrugged, the stony scowl planted back on his face, and motioned Sweeney down the hall. The communal machine, as he called it, was an ancient Olivetti perched on the edge of a card table, surrounded by file cabinets and facing a wall covered with a battered bulletin board. The bulletin board was a chaotic scramble of notes in a dozen different hands, along with yellowed clippings and snapshots. Sweeney sat down at the typewriter.

"How many people use this machine?"

"Hell, half a dozen at least are in and out to use the desk all the time. As I said, Maggie's the only one I allow to use the Mac. I told you though, Blayney hasn't been here since just after he started." The editor's scowl grew a little in intensity and he snatched a few of the yellower clippings off the wall.

"I'm always cleaning up after everybody in this damn office." he muttered, pulling off another eight sheets in a rapid series of jerks.

Sweeney now noticed a color photograph revealed by this fit of tidiness, tacked directly in front of him. The photo was stapled to a sheet of typewriter paper. Squinting a little, Sweeney could read Blayney's name and a date six months old in the corner of the sheet. Sweeney reached up and took the photo down. It showed what appeared to be an Irish soccer team, dirt-stained, but smiling the weary smiles of victory. He scanned the faces looking for Blayney, but the murdered man was not among them. He was about to tack it back on the board when he was hit with what amounted to an electric shock. There in the center of the group of men, holding the ball, with his unmistakable granite features and shaggy gray hair, was Joe Gilmore.

Burke reached for the photo but Sweeney quickly slipped it into his inside jacket pocket and stood to face the darker man.

"The police missed this?" demanded Sweeney, patting his pocket.

"So they missed it. I didn't hide it from them. I'm as surprised as you are."

"You mean you never saw this photograph before?"

The editor shook his head. "This can't have anything to do with the paper. Look, I wish you no harm, but why don't you just leave now and ask your questions somewhere else?"

Sweeney didn't answer. He pulled out the photo and sheet of paper again, glanced from the image to the editor and stuffed it all back in his pocket. "Are you quite sure you can't help me?"

Burke stared at him hard for a second, then shrugged. "You know, I dimly recall now somebody recommending Blayney for the job, after all."

"Who was it?"

"It might have been Joe Gilmore."

"*Might* have been?"

"I said might. I never told the police. Never even hinted at it. And so help me, if you say I said so to Gilmore or anyone else, I'll swear you're a damned liar!"

•

Tingling with excitement, Sweeney raced through the crowded Mission District streets to negotiate the snaking alleys around the southern part of the city. He emerged from the confusing byways where the unbroken blanket of ocean fog rolled over the avenues to rest its edge at the westernmost boundary of the San Francisco State University campus.

Minutes later he was sprinting down the hallway of the Humanities Building, only stopping to catch his breath in front of Rose's office door. He was still gasping as Rose jumped up from her work and closed the door behind him.

"What in God's name?" she started, as she sat him down in her chair.

He held up a palm and with his other hand produced the photograph, placing it on the desk with a loud slap.

"A clue! Let me tell you what just happened."

Sweeney related his adventure at the newspaper office, about how the editor first lied and then admitted that Blayney had been introduced by Joe Gilmore, and about how he'd stumbled upon a photo that Blayney must have tacked on the wall when he first worked there and forgotten when it was papered over.

Rose beamed at him. "Well, it doesn't do my theory a damn bit of good, but let's see what it all means." She leaned forward and took a closer look at the photo.

"Yep, that looks like Joe, all right. A little bit younger, I'd say. But look at the brick houses and the church in the background, next to the playing field. If I didn't know better, I'd say that had to be Ireland and not Australia."

Sweeney scanned the print carefully. He turned it over in search of a date without success. "I wonder how old the photo is?"

"It's hard to say, but if this is Ireland and Gilmore's been here two years and lived in Australia twelve years before that, this has to be at least fourteen years old."

She frowned at the picture for a solid minute. "You know, he looks younger, but not fourteen years younger."

Sweeney sat back in confusion.

"Do we know who any of these other boys are?" Sweeney shook his head as he checked out the other faces. "Maybe I can get a copy to Harry in Dublin and see if he can find anything out." Her voice trailed off as she continued to stare at the photo.

"Niall," she said slowly, "do you notice anything about this boy in the back?"

Sweeney looked again and suddenly the sandy-haired youth grinning from the rear did look familiar. "Why," he began, "with gray hair he could be a skinny version of Joe Gilmore! Or maybe his brother."

Rose nodded silently.

Chapter Twelve

My curse on Sweeney!
His guilt against me is immense,
he pierced with his long swift javelin
my holy bell.

Alone in the quiet of her office, Rose stared for the hundredth time at the pages of Flann O'Brien's *At Swim-Two-Birds* longing for an answer.

Well, Michael Ronan Blayney, old boy, you've certainly succeeded in laying one hell of a curse on Sweeney, she thought to herself. The problem is, how does one lift a curse once one has become the target?

In literary terms, this twentieth century version of the ancient story failed as a parallel if it was merely a one-sided delusion. And of course it was a delusion, since Niall hadn't the faintest idea what was going on until he was literally hit over the head with it. There had been other Sweeneys in Blayney's past. He had disliked all of them. It was difficult to tell exactly what his relationships had been with the others, but the end result had been his writing nasty things about them for whatever publication he was working for at the time. It seemed there was nothing to go on there.

But why the delusion in the first place? Some people found the unpleasant realities of life to be more palatable when cloaked in safely understandable delusions. How often had she heard the pain of a loved one's death explained away by "It's God's will?" A person didn't have to be nuts to cling to delusions. Sometimes the delusion might be the only alternative to going nuts.

Once in a while Rose wished that she had better understood the "gift of faith" that she had for years considered mankind's prime delusion. Life might have been much simpler, if so much confusion could be explained away with tidy phrases like "the Lord moves in mysterious ways." She found herself amused again at the thought of cynical, nonreligious, sexually frustrated Vinnie having deep and meaningful conversations with Christie the Catholic girl. Almost immediately she felt ashamed for feeling so amused. After all, she knew plenty of odder couples who had made lasting relationships work out just fine.

She turned around and tossed the slim volume back onto the crowded shelf behind her as a polite knock sounded on the door. She shot a quick look at the clock. Another hour of scholarly advice and then home to hear what Niall had learned from Dublin, she thought, shouting "Come in" at her side of the door.

•

The telephone connection to Flannery's Bar was better than the last time he'd called, but Sweeney had trouble making out anything over the cacophony of yelling, singing and crashing in the background. Checking his watch, he cursed himself for being a fool, as it must be closing time in Dublin, the time of the most desperate ritual race to pour that last round or two down the throat before the licensee threatened immediate bodily harm to get everyone out of the pub. The noise receded slightly as he managed to convey to the barman that he wished to speak to Brian Byrne. The receiver at the other end was laid down with a clunk and left for several minutes before a familiar voice came over the wire.

"I'm thinkin' I have somethin' for ye, Niall, though I really can't be certain, ye understand," began his Dublin friend.

"Okay, I'm ready," replied Sweeney eagerly, ready with pen and pad to take it all down.

"Wait a tick. I wonder will this cord reach back to the store room? There!" Sweeney heard a door slam and the noise of the last act of the comic opera that was Flannery's receded to a whisper.

"I'd rather this was just between the two of us, boyo. Not often that I wish I had a private phone of me own, but I suppose this'll have to do."

Sweeney agreed while Byrne attempted to get comfortable in the store room.

"Some of this you're likely to know already. It transpires that your man Blayney spent quite a lot of time out in Clare before leaving for America. There was no address I could find but there was a pub where he received mail."

"I know that much. The Glen Bolcain Pub in Inagh, wasn't it?"

"Right enough and true for you! I'm impressed. So, did you speak with the landlord there in Inagh?"

"No, we got the address through secondary sources."

"Well, a man by the name of Walsh owns the place, but I was unable to speak with him meself when I rang as he was away to Galway to supervise the proper replating of a bit of ornamental brass work. His wife, bless her, takes little notice of the comings and goings of anyone but the local neighbors and when I asked about Blayney suggested that I ring your man back in the morning."

Sweeney scribbled madly as Byrne spoke. "Great, Brian. Oh, I almost forgot. My wife wanted me to ask you about Blayney's middle name, Ronan. Was that his mother's name or what?"

"Ah, that's an easy one. That tiny parish where he come from was nearly all of them Ronans. He got the name on both sides of the family. Mother and father were cousins, or something."

Sweeney whistled as he jotted that down. "What else have you got?"

"Well, just in passin', your man Blayney was quite the one for the ladies. An acquaintance spoke of a certain pattern to his conquests. Can you wait a sec?" Sweeney smiled, knowing Byrne must be lighting a cigarette.

"He liked American women and he liked 'em on the young side. No one I spoke to mentioned any serious entanglements that might be of use to ye either here or in Clare, since he was rather less noted for his constancy than for his ability to charm the wee birdies from the branches, as it were."

"Yes, that would square with his behavior out here, too. But you mentioned finding something I might go on?"

"I did, that I did. Before coming back to Dublin a couple years ago, Blayney was livin' in the North, in Belfast in actual fact, workin' at the newspaper jobs you probably know about and keepin' more or less to himself. But there was an incident two years and a bit ago that may be of interest." A short pause indicated another momentary transfer of attention to the cigarette.

"A Belfast policeman was killed on his rounds. Stabbed, he was. No one actually claimed responsibility, but the usual rumors had it an IRA job. Three men were arrested a few days later. Two known IRA hard cases and a another stray picked up as well. And that'd be the end of it but for one thing. The policeman happened to be the son of an English business man. A real mover and shaker he was, as well as a religious nut—plenty in the chips by all accounts. Now, the daddo puts up a reward for the arrest of those responsible for the murder. And do you know the peculiar thing I'm gonna tell ye?"

"No," breathed Sweeney, now too caught up in his friend's story to bother writing any more of it down.

"Two things. The first is, the amount of the reward was never made public. And the second is, the wealthy dad guarantees the anonymity of anyone who supplies the information. Not what you'd call the usual course of action, eh? I suppose it was all quite sensible by his religious way of thinkin'.

"Anyway now, there's no proof you can put your finger on, mind, but in the opinion of a lad I know and who is certain to have been utterly ignored by the police for reasons which need not concern you, your man may have benefited materially by this incident. Do you follow my meanin'?"

"I sure do!" Sweeney gulped. "I follow all right, Brian, but what does that have to do with him getting himself killed in San Francisco?"

"Remember I said there were three men arrested? Well, Niall, only two of 'em ever came to trial—the two hard cases. The third man, the younger one, escaped while being transported from the holding cells to the prison and was never found. Local opinion had it that it was all for the good, since he had nothin' to do wit' it. Not the type. No record anyway. But his name was Kevin Gilmore."

"Gilmore?" Sweeney cried. "Don't tell me. This guy was Joe Gilmore's little brother?"

The voice at the other end of the wire made what sounded like a sharp little inhaling chirp. "And well done, boyo! They could very well be the one and the same."

"But that's not enough of a connection, Brian."

"Kevin was youngest of four boys, the eldest being named Joe, who apparently left Ireland when Kevin was twenty to emigrate to Australia."

"That's what I mean. Joe Gilmore was half a world away from Ireland when . . ."

"Ah, but do you not find it interestin' that in the Belfast murder, the weapon was also a knife and that the knife was never found?"

"But you said that people thought young Gilmore had nothing to do with the killing."

"People, I said. The police thought different. Plenty of innocent men've died in the Block during persuasive questionin'."

Sweeney could find no response. His mind reeled.

"And your cop's father's anonymous reward was only paid out when the conviction was handed down on the other two, and that a mere fortnight before your Michael Blayney up and scampers to America with an airplane ticket he's not likely to have afforded on what he was earnin' from the odd article and poem."

"Wait a minute," replied Sweeney shakily, "while I write this all down."

"Now my source assures me that the police never gave Blayney more than a passin' glance in the matter, at least until him turnin' up dead, as there is nothin' more than a tight-lipped English religious nut to connect him up wit' it. But some interested parties do not require concrete proof in order to go about their business and to my mind it is in that general direction that the answers lie."

"You couldn't think of a more roundabout way of saying that, could you, Brian?" Sweeney tried to sound more annoyed than he felt. His Dublin friend ignored the question entirely.

"I wish I knew what to advise beyond standin' back and lettin' it all eventually blow over. I'd hate to be in your shoes now, lad, and that's a fact!"

"Thanks a million, Brian. I'll phone you back tomorrow to see if that fellow in Inagh remembers anything else."

"Ta, then, lad. Good on ye."

•

Inspector Elliot read the Telex he'd been handed and gave it back to Detective Leigh. "So are you sure which one it is?" he asked gruffly.

"Well, yes sir," replied the younger man, making an effort to sound sure of himself. "We've eliminated all but one solid possibility and that's this one, Roger Sweeney."

"Roger Sweeney. Roger's not much of an Irish name, is it?" He fixed Leigh with one accusing eye.

"I don't know, sir. There's Roger Casement, of course . . ."

"Who?"

"Sir Roger Casement, the Anglo-Irish rebel hero who was caught before the Easter Rising . . ."

"Leigh, I do believe you've been reading." Elliot smiled suddenly. "If you keep taking this job so seriously, you'll end up at this desk someday."

Detective Leigh visibly relaxed and acquired a momentary expression of pride that somehow didn't go with his spotty complexion.

"I only hope that when you do, it kills you faster than it's killing me," finished his superior. "What else do we have?"

"First, about this Roger Sweeney . . . funny how we're working on two Sweeneys, isn't it, sir? . . . um, he's a seriously hard character from way back. An IRA hit man. There are no photographs of him, but we've got a couple of fingerprints from Interpol. From what we have here," he indicated the inch-thick file on the Inspector's desk, "he seems to have been operating unchecked here in the States for a year or more. He's not associated with any unsolved cases in the U.S. and the FBI fingerprint computer came up a blank."

"Tell me the good news."

"Nevertheless, the Blayney apartment bombing fits his M.O. and his physical description matches the one given by Mrs. Sweeney of the man who was watching their house."

Elliot sniffed. Well, at least it was possible he wasn't being played for a fool. But why would an IRA hit man stake out the home of a luckless fiddle player?

"Sir, have you told Mr. Sweeney about the AdTech information yet?"

Elliot sat back in his chair and pointed a finger ominously at his assistant. "No! And no one else is going to tell him, either, until we clear the rest of this mess up. Mr. Niall Sweeney can go on thinking he's under suspicion of money laundering for a while longer as long as he stays out of our hair. Now what else was it you wanted to tell me?"

Leigh opened another file folder and pulled out an odd-sized piece of notebook paper. "You remember we weren't certain what, if anything, had been taken from Blayney's apartment before the bombing?" Elliot nodded.

"I went through everything we got out of the bombed apartment and I found a couple of sheets of this notebook paper, you know, for little pocket ring-binder things? One of them had the holes torn, like it'd been pulled out of the metal rings. Only I didn't find a notebook for them to go into. I'm assuming that Blayney had one and it was lifted for some reason. It wasn't on the body, anyway."

Elliot said, "Good work." And meant it.

•

It took a full minute for Vin Bowen to catch his breath after Sweeney let him in the front door and steered him to the sofa. Sweeney perched on the chair opposite his disheveled friend as he sat there panting, his elbows on his knees.

"I . . . ran all . . . the way . . ." he gasped.

"I can see that. You know, Vinnie, you're not as young as you used to be. You need some training."

"Hey! Be real. I got something hot for you. I thought you might appreciate me getting to you right away."

Sweeney brightened. "The call from Lydia? She actually called from Australia?"

Vin nodded and sucked on his moustache. Sweeney stood up and glanced down the block.

"Rose should be home any minute from school. You want to wait and tell us both?" It was a cruel question, as Vinnie was obviously ready to burst. "Okay, okay, Vin. Give!"

"Lydia sounded pretty pooped but she said she's having the time of her life down there. The gang flew into Melbourne and there was some cock-up with getting all the bikes through Customs, but then everything went exactly as planned and they all started down the coast. She said it was pretty easy going compared to the mountain bike training she'd been doing around here and the scenery was spectacular."

"Yes, yes, get on with it, Vin!"

"Well, one long day got them as far as Laver's Bay, where I told her to ask around for us. So she cycles in and goes into the first pub she finds along the waterfront intending to ask if anybody remembers Joe Gilmore who went to America. She walks into the bar and flags down the barman and guess what?"

"Okay. What?"

"It was Joe Gilmore himself! He never left!"

Sweeney was stunned. "That's crazy. Was she sure?"

"Sure she was! Gilmore is still running the same pub he's had for years. He's never left the town, never shown the slightest interest in traveling even as far as Melbourne. If there was ever a man who seemed rooted to one spot on the globe, Gilmore was it!"

Adding this startling bit of news to the mental image of the photo he'd taken from the newspaper office, Sweeney began to glow with a welcome feeling of satisfaction. Vin sat there, expecting to be thanked for delivering this apparently important development but Sweeney seemed to have forgotten he was there.

Moments later, when Rose mounted the steps and swung round into the living room, there was Vin looking thoroughly deflated while her husband beamed up at her like a cat that had just consumed the world's fattest canary.

•

"But what did she say to this Joe Gilmore in Laver's Bay?" pressed Rose, having moved the two men to the kitchen table. "I mean, she didn't do anything stupid like saying 'You can't be you! You're in San Francisco!', did she?"

"No, she said didn't talk to him at all. Just ordered a couple of beers for herself and Omar and tried not to stare. She used to come in the Bag with me often enough to know Gilmore by sight, all right. There were fishing trophies all over the wall next to the bar and she wandered over and checked out the plaques. It was his name all right. And all the customers were calling him Joe. I don't know what else to tell you."

Rose rubbed her forehead. "Thank goodness for that. Until we can figure out what's really going on, we don't want to mess things up by spooking the wrong person."

It was plain to Rose that Sweeney had not yet shown the photograph to Vinnie. Her eyes met her husband's for an instant and she tried to suggest telepathically that he keep it that way for now. But he seemed too caught up in thought to jump up and want to explain anything to his helpful friend.

"You be sure to thank Lydia for us when she gets back, Vin," said Rose. "And we'll cover the phone call. It was mighty decent of her to go out of her way like that."

"No sweat, really. She'd rather eat seafood than anything in the world. And South Australia is seafood heaven from what she said. One thing *our* Joe Gilmore said that was on the money was about the fishing in Laver's Bay. Sounds like it is the best in the world."

"But what are you going to do now, Niall? Gilmore can't be in two places at once. One of 'em's got to be a phony. But even if the one here is a phony, that doesn't change anything about who was where on Friday night, does it?"

Sweeney and Rose just looked across the table at each other, thinking independent thoughts. At the moment, all Sweeney really wanted was for Vin to get lost so he could fill Rose in on the astonishing news he'd received from Brian Byrne.

Vin, however, seemed delighted to be centrally involved in the investigation. He leaned back and helped himself to a cold beer from the fridge.

"You know, I've been thinking but I just can't figure it. You remember, we went over it before, about who had left the bar and who hadn't, and aside from tossing Blayney out the door after the fight, Gilmore supposedly never left the back of the bar until the body was discovered. So how could he be the murderer? Seems like we're wasting our time worrying about him if he never had an opportunity."

Sweeney remembered how Annie and Gilmore swore he never left and how none of the others around the music table were near the front when he chucked the defeated Blayney out the door. The fight had attracted the total attention of the pool table contingent and everybody standing at the bar. The ones at the bar had backed up the story, but perception of elapsed time while standing at a bar had to be suspect. Did it really just amount to Gilmore's word that he didn't have time to haul Blayney around the corner and carve him up?

Sweeney beetled his brow and went over the cast of characters again in his mind. "Yeah, I suppose we still have to try to figure who left the bar after the fight as the possible suspects. That would be all the musicians except me, wouldn't it? Marjorie and Rod left together, then Kilbride and Charlie the bodhran player and Peter all left when I wasn't paying much attention to them, but I don't know who left first. Did you see any of them leave, Vin?"

"No, remember I came back after taking Christie home right when the fight started. I found out about how it turned out when I got back, but by that time all the others were gone. That was long before you left for the car and found Blayney."

"The poor kid was so upset," said Rose, "I'd have thought you'd want to stay with her and comfort her."

"I did, but by the time I'd walked her home she was a little calmer and quieter. When I asked her if she wanted me to stay she said I'd better not. She was afraid of waking her mother up. So she tiptoed in and I left her there and came back."

"Any chance you saw one of the others walking down the street when you came back? Can you remember anything at all?"

"Not really, because after dropping Christie off at her house down the other end of the block near California Street, I just walked back up California and cut across Eighth to the Bag. It was the same distance either way. There was nobody walking down there that I knew."

"So you really weren't gone that long." remarked Sweeney, trying to piece together parts of the Friday night that still remained blurry.

"Nope. Eight blocks down and eight blocks back. And it was too chilly a night for a slow stroll. Besides, I was worried about you!"

Ten minutes and many "thank you's" later Rose hustled Vinnie out the front door and strode back to the kitchen to where her husband was nosing around in the fridge looking for another beer.

"I think Vinnie got the last one," she offered. With one last look behind the mayonnaise he was forced to agree and drew himself a glass of water at the sink instead.

"Good thing you didn't clue Vinnie in on the photo from the newspaper office. We'd never have gotten rid of him. And I need some quiet time to figure what to make of that photo combined with Vinnie's little Aussie news flash."

"So, you've abandoned your notion of a deep, dark mythic plot full of bells and spears and curses?"

"Not in the least! Blayney's delusion is central to the case, whether you or the police care to admit it or not. Just give me time and I'll figure it out."

"We may not have all the time in the world, you know. If all the other leads get cold, the police may end up hauling me in as the only remaining suspect just to keep this case out of the unsolved file."

"They wouldn't," said Rose, not sounding entirely sure.

Sweeney clattered out of his chair and skipped for an instant down the hall, returning with the mysterious photo of the Irish soccer team and a well-scribbled note pad.

"I talked with Brian Byrne in Dublin again before you and Vin got here," he said excitedly. "He didn't tell me anything new about Blayney's literary obsessions, but listen to this!" And he read aloud his notes on Joe Gilmore's young brother and his brush with the law and subsequent disappearance. Rose's eyes grew wider as he added the facts about the other murder, the other missing knife, the private reward and the nameless tipster's suggestion that Blayney was the paid informer.

"Wow!" was all she could think to say when he had finished. She reached over and picked up the photo again. "Gilmore's got the sort of face that ages well, don't you think?"

"I never gave it much thought."

"No, really. There's a sort of Irish face that sets up early and then just stays the same for the next forty years, adding little crinkly lines. I'd say Gilmore has a face like that."

Sweeney looked down at the photo over Rose's shoulder. "Yeah, could be."

"So look at this guy in front here, Gilmore. Suppose this photo really is fourteen years old, since it sure as hell looks like Ireland to me and we know that fourteen years ago is the last time Joe Gilmore set foot there. Add fourteen years of crinkly lines in the face and what do you get?"

"You couldn't really tell in the shot like this."

"Exactly! And what would you get if you added fourteen years of crinkly lines to the face in back?" she inquired, pointing to the sandy-haired kid in the top row.

"You'd get a slightly older-looking guy who looks like he could be a blond version of Joe Gilmore."

"You can get gray hair dye, you know," suggested Rose softly.

The penny dropped. Sweeney tugged at the back of Rose's chair.

"C'mon! If you're right, we really are ahead of the cops for once. It's time we got the real story!" And he stormed toward the door, whisking his coat off the hook as he passed.

Rose stopped him at the end of the hall.

"But what in God's name are you going to ask him?"

"I don't know. I'll think of something in the car. But if I can come up with the $64,000 Question, you'd better be there with me to hear the answer."

Chapter Thirteen

Today the late afternoon was uncommonly quiet on the block of Clement Street as Sweeney parked opposite the Bag of Nails. The book stores and boutiques and Asian markets were all packed together farther down toward the Pacific, while here at this end the various restaurants were enjoying the welcome lull between the lunch rush and the dinner trade.

A gentle wisp of salt air licked at their faces as Sweeney and Rose crossed the street, warning of the fog's return at sundown. The green scalloped awning above the door of the bar rippled quietly as they swung open the door and entered.

Quiet. Sweeney had never seen it so quiet, though he had rarely stopped by the Bag of Nails before the end of his normal work day. Only one solitary regular was seated at the bar, a sad elderly fellow with an overlong fringe of wispy hair connecting his ears. Joe Gilmore seemed to be ignoring the single customer as he stacked glasses down at the far end of the bar. Sweeney looked around for Annie Simpson but she didn't seem to be around. The pool table was deserted. The juke box was playing Van Morrison.

Raising his eyes from the arranged pint glasses, Gilmore silently acknowledged their entrance. They chose a pair of stools directly in front of the tall, squarely-built barman, between the cash register and the tap handles.

Gilmore smiled casually and nodded greeting. "Afternoon Niall, Rose. What'll you have?"

Sweeney indicated Guinness and a pair of massive hands slid the two black glasses over the smoothly-polished reddish wood of the bar. There was an unusual tenseness about Gilmore, Rose thought. It couldn't have to do with why they'd come in, though, she told herself. How could he know what they had stumbled upon?

"So, things gettin' back to normal, Niall?" ventured the quiet, husky baritone.

"Normal? No." Sweeney shook his head slowly, his eyes remaining on the gray-haired man. "I'm still out of a job. And more importantly, I'm still being tagged for a murder I didn't commit. Not normal at all, really."

He took an unhurried swallow from his pint and wiped his moustache on the back of his hand. Gilmore stood there impassively.

"You know, Joe, I've been trying and trying to find a way to get my ass out of this sling. Haven't had a hell of a lot of luck so far. But I remembered something you said the other night and thought I'd drop by for a chat."

"Somethin' I said?" responded Gilmore, sounding slightly amused. "I know barmen have the reputation for bein' the poor man's shrink, but I ain't no psychic medium. If the cops haven't found that bastard's killer by now, it's a psychic you'll be needin', not advice from me."

Sweeney lowered the ends of his moustache in amiable disagreement. "Maybe not. Remember when I asked you after the fight about calling the cops to get Blayney? And you said something about them never being around when they're wanted? Then I remember you saying that they never arrest the right man anyway?"

Gilmore's gray features turned a shade grayer if possible, as if molded in hardening cement.

Sweeney hunched forward and smiled. "You sound like an experienced man of the world. In fact, I think you may just be the only person I know who can give me the advice to get me out of my unusual and very unpleasant predicament."

At this moment, Annie Simpson emerged from the back store room carrying a broken case of whiskey bottles. With a startled expression, she quickly surveyed the scene and scurried behind the bar, nearly dropping the box on the floor.

"That's all right, Annie girl. Stay put for a second." Gilmore moved out and around to where the only other customer still sat, behaving like part of the furniture.

"That's it, Mulreavy," he said, clapping a friendly but firm hand on the old man's shoulder. "Time to go home, lad. We'll be seein' you later."

Mulreavy was ushered stumbling out the door before he could protest.

"New business hours," Gilmore finished, closing the door and throwing the deadbolt. Very slowly, he walked back to where Sweeney and Rose sat, staring at the floor.

Standing before Sweeney, the tall, powerful man stopped, his hands in his pockets. "Now what's all this about? What is it you want?"

It was Rose who spoke first to the grim barman, as calmly as she knew how. "You wouldn't want another man to have to go through the horrors you've had to go through these last two years, would you, Kevin?"

Gilmore and Sweeney both turned to Rose, equally startled. Behind them, Annie uttered a stifled cry.

"Please believe me, Kevin . . . and Annie. Blayney may have blackmailed you with his knowledge of your past, but we only want your help to prevent a terrible injustice." She reached out and touched Gilmore's elbow. "You can be sure that what we've learned will never go further. We just stumbled on it as it is. We won't prevent one injustice by precipitating another."

Annie now had her arms around the gray-haired Irishman, her face buried in his chest. He stood quietly for a few moments and spoke.

"I'm not a murderer."

"If what our friends tell us is true, then . . . no, you're probably not." It was her turn to wash a long swallow of Guinness down a throat that had turned desert dry. "We really only have their word for it, you know. But maybe it doesn't matter."

Gilmore was still obviously so tightly wound as to be near the snapping point. "Friends? You say the police don't know. How did you . . . ?" he trailed off as Rose quietly began to relate the tale of the photo at the newspaper office, the extra-legal Dublin rumor mill they'd tapped into, and finally the ridiculous long shot of Lydia dropping into the bar in Laver's Bay. She omitted the part of the tale that had Blayney informing for the reward money.

"You have been busy, haven't you?" he grimaced, with no humor in his eyes. "And now that you know all that, you think that you can make me admit to killin' Blayney?"

"Oh, you didn't kill Blayney, of that I'm certain," replied Rose. Sweeney glanced at her, not looking at all certain. Gilmore and Annie seemed to share his skepticism. "It's really simple enough. We were worrying for a while about who could have popped out the front door and knifed Blayney and then come back to the bar. Well, even if the murderer hadn't gotten splattered with blood, there'd have been blood all over the knife, and a bloody knife would have been impossible to bring back in unnoticed."

Sweeney objected, "But anyone could stick it in a pocket . . ."

"Nope," said Rose. "Remember how thoroughly the police searched the bar. They didn't find the knife, but they sure as hell would have found a bloodstained pocket or a rag or something. Just one drop would have done it. And not one of you had time to change or try to wash your clothes."

"But that would mean none of the other musicians could have . . ." began Sweeney as Rose turned back to Gilmore.

"No one else had all the information in one place. We're the only ones who put two and two together. Our friend in Dublin swears that the Irish police never made the connection between Blayney and the cop killing you were accused of being involved with. That was what Blayney was counting on, wasn't it?"

The gray-haired man stared at the intense woman, conflicting emotions dancing behind his eyes. Rose suddenly realized that for all her assurances, Gilmore really had no reason to trust them. Not with the rest of his life. She reached over and pulled the photograph from her husband's inside jacket pocket and handed it to Gilmore.

"This is the snapshot Niall took from the newspaper office. If it told us what we wanted to know, it'll tell others. I imagine you can find a safe place to keep it."

Kevin Gilmore gazed down at the photo for the space of a dozen heartbeats and nodded, while the lines of tension slowly relaxed around the corners of his eyes and the visible pounding of blood in his temples subsided.

"I'll never see them again," he whispered almost inaudibly.

"He was sure he was the only one who knew the truth about you. So he used it for blackmail."

"No one in our crowd in Belfast trusted Blayney. He was a strange bastard from the start, always on about the heroes of the past. An angrier man you never met, but it was an unfocused sort of anger, if you know what I mean. Not the sort of bloke to trust with secrets. So he was always a bit on the outs and I guess he knew it."

"But what was your crowd?" asked Sweeney, emphasizing the last word.

"Jesus, what do you mean, 'crowd'? I laid bricks. I loaded boats. I was a printer's apprentice. I collected the dole. I lived in the house I was born in and drank in the local at the corner. It was none of my concern that the pub became a gathering place for crazy bastards who think they can create a free and united Ireland by killing a policeman or blowing up a bridge." He spoke with the hard and steely edge of truth.

"What about the Belfast murder?"

"Nothing to tell. I was in the wrong place at the wrong time. I had nothing to do with it. I only saw it done. Someone spotted me running away and the Army picked me up along with the other two what done the knifin'.

They never asked me for a confession or an alibi. They just started beatin' me. They were two days and nights at it before they pitched me in the back of the van to be arraigned. By that time they'd broken both my cheekbones and three fingers. I was unconscious so they didn't suss I needed a guard in the back with me."

Rose suppressed a shudder.

"The van was stopped in heavy traffic when I took a fool's chance and kicked out the back door. I managed to get away in the confusion and laid low with a friend who got me across to Scotland in a small boat. They hid me in a container ship to Australia. I almost starved on the way, but managed to get safe ashore in Melbourne. Somehow, they'd gotten word to my brother Joe and he had a safe place ready to put me while I got my strength back."

Annie looked up and sniffed. "It was the real Joe's idea about changing identities," she said. "He'd found the perfect place for himself and knew he'd never leave. So he dyed Kevin's hair gray and gave him his passport and enough money to get started here. None of the authorities gave him a second glance. He just vanished into thin air."

"Yes, the family resemblance is uncanny," said Rose. "Why'd you pick San Francisco?"

"It was just a place. I'd never been there, Joe'd never been there, there were plenty of Irish immigrants for company. Seemed like a likely spot. And my luck seemed to change the moment I arrived. I chanced on this job and Annie at the same time." He looked down at the blonde woman's troubled face with evident pride and tossed the photograph onto the bar.

"But what about Blayney?" insisted Sweeney. "What was your connection with him here?"

"Blayney? Damned if I thought there was any connection at all! He showed his face in here six months ago and let me know he knew I was a fugitive. To hear him tell it, he was in on the Belfast murder himself and even knew where the murder weapon was. Well, whether I was innocent or not I knew what sort of treatment I could expect should they cart me back. Blayney started askin' favors, like, and well, I helped him out to keep him quiet."

"Like recommending him for the job at *The Irish-American*?"

"That, and covering a bit of rent. That was all he'd asked so far, though I always knew he was holdin' out for somethin' big time. Just bidin' his time, like. I told you he was an untrustworthy son of a bitch. And why did he have that go at you, anyway?"

"If I knew that, I'd be a lot happier," admitted Sweeney.

"You sure you didn't kill him?" Gilmore cocked his head sideways.

Sweeney flushed. "What?" he nearly shouted.

"Forget it. I admit I thought you done it at first, but now that I come to talk to you, you don't strike me as havin' it in ya. Though I tell you I can't say I'm sorry that somebody took care of the job."

There was the sound of nervous throat-clearing.

"You say he mentioned the knife that they never found in Belfast?"

"Yah. Said he had it safe. Ha!" he laughed mirthlessly. "Safe for who?"

"Is that why you hid the knife he dropped the night of the murder," asked Rose evenly.

Gilmore and Annie both stiffened.

"It wasn't the knife that killed Blayney because it never left this bar. Was it the knife that killed the policeman?" Rose was suddenly sorry she had broached the subject. This man had a breaking point, and it was obvious that he had the strength to snap them in half as easily as a pair of pool cues if he thought he had no option. But Gilmore merely flushed and lowered his eyes, unclenching his vice-like fists.

"I honestly don't know," he said finally. "A switchblade's a switchblade. It might have been about the right size, though. My guess is that it wasn't the one. But I didn't know that on Friday. Jesus, I need a drink."

He lumbered around to pull a bottle of Jameson from the ranks of green bottles and pour himself a generous three fingers into the bottom of a half-pint glass. He downed it in two swallows.

In a small voice, Annie said, "Kevin . . . I mean Joe had told me all about the knife, the same as he'd told me about everything else. When the fight broke out and the knife went clattering across the floor, I nearly fainted for the shock! Joe hadn't seen it, but all I could think was that it meant his being sent back to die in prison."

"So you picked it up and hid it."

Annie nodded mutely.

"But if it was you who picked it up, how come the cops never found it when they searched the bar?" put in Sweeney, confused.

Gilmore looked at Annie for a moment. "Why not?" he said, half to himself, putting one finger under the cash register and another up underneath the Guinness tap two feet away. There was a tiny ping, and a narrow hidden drawer slid silently out from Gilmore's side of the bar.

"Works like the safety trigger on a printer's guillotine cutter. You need to push two buttons at the same time to release the catch, so no one is likely to open it accidentally. As you can see, I was right. The police missed it." And reaching into the drawer he lifted out the black-handled switchblade and laid it down on the bar. Sweeney and Rose stared at the evil-looking relic that had been the source of so much fear to everyone there.

"But why the drawer?" began Sweeney.

"Why? What do you think? When I first got here I couldn't be sure they wouldn't be comin' after me. I fixed up the drawer and kept a pistol handy. All I knew was they weren't gonna take me back." Annie put her arms around him again as he poured himself another drink. Rose could just see from her vantage point that the pistol still lay in the secret drawer where he'd placed it two years before.

"Nice job," said Sweeney admiringly.

"Speaking of nice jobs," interjected Rose, "who does your hair, Kevin? That's one authentic-looking dye job you've got there."

This question evinced the first honest, if hesitant laugh from both Gilmore and Annie.

"First of all, enough of the 'Kevin' stuff, if it's all the same to you. I'm Joe now, forever and always. My Aussie brother won't mind and I think Annie prefers Joe anyway." Annie hugged him and nodded.

"And about the hair," he said, glancing over his shoulder at his reflection in the bar mirror and running his fingers through the thick silver mop, "This is me color now. Premature gray runs in the family, see? I kept it dyed for about a year after I arrived when I noticed it was growin' in the same color. No need for Annie's secret salon treatments any more. It caught me about five years younger than brother Joe. Must've been the fear of the fugitive brought it on so sudden. But I'd rather it took the years off my hair than off my life!"

Sweeney toasted that thought with the last of his pint of Guinness. Running over this astonishing conversation in mental quick reverse he noted how easily Rose had taken over control and maneuvered Gilmore into his amazing admission. Earlier in the car, he'd racked his brain to come up with the clever and subtle questions for Gilmore that would lead them out of this confusing darkness swirling all about them. But he'd never asked them. And a good thing, too. Rose had blithely taken charge and done better than he'd dreamed without a second thought. No, they hadn't found the murderer yet, but he was damned proud of the remarkably perceptive woman he'd married.

Replacing his empty glass on the bar, Sweeney suggested that Joe put the knife back in the drawer and the less said about it the better. They all agreed. Together the knife and the old photo slipped into the shadows and the drawer disappeared again with a click. Gilmore automatically reached to his right and flipped the remote switch to turn off the sound of the juke box.

Sweeney realized that he'd had no idea that the tinny music had been playing ever since they'd arrived.

Rose sat quietly and pondered. So, now they were certain that Blayney's knife hadn't been used to kill him. That meant there was another knife somewhere waiting to be found. And Gilmore's and Annie's fearful behavior as regards the weapon was explained. Or was it?

She remembered Niall recounting to her his afternoon of conversations with Vinnie and Marjorie McAulliffe. They'd gone to the bar to get Marjorie's address first and Niall had said he was certain that both Annie and Gilmore were scared to death of something. But they couldn't have been frightened of the police arresting them for the murder, since they really hadn't left the bar and presumably could prove it. And they knew the knife wasn't the murder weapon. It had been fair enough to assume that if they just sat tight, the real weapon and murderer would turn up and it would all blow over quietly for them. With experiences like he had under his belt, Gilmore would know he could tough out such a wait, now that the only person besides his devoted girlfriend who knew he was a wanted man was dead and forever silenced.

The only other person, that is, besides herself and Niall. And she'd handed Gilmore the only concrete evidence they had found to connect him with Blayney. That should satisfy the poor wronged man that they truly meant him no harm.

But what if there was still someone else? Niall hadn't killed Blayney and, unless her gut feelings were dead wrong, it seemed now that neither Gilmore nor Annie had either. Could it actually have been an act of IRA revenge after all? And if so, was the killer still hanging around the city? And was Gilmore now under some different kind of pressure?

Rose felt like steering back toward the violent beginning of Gilmore's strange odyssey.

"Joe, the other two who were arrested with you for the killing of the policeman. Did you know them?"

He plainly didn't like talking about it. "To talk to, maybe. That's all. They were hard characters. They didn't mix."

"Were they Provos?" She searched his eyes.

He merely shrugged. "I had no politics. I kept out of political conversations, for all the good it did me in the end. Everybody said it was an IRA killing. Who am I to argue?"

"And whatever happened to them? Do you know?"

"What do you expect me to say? They been tried and sentenced and they're done for. Nothin' I say'll change a damn thing for 'em now, will it? I told you I have no politics and that's God's truth!"

"But if that murder was planned and executed by the IRA, they'd know you weren't involved, wouldn't they?"

Gilmore's face again became the granite mask behind which he had challenged them after bolting the barroom door.

"What are you asking?"

"I'm not sure." She found herself thinking aloud, remembering that for some reason she'd held back from the two of them Brian Byrne's belief that Blayney had received thirty pieces of silver for crucifying a pair of Irish martyrs. Or was it a fat bounty for the destruction of two dangerous wild animals? She couldn't know if Niall knew Brian Byrne well enough to read any subtle editorializing.

"Suppose," she began slowly, "Blayney really knew more about the Belfast affair than you think he did. And suppose he did something stupid and was in part responsible for the IRA murderers—and you—getting caught. Or even worse, suppose he deliberately ratted on them for some reason. Maybe even money. Do you think if the boys back home ever became convinced he'd done any of that that they'd send somebody after him for revenge?"

"That's a lot of supposin'."

Sweeney grasped at the straw Rose had tossed out. "But don't you see, Joe, if Rose is right, this was a political assassination and nothing to do with either you or me. Why, the IRA can't care about you even if they knew who you really were. And that's impossible."

"Impossible? What the hell are you doin' here, then?"

"All right, all right! I'm sorry." He threw up his hands, despairing. Rose broke in, trying to sound soothing.

"Really, Joe, we're awfully sorry about all this. But of all people you must be able to see that the police aren't going to let us live in peace unless they're convinced Niall is innocent. And the only thing that's likely to convince them is for the real murderer to be found. If neither of you have an idea who it might be, then Niall and I have got to come up with something damned clever, damned quick!"

But Annie and Gilmore seemed to have receded together behind an invisible barrier. There was fear here, but it was apparent to both Rose and Sweeney that no matter how much they wanted to help these two troubled people or how much they believed that the fear was somehow tied up with the answer to their own troubles, they were to be utterly shut out.

•

Across the street, a neatly-dressed man sat alone at the window table in the coffee house as the evening foot traffic increased and the shadows lengthened. Average and unremarkable, the man had sat there expressionless, smoking and nursing his coffee when Sweeney and Rose had entered the Bag of Nails. He had watched as the door had been locked against the thirsty paying public. He had waited. And he was still watching expressionless when the couple emerged again and drove off.

Chapter Fourteen

With Rose at the wheel, the two rode together in silence as they traversed the wooded hill at the east end of Golden Gate Park and turned with the traffic up toward Divisadero and the comfort of their own neighborhood.

Sweeney finally let out a long breath and spoke first. "Well, what do you think? Does that editor Burke know the truth about Gilmore?"

"I don't know. Why do you ask?"

"I was just wondering why he lied at first about Gilmore recommending Blayney for the job?"

"Hm. It could be just natural reticence. There are plenty of people in the Irish community around here who'd just as soon keep their activities quiet. He's in a position to know plenty of them."

"Yeah. Most of it is innocent enough, like construction work done under the table. Chances are Burke is just a man who likes to keep his mouth shut." He rode another block without any additional theorizing.

"Still, Gilmore is frightened of something, and that means either that someone else out there is onto him or that he thinks someone's onto him."

Rose could think of no good reason to argue the point. Another thought, though, was nagging at her quietly. "Joe said he'd given Blayney some money, didn't he?"

"For rent. Yeah, that's right."

"But why did he hit Joe up? If Brian Byrne was right, Blayney had a wad of bounty money, didn't he?"

Sweeney tugged at his moustache pensively. "Yeah, but it might not have been much. Say a few thousand. That's quite a pile of money by Irish standards and it looks like it was enough to justify tossing a couple of guys to the sharks. Maybe he thought it was enough to start a new life, got over here and found out the cost of living was outrageous. He couldn't go back, certainly. Maybe he lost it gambling. Who cares?" he shrugged.

"Hm," repeated Rose, remembering that the police had never mentioned finding a huge, mysterious pile of cash.

They turned up Hartford Street, where the crisp air determinedly kept the ocean fog at bay and moisture glistened on the eaves, reflecting the last light of sunset. As they stopped in front of the house, Sweeney pulled himself out of the car and leaned against it heavily while Rose walked around to join him on the sidewalk.

"It's been a full day, don't you think, love?" she inquired, noticing how tired and taut the once-ebullient lines in Niall's face had become.

Sweeney just stood there, his lips pressed together. He shook his head, trying to order his thoughts. "Shit! There's got to be something else we can do!" he declared. "It just keeps rolling around in my brain. If Gilmore and Annie are in the clear, it must've been one of the other musicians. Nobody else could have gotten hold of the . . ."

"Ha!" injected Rose, her index finger in the air. "See? Blayney's knife doesn't matter any more, you stubborn lummox! It could have been anybody! Now, why don't you just come in and relax and maybe let it rest?"

Sweeney acquiesced moodily, climbing the stairs behind her and plopping down in the blue chair in the living room with a resounding thud. So it didn't have to be one of the players. Still, it might be one of the players. He'd only talked with Marjorie. Maybe he should have a chat with Rod Hesse just for laughs. He just couldn't relax. His skin crawled.

"You want something for dinner? There's not much to eat in the house," called Rose from down the hall.

Sweeney got back up and put his jacket on. "No thanks. I'm not hungry. I think I'll go for a walk. I'll pick up something down the street on my way back."

The front door closed quietly. Rose stared into the nearly empty refrigerator. She wasn't hungry either. She wandered back into the unoccupied front room and spent a minute idly moving knick-knacks around and straightening books. Mad Sweeney and Saint Ronan kept dancing around in her crowded brain, thumbing their noses at her. Maybe it was time she admitted she was all wrong and abandoned her loony theory.

Since Saturday morning she had carried Seamus Heaney's *Sweeney Astray* from home to school and back again, hoping for a sweet, golden moment of inspiration. She dug the small volume out of her bag and propped it up on the mantelpiece, glaring at it. It was a ridiculous idea, she had to admit. Sure, there might have been delusion both in the legend and in the real life and death events of recent days, but it was all different sorts of delusion wasn't it?

And anyway, she couldn't get away from the cold, hard fact that in the legend it was Sweeney who was mad, dazed and confused, while last Friday it was Michael Ronan Blayney who had clearly behaved like a madman, even if her victimized husband, the designated Sweeney, had been a little dazed and confused himself. As he'd had good reason to be.

She took the book down and began leafing through it again aimlessly. The curses at the beginning had sounded like such a promising link, since Blayney had initiated his attack on Niall with similar invective. Her eyes sparkled when she recalled how she'd almost convinced Inspector Elliot that she'd hit upon the key to the mystery. Almost.

Oh well, if the beginning of Mad Sweeney's story was in some way parallel to the beginning of Blayney's, then maybe the end for Blayney was somehow parallel to the end of Sweeney. She riffled to the back of the book, not particularly hopeful. Strained logic be damned.

Rose had never much liked the end of the story, since after all those years of madness and torture, Mad Sweeney still lost out at the last to the church. That was hardly a fair and fitting ending, she thought. She felt certain that there had once been a more satisfying, pre-Christian reading of the legend that brought Sweeney back to a position of, at the very least, human dignity, after being so thoroughly punished for his admittedly rash acts.

Leafing backwards, she found herself reading snatches of Mad Sweeney's final poem, spoken as he lay dying. It was supposed to be his final confession but she thought it still rang with the voice of the proud, uncompromising spirit. The dying madman still spoke as the pagan, forever locked to his beloved stony homeland and all the living things with which he shared it and from which he drew power from it.

> *There was a time when I preferred*
> *the blackbird singing on the hill*
> *and the stag loud against the storm*
> *to the clinking tongue of this bell.*
>
> *There was a time when I preferred*
> *the mountain grouse crying at dawn*
> *to the voice and closeness*
> *of a beautiful woman.*

There was a time when I preferred
wolf-packs yelping and howling
to the sheepish voice of a cleric
bleating out plainsong.

You are welcome to that cloistered hush
of your students' conversation;
I will study the pure chant
of hounds baying in Glen Bolcain.

Of all the innocent lairs I made
the length and breadth of Ireland
I remember bedding down
above the wood in Glen Bolcain.

Was that the speech of a last-minute convert? Rose didn't think so. A glance at the clock shocked her out of her poetic reverie as she suddenly remembered that she was late for her one English Lit evening discussion session of the week. Whisking all of her class materials into her briefcase, she sprinted twice up and down the hall before she'd bundled all the appropriate clothes back on and bounded out the door to the car below.

•

Twenty minutes later found Sweeney pacing down the Stanyan hill, going no place in particular. The backs of his calves ached pleasantly and the crispness of the air held a refreshing power, having pushed his worries into the background at least for a short time.

Stopping to get his bearings, he realized that he was standing less than a block from Marjorie and Rod's apartment. Since it seemed that his feet had made a decision for him, he turned the corner and knocked on the door.

"Hi," greeted Rod. "Marjorie said you'd been by. Want to come in?" he added almost as an afterthought.

"For a second." The floral scent in the hallway was as strong as during his last visit with Vinnie, but the perfume had altered slightly. It seemed that Marjorie had inherited an extra bouquet of roses today from the flower shop.

"I guess Marjorie told you I came by to thank her for helping clean me up the other night. I found myself in the neighborhood and thought I'd thank you, too . . . you know, for stopping the fight the way you did."

Rod shuffled his feet uncomfortably. "No problem. Glad to do it, really. Don't like to see anybody get beat up."

He led Sweeney back down the hall to the kitchen where, apparently, he and Marjorie did all their entertaining. Rod noticed Sweeney looking around for signs of Marjorie. "She's out at the store. Should be back soon if you'd like to wait around."

"Oh, I don't know if I'll stay long. I'm supposed to pick up some groceries myself. I understand the police were around asking you guys questions, too. Hope they weren't too much of a pain."

"Nah. The Inspector came over to ask me if I'd killed Blayney for being impolite to Marjorie. I said no. That was about the size of it. He never came back, anyway. Fine with me."

There was something ineffably believeable in Rod's casual response to the question. Sweeney wanted to believe him. Looking at him for a long moment he discovered that he felt relieved. "What do you think about the other musicians, though?" he asked.

"What do you mean? Do I think one of them killed the guy? Christ, I don't know. They had nothing to do with him, any more than Marjorie or I did. Besides, they all left about the same time. Nobody felt like playing tunes after he conked you and Gilmore tossed him out. What mayhem!"

Sweeney agreed wholeheartedly. "But are you sure they all left when you did?"

Rod didn't seem to care. "Yeah, the two of us walked out as soon as we'd cased up the instruments. We saw Peter get in that old VW bus of his and drive away while we were loading the car. And Kilbride was walking up toward Arguello with two other Irish guys who'd been playing pool. I think they're all related or something."

"And Charlie?"

"Charlie . . . ? Oh, the kid with the bodhran! Ah, he'd left already. I didn't say peep to him all night. He doesn't know anybody, does he?"

"Not me, anyway," replied Sweeney and they both laughed.

Rod stood and stared out the window into the backyard complex of gardens and fences and washing lines. "Marjorie told me you were asking a lot of questions about Blayney." Sweeney sat up, no longer entirely relieved, wondering whether the undercurrent of violence he'd once seen well up in Rod was showing any indication of returning with the change in subject matter. But the muscular guitarist simply stared as he spoke.

"The guy had one foul mouth. I never liked him from day one. He had a way of getting under your fingernails like an infected splinter." Sweeney found himself wringing his hands in involuntary response to the uncomfortable mental image.

"And yes, I knew about Marjorie going out with him when I . . . when we . . . when we'd had our little misunderstanding. But I know nothing happened. Still, he had that way of hinting that was so sick! He just couldn't leave it alone. I knew I was going to have to haul off and flatten him one day. And I was fixing to the other night. But I never got a chance to do it properly. He'd have gotten more than just a quick crack on the head from me if Marjorie hadn't intervened and then . . . all the rest . . . you know." He looked a little sheepish and perhaps a bit ashamed.

Sweeney got up to leave. "Funny how things turn out, sometimes, isn't it, Rod?"

"Yeah. Funny."

•

The discussion group dispersed at nine o'clock in a general glow of good feeling. Rose had ended up as referee between one student's spirited denunciation of Hemingway's sexual imagery glorifying both battle and bullfighting and another student's rebuttal on the grounds of unfair feminist revisionism. She'd thoroughly enjoyed it, since no one had ever gotten around to asking her personal opinion of Hemingway . . . always a sore subject in the English Department.

Violet Reese had made a comment or two during the discussion but had avoided the full-scale verbal fisticuffs toward the end. Rose thought of her as one of her more sensible and sensitive young students. As they left the classroom, they found themselves walking together and Rose offered the friendly girl a lift home.

"You know, I'm really very pleased that Christie's going out with Vincent," said Violet as they climbed into the cluttered car. "It's very good for her. I mean he's very good for her."

Rose appreciated being taken into such a sisterly confidence. "I certainly have every expectation that Vinnie will be the perfect gentleman, Violet."

"No, that's not what I mean. I mean she really hasn't dated anybody at all for the longest time. Not since Daddy died. Vincent has helped her come out so much in just only a few weeks. You wouldn't believe the change."

"Well, to be honest, I didn't know Christie until quite recently, so I'll have to take your word for that. But Vinnie has excellent taste."

Violet flashed an earnest grin.

"I suppose the death of your father was hard on both of you," Rose added casually.

"Oh yes, it was a terrible shock. Mother's never been very strong since I was little, but I think it hit Christie the hardest."

Rose became more interested. "This happened before she went on that trip to Ireland?"

"No, it was right after, maybe two or three months, I think."

"I'm sorry."

"Oh, that's all right," Violet responded in quite a positive voice. "I think it's better to be able to talk about things like that. After all, we're all mortals aren't we?" Rose was forced to agree. They chatted amiably about growing up as kids in San Francisco, from Violet in Catholic school to Rose in college, and finally pulled up in front of the Reese's house on Eighteenth Avenue. It was a quiet block, once a simple middle-class neighborhood like a hundred others, now slowly being gentrified as the children who had been born here grew up and moved away.

As Violet got out of the car, Rose remembered leaving the question of food in a muddle when she had run off to school.

"Violet, do you mind if I pop in and call Niall. I may have to swing by the store and pick up some groceries."

"C'mon in," the girl cried eagerly. "I'll make some tea. Oh, but . . ." she flashed a troubled look at Rose as if she'd just been reminded of something. "I wonder if you'd do me a favor and not mention, you know, last Friday night in front of Mother?"

"Sure, if you like."

"Mother never knew that Vincent took Christie out to a bar, and certainly not that bar where the guy got murdered around the corner. Mother gets upset so easily sometimes, and I'd hate for her to get all strict and stuff and tell Christie she couldn't see Vincent . . ."

Rose indicated that the subject was closed and Vinnie's escutcheon would remain unblotted. Violet brightened instantly.

"Oh, and Mother is a little deaf, so if she's up and wants to talk, please be sure to talk sort of loud, okay?"

Rose tried to reach Niall on the phone but received no answer. Mentally assembling a short shopping list, she accepted the proffered chair in the front sitting room as Violet trotted into the brightly-lit kitchen facing the entrance hall and popped the kettle onto the stove.

The house was immaculate, decorated as a model San Francisco home of the 1930s. Rose's eyes followed the delicate floral wallpaper pattern up to where it met the ornate picture rail, above which the plaster of the walls was smoothly rounded to meet the ceiling, even in the odd angles above the bay window. The lamp light was reflected in a pleasant, softened glow.

Framed pictures occupied nearly every available space in the sitting room and up the stairway, which rose to the right of the hallway and the conveniently centralized kitchen. Rose noticed three large picture frames grouped together above the fireplace and suppressed a smile. Niall had pointed such a trio out to her at the first Irish bed and breakfast they'd visited on their trip together. Afterwards she swore she saw them in every parlor in the country. Jesus, the Pope and John F. Kennedy: The Holy Trinity.

Violet was finishing fussing in the kitchen. The white enameled gas stove must have come with the house, thought Rose. Home designers of the early twentieth century did not skimp on the size of kitchens, and a good thing, too. Lovely old appliances like these would be utterly out of scale in a modern efficiency apartment, even if the movers could have gotten it through the doorway. Salt, pepper and spice boxes were arrayed neatly along the warming tray up top, while a magnetic strip held assorted cutlery on the side of the stove facing the entryway and hand-knit oven mitts dangled from handy hooks on the wall. A slightly envious Rose made a mental note to go home and sandblast her own stove.

Violet brought out a small tea tray with three cups as her mother descended the stairs in a light gray cardigan over a simple long blue cotton dress. She was a small, slender woman. The girls evidently got their height from the father's side of the family. Still, the similar sparkle in the eyes was an unmistakable family trait. Violet made the presentations and Mrs. Reese expressed delight at the meeting.

"I rarely get an opportunity to meet my daughters' teachers anymore," she said, stirring her tea. "College is so much less formal than it was in my day."

Rose agreed, remembering to speak clearly as Violet had asked. "Personally, I prefer being on a first-name basis with my students. I find that informality isn't what makes or breaks a student. These days the competition is so fierce that each student has much more individual responsibility to perform than even as recently as when I was going for my degree. Too much formality on top of that is just a little too forbidding."

Mrs. Reese smiled indulgently. "Ooh, but you would have gotten quite an argument from Dominic, my husband, about that," she said. The red-headed daughter slurped her tea and rolled her eyes in agreement. "He believed that the old wisdom was best and that learning proper formality was necessary for a proper education. I've always thought the same, but what can a mother do alone with two modern-minded daughters?"

"I don't think you're doing too badly. By the way, where's Christie tonight?"

"Vinnie took her out to a movie," said Violet. "She has no night classes this term."

"Christie tells me that your husband is the fine fiddler she played me on the phonograph. Why, he's quite good. It's really very lovely." Rose politely accepted the praise.

"My husband, rest his soul, would be pleased to know that such fine traditional music was still being played here in San Francisco. And it's lovely that Christie has become so fond of it. It was very important to Dominic that the girls learn more about their heritage." Very Irish-looking biscuits made a circuit around the table.

"My people are from Boston, but Dominic was born in Cork and emigrated to America as a young man. That's where I met him. Boston, that is. It's a blessing that he lived to see Christie going back to visit for the first time. He was terribly pleased with her. We would have sent our younger one on a tour the following year had he not been taken from us so suddenly."

She and Violet exchanged identical disappointed smiles.

"I've never traveled anywhere with a tour," admitted Rose. "I always thought I'd do better finding interesting things on my own."

"Ah, but you're a bit older and knowledgeable about things. And married," the mother added pointedly. "That kind of travel is not such a good idea for the younger girls." She stated it as unalterable fact.

"Our church put together a marvelous, well-chaperoned tour to help introduce the girls to the best historical and cultural aspects of Ireland without worrying about the unfortunate sides of Irish life."

Rose detected from the tone of "unfortunate sides of Irish life" that if her fiddling husband and Mrs. Reese were ever in Dublin at the same time, they'd never run into each other. Still, there was something to be said for getting one's feet wet before diving bodily into another country or culture. They chatted about her holiday with Niall and about the more polite aspects of his long stay in Dublin on business.

"Was it a large group?" Rose inquired conversationally, steering the subject politely back to her hostess.

"No, only twelve girls from eighteen to twenty years old. The Sisters here at Sacred Heart are marvelous guides. Many of them lived for a time in

Ireland, and Sister Mary Frances was born in Wicklow. Violet, why don't you show Mrs. Sweeney . . . Rose, that is . . . the photo album."

Rose was pleased that Violet didn't seem the least embarrassed by this request and shifted forward to lean over the brocaded binder propped open on the low coffee table.

"I think these are some of the most beautiful photographs anyone in this family has ever taken. Here's a group of them in St. Stephen's Green. Here you can see the Rock of Cashel above, there . . ."

They leafed through half a dozen pages of green and rocky backgrounds, huge stone Celtic crosses looming over stone-bounded church yards, and candid snapshots of girls who were quite obviously having the time of the lives. They finally came to a group shot, evidently the requisite class photo. Rose could easily spot Christie in the back, among the taller girls.

"Which one is Sylvia?" asked Rose.

"Sylvia?" repeated Mrs. Reese. "Oh, I don't think there was anyone in the group named Sylvia." She turned the book around to face her and looked again at the photo.

"No, no, I've known all these girls for years. Never a Sylvia. Why do you ask?"

"Oh, no reason. I must have misheard the name." She accepted another cup of tea from Violet.

"Are you feeling all right, dear?" Mrs. Reese asked her daughter. "You don't look well."

"I'm fine."

"It's funny," Mrs. Reese began, as if prodding an old memory, "I recall when the girls were no bigger than two buttons. Christie had a little playmate named Sylvia. An imaginary playmate. Violet, you should lie down, dear," she turned again to the pretty red-haired girl who had placed her teacup down on the coffee table and was now shivering almost imperceptibly.

Rose could see that the mother was right. Violet did not look well at all.

Chapter Fifteen

In the distance Rose could hear the ferocious roar of the water that dashed itself into arcs of white mist and detonations of refracted color upon the jagged rocks a thousand feet below the crest of the high cliffs. Oddly shaped trees posed at intervals along the meandering green banks of the lake which stretched off into the distance, becoming the same dull gray as the sky. She picked her way carefully among the smooth stones and boggy patches, the watercress glistening in the cold, damp air, the tiny white blossoms winking like distant stars.

The man drinking at the water's edge seemed unaware of her approach until she stood scarcely more than a pair of arms' lengths behind him. His gaunt body was caked with earth and moss. Twigs tangled in his thin black hair. The red cuts and puncture wounds covering his arms and legs seemed not to concern him. A red and silver fish jumped far out in the lake and he started, bird-like, cocking head to one side. Rose could see one eye staring out toward the sound, round and filled with terror. The man blinked once, then again, sniffed at the air and slowly stood, completing his turn and standing naked before her.

Rose stood transfixed. The pools of his eyes were deeper and more troubled than the waters of the lake below the roaring falls. Here was unnamable and unquenchable sadness.

"Do you remember, lady, the great love we shared when we were together?" said the man in a voice so tormented that it brought unbidden tears rolling down Rose's cheeks. "Life is still a pleasure to you but not to me."

For a moment it was if she could feel the unutterable pain of the cursed exile. She began to raise her hand toward him but he started like a wild rabbit. She heard herself recite:

> *Sweeney, your sorrows are well known*
> *and I am not the treacherous one:*
> *the miracles of Holy Ronan*
> *maddened and drove you among madmen.*

But he backed away, his staring eyes fixed upon her, and clambered into the branches of a bare thorn tree. Unmindful of the blood which now dripped from his feet and hands, he continued until he'd reached the topmost branches, there swaying against the cloud-filled sky.

Safely out of reach, the mad man now looked down at Rose with a slightly altered expression. He passed a hand over his eyes, as if banishing a faroff vision and realizing for a moment that it was someone else now who stood beneath his perch.

"I freeze and burn," he said.

"I cannot help you," said Rose.

"My hearth grows cold. My fire dies."

"I know," said Rose, consumed with sadness. But Mad Sweeney's expression became almost wistful as he turned his gaze toward the far cliffs and spoke.

> *Of all the lairs I made*
> *the length and breadth of Ireland*
> *I remember bedding down*
> *above the wood in Glen Bolcain*

As he recited the verse he lifted up out of the tree and flew in ascending spirals up into the roiling clouds. The verse echoed again and again in Rose's ears, and as it echoed the sound changed until the words were being recited by another voice entirely.

Rose bolted up out of bed wide-eyed, soaked with sweat. She rubbed her eyes and lowered her feet to the floor, shuffling in search of her slippers. The electric clock made it nearly two in the morning. Niall stirred in response to the unusual disturbance, rolled over and opened one eye.

"Is it time yet?" he mumbled unenthusiastically.

"Time for what?"

"To call Brian. Thought I'd set the clock. I didn't hear it go off." He, too, sat up and scratched his head.

Rose stripped off her wet nightgown and fished her bathrobe out of the pile of clothes unceremoniously dumped beside the bed.

"It'll go off in a minute. I'll tell you what . . . I'll make you a cup of coffee and keep you company." She shuffled off to do just that, immensely relieved to have returned to a normal, human world.

A few minutes later Sweeney sipped at his hot coffee, thinking again about the previous day. "So you didn't catch Vinnie again last night after class?"

"No, I just dropped Violet Reese off at her house. Vinnie had taken Christie out to a movie."

"I've been thinking . . . what are we going to tell Vinnie about Gilmore, you know, being in two places at once?"

Rose poured herself a cup of coffee and sat down. "I don't think we have to tell him anything, do we? Lydia will have forgotten about it before she gets to Adelaide and she and her new flame will probably have different watering holes to hang out in. She was never that fond of the Bag of Nails."

Sweeney grunted in assent.

"And as for Vin, he knows that Irish families can be big. Just tell him Lydia was wrong and it was Joe's cousin in Laver's Bay. Say we all had a big laugh about it and that was the end of it."

"I suppose the simple answers are always best." He sat awhile in thought, considering that precious few simple answers had been offered to him since Friday.

"It oughtta be late enough in the morning, Dublin time, to catch somebody at Flannery's," he finally declared, pulling the kitchen phone over to him and searching out the address book with the long series of numbers that would connect him with his friend across the Atlantic.

"I'll go plug in the extension," said Rose. "I'll just listen . . . let you do the talking." And she took her coffee cup with her into the bedroom.

The line crackled and connected. Paddy himself answered and brusquely deigned to ferret Brian Byrne out from wherever he was. Byrne's always-leisurely voice finally drifted to Sweeney over the wire.

"Ah, Niall, are you still needin' help?" Sweeney sadly replied that his troubles were no less profound today than they'd been when he'd last called.

"Mm. Well, I did ring back Mr. Walsh, the owner of the pub in Inagh. He's back from Galway."

"Great! What did he say?"

"Ah well, it wasn't pleasant, boyo, that's a fact. I was hopin' you'd squared it all up by now. I don't see that it can be any more helpful than any other nasty gossip, but you can have it just the same. When I asked Mr. Walsh about Michael Blayney I was caught in a wee floodgate. How was he ever to forget the man who brought such shame on him, he says. It was two years ago and more and still clear as if it were yesterday, he says."

Sweeney waited anxiously while Byrne coughed and lit a cigarette. He could hear Rose breathing as she listened on the extension.

"So he comes in as usual early in the evening with a young girl in tow and he's quite the gentleman, with singing some song or other with the musicians and buyin' rounds friendly as ye please, he says. Then he and the girl go off and not an hour later she's burstin' back in screamin' that she's been attacked!"

"Raped?" exclaimed Sweeney.

"That's right. Quite hysterical, she was, and roughed up as well. Your man Walsh says such a thing had never happened at his establishment in living memory. And when Blayney comes tippytoin' back into the bar she starts screamin' so, he took off like hell wouldn't have him and never come back, even for his mail. And he bein' a regular and all."

"So, what happened to the girl?"

"Well, then. They finally calmed her down and she phoned someone in Dublin who came and picked her up and took her home, wherever home might be. Said she'd see her own doctor and report to the authorities there. Tall she was, he says, like most American girls."

"She was American? Did he remember her name?"

"He did. He said it was Sylvia."

That was all. Byrne apologized for having made no further headway toward clarifying Blayney's political connections and rang off.

Rose returned to the kitchen quietly, coming up behind her husband and gently wrapping her arms around his neck as he sat staring out the window into the darkness. Her arms dropped down to his waist and she squeezed him very tightly, saying nothing.

"Well, I really don't know what to make of all that," he said.

"Don't worry. Let's get some sleep now. We can think about it in the morning. I'll turn off the alarm. You sleep in."

Sweeney's breathing was regular within moments of his returning to the warm bed. Rose lay beside him, staring at the ceiling. She had one thing to do in the morning now. After that . . . well, she hadn't thought it out any farther.

She thought she knew the identity of Blayney's murderer and the reason for his death. But what in God's name was she going to do with the knowledge?

•

Rose sat in her office, haggard after a sleepless night. Niall had still been sound asleep when she'd slipped off early to school. Her aching eyes followed the second hand round and round the clock face, noting that she now had less than a half hour before her one-hour literature section, after which she could run home and . . . do what?

It was not the heroic finish she'd envisioned for herself in the wake of the catastrophes that had befallen her beloved Niall a few short days before. It was not heroic at all . . . if she was right, that is. She ran over her train of thought again for the hundredth time. Maybe she was wrong. Maybe she'd missed something, or made something up. She tried to think, her elbows on the desk and her fingers gripping at the roots of her hair.

It was only a guess, she kept reminding herself. There was no real proof. But she couldn't help coming back again and again to the way Blayney had died. The particular placement of the wound and the choice of the knife in the first place. These had to have been deliberate. And put together with what she now knew to be true—the thought made her shudder violently.

There was a knock on the door.

Rose raised her face from the blankness of her desk to see Violet Reese enter with an armload of books.

"Can I talk with you a minute, Rose?"

"Certainly, Violet," answered Rose, indicating the empty chair. "You look troubled. Is there anything wrong?"

Violet sat down, still clutching her books nervously. After a couple of false starts she said, "It's about last night . . ."

"Having tea with your mother, you mean?"

"Not the tea as much as the conversation." She gathered her courage and continued. "It's just that . . . well, Mother's very frail and I don't want to upset her and . . . last night you asked about Christie's friend Sylvia, and I wanted to ask you, um, never to mention her again. And maybe you could ask Vincent, too." Her eyes gleamed urgently.

Rose sat back and considered the nervous young girl for a moment, then smiled gently.

"You and your sister are pretty close aren't you? I admire that. I always wanted to have a sister, but I was an only child. You know, there are some things that a girl will never tell anyone in the whole world except a sister. That's a unique and special relationship."

She paced her words slowly and calmly. "I've got Niall, of course, but that's not quite the same thing. There are plenty of things I've done that I don't think I'll ever tell Niall."

Violet flushed and hazarded a tiny smile.

"I'm sorry if I accidentally said something embarrassing in front of your mother, but surely mentioning an imaginary childhood friend can't really upset her, can it?"

Violet's response was sharp. "But how did you even know about Sylvia? And you asked about her when you were looking at the photograph album!"

Rose let the question and the accusing tone pass and continued at the same measured pace.

"Violet, let me tell you a story. When I was a little girl I was something of a tomboy. I used to get into trouble all the time, coming home with torn blouses and skinned knees. When I was about seven I accidentally left the hose running in the back yard. It ran for an hour before my mother found it. By that time it had flooded the whole basement and ruined the carpet. Oh, was my mother furious! I knew I was going to catch it, but when Mother called me over and asked me if I'd done it I said no, as innocent as you please. I said it was my friend Alice. Trouble was, I didn't have a friend Alice. Mother asked me where Alice lived and I pointed down the street, thinking that would be the end of it. But that evening mother called me in and made me admit both to flooding the basement and worse: to lying about it. It was terrible. I cried myself to sleep that night. But I never again blamed anything I'd done on Alice.

"I've sometimes wondered what would have happened if my mother had believed that the nonexistent Alice really had flooded the basement. I might have had someone to blame something else on one day and get out of another licking."

She stopped and gazed seriously at Violet. "Was Sylvia that sort of imaginary friend for Christie? Were your parents more inclined to believe that Sylvia had misbehaved than that your sister had?"

Violet nodded. "But don't you see, Rose, as far as Mother is concerned, Christie and I never grew up. We're still perfect little angels to her, and since Daddy died, I couldn't bear for anything to make her doubt that."

"But Violet, are you more upset that I mentioned Sylvia to your mother or that your sister has brought her back to life again in the first place?"

Violet thought for a moment. "The fight in the bar really upset her, Rose. She's just afraid mother will find out she was there. She told me about the fight and being so scared and Vincent bringing her home and all, you see. She never goes to places like that and she was afraid that if Mother found out she'd be grounded and forbidden to see Vinnie or worse."

"That would be too bad," agreed Rose. "Did she tell you all this that night? I mean, when she came home?"

"Well, I came in first, after going to the movies sort of late. Mother was in bed and I ran upstairs to get changed. I heard Christie slam the door maybe five minutes later. I came downstairs and she was doing the dishes. Said there'd been a fight and that she'd left and . . . that Sylvia'd taken her home."

Rose took a deep breath.

"I know how upset she must have been," said Violet, "cause she hadn't mentioned Sylvia for years since . . ."

Rose finished the sentence. "Since she got back from Ireland, right?"

A silent tear glistening on her cheek was Violet's only response. Rose came around the desk and sat down on the front edge next to the young girl and took her hand. She had come this far and there was no turning back. Now, whatever happened, she had to know the whole truth, though it terrified her to think where the whole truth would lead.

"Violet, I hope that you came to talk to me because you believe I'm your friend and I'll do all I can to help you and Christie."

Violet still appeared apprehensive, but nodded her assent.

"First, let me assure you that neither I nor Vinnie nor anyone else will ever utter the name Sylvia in your mother's presence or, for that matter, to anyone else. Cross my heart. For that matter, this entire conversation will be our little secret. Swear to God." Inwardly, she realized that swearing to God likely meant two entirely different things to the two of them.

The frightened young girl blew her nose into a tissue and whispered thank you. Rose could no longer avoid addressing the last possibility. She suppressed another shudder and tried to continue calmly, hoping that her voice carried more certainty than she felt.

"But this is a strange world, Violet. And it's a much smaller world than you'd ever believe sometimes. Before you go will you answer me one question even though I can't tell you why I need to know the answer?"

Violet sniffed and nodded.

"After Christie returned from her trip to Ireland, were you the only person she told that she was pregnant?"

Chapter Sixteen

Rose found Niall in the same kitchen chair from which he'd called Dublin in the middle of the night. The morning newspaper was scattered across the table and the air was heady with the aromas of coffee and toast. He looked up as she entered and cinched up his bathrobe as he got up to pour her a mug of coffee.

She sat down and held the mug in both hands, letting the warm steam bathe her face. "I think I've solved the mystery, Niall," she said quietly. He responded with a slow smile—an expression of hope mixed with detached amusement.

"So, old Mad Sweeney was the key, after all, was he? I'm still not sure you'll be able to convince Inspector Elliot, though."

Rose considered just how to begin. "Funny enough, Mad Sweeney was a key, Niall. I had to wake myself out of a nightmare last night just before you called Brian Byrne. I met Mad Sweeney and we talked a little and . . . he recited part of a poem to me that connected up with some things we'd learned before and something else I was told last night."

"Doesn't sound like too bad a nightmare."

"No, but it was so sad, somehow. I couldn't help crying the whole time and I had to wake up." She blinked back the memory. "Then it was as if it all came true when you made the phone call. And somehow it was even sadder."

"What do you mean?"

"In my dream, Mad Sweeney recited the verse about his never forgetting the night he bedded down above the wood in Glen Bolcain. You remember?" Sweeney nodded, knitting his brow in an effort to remember clearly.

"Then Brian Byrne told about Blayney raping the American girl."

"Right. A girl named Sylvia. What does that have to do . . . ?"

"Niall, he bedded her down in Glen Bolcain! Don't you see?"

He didn't see. "But what does that have to do with us?"

"Last night after class, when I took Violet home, I stopped and talked a little with Violet and her mother. They showed me some snapshots of Christie's church tour to Ireland and I asked about her friend Sylvia."

"Sylvia!" cried Sweeney, finally remembering. "Good grief, I must have been asleep. Christie told me about her friend Sylvia the first time we talked in the bar. So," he leaned over with reignited interest, "you think that it was Christie's friend Sylvia who was raped by Blayney?"

"No. There is no Sylvia. She was a make-believe friend invented by Christie when she was a little girl. It was Christie Reese who was raped two years ago by Michael Blayney above the wood in Glen Bolcain."

And as Sweeney sat in stunned silence, Rose recounted to him how she'd learned the truth about Sylvia. She then told him about the illuminating follow-up conversation she'd had at school with Violet this morning.

"I don't know what to say. I'm not sure I can believe it. But even if it's true, are you suggesting . . . ?"

"I'm not sure, either. Let me try to explain what happened from the beginning, according to what I think we know. Violet supplied all the details I was missing." The sound of her own voice seemed to her to be coming from a great distance.

"Christie was brought up in a devoutly religious home, with a very strict father. After two daughters, her mother had miscarried and almost died, the result being that they could have no more children. The mother was physically frail from then on. Violet didn't say it in so many words, but it seems her mother projected her own guilt about the miscarriage on the two girls, making them feel as if they had to achieve as much as the umpteen unborn brothers and sisters might have." Sweeney swallowed hard, quietly thankful he'd been spared that sort of pressure growing up.

"The father was a complete authoritarian and severely punished bad behavior from a very early age. The girls were also instilled with a particularly strong consciousness of sin and fear of Hell from this upbringing. But kids behave like kids sometimes in spite of the fear of Hell, and Christie had an adventurous spirit. She began to get into trouble early and invented an imaginary friend Sylvia to be the fall-girl if her father should ever disapprove of her games. By the time she was a teenager, she'd apparently perfected other forms of adolescent deceit and Sylvia sort of faded out of the picture as no longer needed."

"What about Violet? You say she knew about Sylvia?"

"Oh yes, from the beginning. It was a little sisterly joke at first. But Violet remembered when they were about nine and ten that Christie was hauled up for something shameful in front of her father and refused to admit she was lying about Sylvia. She steadfastly insisted that Sylvia was the culprit, even in the face of some obviously damning evidence. Violet was forced to watch her being thrashed and the memory apparently burned both of them. Violet never said a word about Sylvia to anyone after that. And, as far as Violet was concerned, that was the end of Sylvia. Until two years ago."

"Two years ago. Christie's trip to Ireland."

"Uh huh. Most of the church tour went the way you'd expect a church tour to go. Then, while they were in Clare, Blayney happened on Christie and a couple of the others and turned on the charm. She stole out alone and met him, thinking they'd go out to hear some music in the village. She was too green to notice that the shandys she was brave enough to let him buy her were heavily laced. A few rounds later and . . . Brian Byrne finished the story on the phone last night."

Sweeney felt the hair rise on the back of his neck. "And she lied about going out west. I remember she said the tour hadn't gone that way. But after she came back in," he protested, "Brian said she called a friend in Dublin who came and picked her up."

"There was no friend in Dublin. She called a girl in the tour group. They were all staying nearby at a large B & B. And she never reported the incident to anyone."

"So this other girl knew about Blayney, too?"

"No, apparently not. Christie had her wits about her enough to tell her friend that she was only afraid of the sisters learning that she'd been out after curfew against all the rules. She locked the rest away inside."

Locked the rest away inside, repeated Rose to herself. And wasn't that exactly what happened to the poor girl?

"Two months passed and Christie began to feel sick. Fearing the worst she went secretly to the Planned Parenthood clinic and learned that she was pregnant."

"Pregnant! But, how'd you know that?"

"I didn't. It was just this nagging sense I had that the particular way Blayney was killed was important. I was faced with a possibility, so I bluffed Violet and she admitted it was true. Anyway, this was the worst possible news for the 'perfect' young unmarried daughter of two devoutly religious parents. It wasn't until then that she told Violet about it."

"So, Violet knew about the rape?"

"Yes, but only the fact of it. She had no idea who the man was. Christie never mentioned his name. She still knows of no connection between Christie and Blayney. Anyway, the girls talked and talked and finally agreed that no matter how mortal a sin it would be to get rid of the baby, if their father found out about it, it would surely kill him! That was too horrible an alternative. So Violet helped Christie take care of it quietly."

"You mean an abortion?"

"Yeah. Not so amazing, really. Even Catholic girls get abortions sometimes. It was early enough and the rules around here are 'no questions asked,' so no one ever knew except Violet. Unfortunately, things didn't work out the way they'd planned. Two days after the abortion, the father drops dead from a heart attack."

"Jesus," intoned Sweeney.

"Exactly. Christie lost it. She was certain that her horrible sin had killed her father after all, that it was God's swift punishment upon her. But Violet really didn't know what to do when Christie started talking out of her mother's earshot as if it had been Sylvia who had had the unspeakable abortion, and not she! Violet kept her going to mass and confession in hope that she'd be able to put it all behind her and, as far as the younger girl could tell, weeks later she seemed to have finally calmed down and gotten over it."

"And I suppose their mother had enough torment of her own to prevent her from noticing all the extra guilt that Christie was going through," added Sweeney with a sigh.

"Yes, all that churchgoing didn't clue the mother into anything weird at all. She just thought that the shock of Daddy's death had brought the girls closer to God and was one of the things that she, the grieving widow, still had to feel thankful about. Eventually, Christie stopped mentioning Sylvia around Violet so her sister gradually stopped worrying so much about her. Until I mentioned Sylvia last night, that is. Violet couldn't disguise her shock when I mentioned the name. I was trying to find a good way of asking her about it when she came by my office this morning and beat me to it."

They sat together in silence for a few minutes, digesting it all separately. Sweeney was picking through his scattered memories, plugging in scraps of disparate information that now, in the light of what Rose had told him, filled out a more complete picture. But the question of what had happened late Friday evening was still unanswered. He still couldn't connect up the rape, the imaginary friend, the abortion and the sad death of a young girl's father with the mysterious and violent death of Michael Blayney.

Rose seemed to sense her husband's frustration and took up her story again.

"It must have been an incredible shock to Christie to see Blayney again in San Francisco. Certainly she'd been able to bury him so deep, the memory of the name and face and voice would never have welled back up to her conscious mind by themselves. It was an extraordinary coincidence that they should have been there at the same time."

Sweeney recalled reading the *Irish-American* review earlier that evening with Vinnie and Christie. Christie had tried to read it herself but Vin had grabbed it and had read bits aloud. So she hadn't noticed the name of the reviewer then. And she must have been coming out of the ladies' room when Blayney started the fight. That's when she screamed. She had screamed not in fear for Sweeney's safety, but because she had recognized the man who, by the extension of his foul and brutal attack on her two years earlier, had caused her to believe that she had killed her father!

He still resisted the conclusion. "But Vinnie took her right home. He walked her there and walked back to the Bag and hung out with me for a while."

"Remember what he said, though? He said that when she'd calmed down at her door, she'd told him to go home and not disturb her mother?" Sweeney nodded. She'd tiptoed in quietly.

"But Violet told a different version. She said that Christie had slammed the door when she got home. That when Violet had gone back downstairs after hearing the door, Christie was doing the dishes."

"Are you saying that Vin was lying?"

"No. Christie came home twice. It was the second time she came in the front door that she wanted to be noticed. That's why she slammed the door, so that even her slightly-deaf mother would sit up and remember."

Sweeney felt fingers of ice trace along his shoulder blades.

"The knives stuck on the side of the stove must have been the first things Christie focused on when she came home. That side of the stove faces the front door, where she stood, having gently closed it on Vinnie. Her confused and terrified mind was being pulled back to the night of Blayney's vicious attack on her, the night she'd tried so hard for two years to bury and forget. From the timing of what actually happened, it could only have been a matter of seconds before she grabbed one of the knives and was back out the door to look for Blayney. She must have turned back up the way she and Vin had come. Vin had walked around the other way, so he never saw her on his way back to the bar."

"Blayney had sat dazed where Gilmore had tossed him in a nearby doorway for a minute or two while he gathered himself enough to stand back up. From what we know of him, he probably considered going back into the bar, but for some reason thought the better of it and decided to go home. He was pretty banged up, after all. So he staggered two blocks to the corner of Tenth and turned down the street toward his apartment just as Christie walked up through the fog from the other direction and saw him there."

"What the hell was she thinking she'd do?" cried Sweeney. "She didn't know where Blayney lived."

"No, but she didn't know he'd been tossed out of the bar permanently, either. I think she thought she'd still find him there. But he'd walked two blocks in her direction when he met her. The timing is right. That was the exact moment she appeared and saw him."

"While Vinnie was walking up a parallel street, not two blocks away."

"Yeah." Rose nodded to herself. "I think we can guess the rest. She approached him as he got to his stairway. I don't know if he recognized her as a previous conquest. It doesn't really matter. Doubtless he said something meant to be charming. God knows what. I'm willing to bet it was similar to the line he gave Christie the night he raped her, though. I bet that it was the trigger mechanism. The poor girl snapped, pulled out the knife and gave him one well-placed swipe across the middle." She shuddered uncontrollably.

"Even the method points to her. This was no clean and efficient political killing or a junkie mugger in an alley. It was an abortion and a death in payment for an abortion and a death."

Sweeney discovered that he was squeezing Rose's fingers tightly. "Vinnie did tell me she had a hell of a backhand."

Rose continued softly. "Then she turned, tripped, fell once against your car and ran back home. I expect she peeked into the house to make sure no one was downstairs, then came in and washed off the knife, went over and slammed the door to signal her return to her mother upstairs, and was washing the rest of the dishes when sister Violet came down to chat.

"So the murder weapon . . ."

"Is stuck on a magnet on the side of a stove eight short blocks down the street from the Bag of Nails. The police will never look for it there."

"And after she'd killed Blayney she had to keep Sylvia alive. She kept dropping her name into conversations, probably to keep convincing herself that the imaginary girl really existed."

"She never entirely lost Sylvia after her father died. You said she mentioned her earlier Friday evening, didn't you?"

"Yeah, she did," he remembered. "She must have been feeling vaguely guilty just being in the Bag of Nails, even with as squeaky-clean a date as

Vin Bowen. But you think that keeping Sylvia alive, she could tell herself that it was somebody else who had strayed in Ireland, had been raped, and all the rest?"

"Including killing Blayney."

"Even including that. What do you think, Rose? Do you think she's . . . I don't know . . . schizophrenic or anything?"

Rose just sighed. "Hell, I'm no expert, but I don't think so. More likely she's just a very guilt-ridden girl who handed out what she saw as appropriate Biblical justice to a dreadful man who had done her irreparable harm."

Her husband's next question was one she'd been putting off thinking about. "What are we going to do now?"

"About Christie? I honestly don't know." Her voice acquired an edge. "We can't just call Elliot and have her arrested, can we? Knowing what we know? She certainly wasn't in her right mind when she did it. And even given the two year wait, I think she gave him what he deserved. It was justifiable homicide!"

"I doubt a jury would see it that way, though. More likely, she'd end up in a mental institution. And that would break her mother's and sister's hearts. To say nothing of Vinnie's! Haven't they suffered enough already?"

Rose walked over to the stove and called up a blue flame under the kettle, fumbling blindly for a coffee filter. She stood there for a full minute in silence.

"I can't tell the police," she declared firmly. She looked over and met his eyes. "I can't do it!"

"No, love. I don't suppose you can. And I can't either, though I have no idea where it leaves me."

A moment later another thought occurred to him as well. "And what about Vinnie? What the hell are we going to tell him?"

Tears welled up in Rose's eyes. So this was the thanks the world was going to give her for solving the goddamned mystery.

•

The day came and went on Hartford Street, only this day was not like any other recent day. There were no eager errands, no leads to follow, no clues to pick over. There was not even a desire to think about the situation any more, in this world that had caved in so thoroughly on the carefree fiddler and his almost irrepressible wife. There was no hope today.

Sweeney brooded at one end of the house while Rose sat scratching vague comments on English papers at the other end. Inspector Elliot had come over and admitted (how long ago was it now?) that he probably wasn't involved in the AdTech money laundry scandal after all. But that was after he'd been booted out of his job and the ex-boss refused to listen to reason. Now Rose seemed to have figured out what happened on Friday night and no matter how they turned it, twisted it, shook it, or cursed it, the answer seemed certain to ruin the lives of more than one innocent bystander. And if they kept the answer to themselves and Inspector Elliot came back to Sweeney demanding that he defend himself against a charge of willful murder? What then?

No, it was not a good day at all.

The evening crept in, the darkness welling up from the east to meet the bank of fog welling up from the west. Sweeney and Rose had not spoken for hours by the time Rose looked up from her work and noticed that it was past midnight and the distant foghorns were echoing plaintively.

She plodded down the hall and found her husband standing at the fireplace in the living room, playing with the junk on the cluttered mantel, equally oblivious of the time.

She came up quietly and scratched him on the back of the neck. "It's awfully late, Niall darlin'," she whispered. "What do you say we call it a night and pick this back up in the morning?"

"What do you say we pack our bags and get the hell out of here?" A low foghorn sounded once more in seeming support of the idea.

"What, now? This minute?"

"Sure! We can hop on a plane and be in Ireland in the morning. We can find a cheap reconditioned workhouse in Clare and survive by playing Irish music to American tourists."

Rose laughed, half because Niall sounded like he almost meant it.

"Right!" she agreed peremptorily. "You can, you mean. Only two problems with the plan." She counted on her fingers. "First: I don't play Irish music, so if you expect me to make a living digging peat or knitting Aran sweaters instead, you've got another think coming. Second: The only thing we own that's worth enough to cash into a pair of tickets to Ireland is your fiddle! We'd end up like O. Henry's watchless man with his watch fob and his bald wife with her comb. You'd be an itinerant fiddler without a fiddle. And me . . . I don't know what I'd be. Aside from that, it's a great idea!"

Sweeney clasped one hand around the small of her waist and pulled her to him, cupping her face in the other palm. "All right, then. I'll settle for the other plan."

"What other plan?"

"That we call it a night and start again in the morning." With his soft but weary gaze locked on her large brown eyes, Sweeney trailed his fingertips down Rose's neck, tracing the contours of her breasts in a slow figure-eight, his hand coming to rest over her heart. Rose sighed, her heartbeat thundering in her ears.

"It seems like years since you looked at me like that."

"No, not years. But for longer than I should have. For that I humbly apologize. I guess I forgot for a little while what's really important to me." He began unhurriedly to unbutton her blouse. "Do you know what?"

"What?"

"If I had to choose between my fiddle and you, I think I'd choose you."

Tears glistened on her cheeks as he kissed her.

Chapter Seventeen

Rose lay in the warmth of Niall's arms, listening to the distant, scattered conversation of the foghorns. It was true that sex didn't solve any long-term problems, but it was one hell of an efficient short-term distraction. And anyway, to quote some literary character or other from her youth, "nothing is so urgent today that won't be urgenter tomorrow!"

A foghorn sounded again and Rose felt Niall's finger slowly meander along the bump of each vertebra from the small of her back to the nape of her neck. She shifted over luxuriantly and was about to make a chiropractic suggestion when the phone rang.

Sweeney sat up and switched on the bedside lamp. It was nearly two o'clock in the morning. The phone rang again. He reached out and grabbed the bedroom extension.

"Niall? Is that you?" spoke the unmistakable clipped accent of Joe Gilmore. Sweeney answered that it was.

"You've got to get down here right away," declared the voice, clearly alarmed.

"What's happened, Joe? Why the hell call me at two o'clock in the morning?"

"Listen, there's no time to explain! Just get yourself down here to the bar as fast as you can!"

"Does this have something to do with what we talked about last . . . ?"

"Yes!" Gilmore cut him off. "Hurry, damn it! And make sure you're not followed!" The line went dead.

Rose propped herself up on her elbows with a quizzical expression on her face. Sweeney jumped out of bed.

"C'mon! Something weird's going on. Maybe you can figure it out faster than I can!"

They parked directly in front of the Bag of Nails, the street being deserted except for a few restaurants still stacking the day's trash out in front for early morning pick up. The damp westerly wind stung their cheeks with a gust that was chilling rather than refreshing.

Pulling open the front door, Sweeney and Rose entered the bar. The light was subdued, as the fluorescent banks over the pool table and at the end of room in front of the stage have been switched off. All that was left to illuminate the long room was the flickering of the juke box and the softened bar light.

Annie was mechanically picking up dirty glasses from one of the untidy tables. Joe stood behind the bar but made no move toward them.

"Lock the door, Niall," Gilmore said. It was a cold command, not a request. Sweeney flipped the deadbolt, turned and proceeded past the pool table toward the grim bartender.

"What did you mean make sure I'm not . . ." He froze in his tracks. Another man emerged from the blackness of the store room, an automatic pistol in his right hand and a cigarette dangling loosely from the corner of his mouth.

The man was about thirty, average height with narrow hips and small shoulders. He wore a well-tailored gray suit, his pocket handkerchief the same light brown as his conservatively-cropped hair. His eyes held no warmth. Indeed, Sweeney could only remember seeing such an expression once before in his life, in the eyes of Michael Blayney. In his hand the man hefted the pistol with the quiet, unruffled ease of one who is comfortable around guns.

Rose felt suddenly cold all over. This was the man she had spotted watching the house. She was certain of it!

"Glad you decided to make it," he said in a soft, yet somehow cruel Irish accent that Sweeney couldn't quite place.

"Who are you? What do you want?" demanded Sweeney nervously, never having had a loaded gun pointed at his heart before.

The man with the gun ignored his question, clearly intending to dictate the pattern of conversation. "Good evening, Mr. and Mrs. Sweeney. I asked Joe to invite you here for a little chat. You see, we've already come to a useful understanding, Joe and I, and we . . . I . . . thought it was time for an understanding with you as well.

"Who the hell is this, Joe?" Sweeney flushed both angry and embarrassed. Gilmore remained motionless at the bar, leaning squarely on his elbows, his face betraying no emotion. Farther down the bar, Annie stood equally still.

"His name is Roger Sweeney."

Sweeney's eyes darted back and forth between the two men, the square and steely bartender and the shorter, neatly dressed, drab-looking man who now stood before them, the cold barrel of his gun fixed upon the apprehensive newcomers. Was this the Other Sweeney that Inspector Elliot said he was so anxious to talk to?

"Yes, ole cuz," he said easily, as if answering the unspoken question. He took a few steps toward the bar and stopped behind an empty table. "I suppose we are distant relations, though I'm afraid we can't allow that to affect our . . . business."

Sweeney couldn't suppress a question, turning again to Gilmore. "Joe, you knew about this guy?" The defeat washing over the barman's expression was an eloquent enough answer. This, then, was the real source of the fear and silence Joe and Annie had left them with at their last meeting. And it must have been for the newcomer's benefit that Joe had told Sweeney not to be followed.

"I'm what you might call a professional political fundraiser." The corners of the gunman's mouth elevated in a snakelike smile, his eyes utterly emotionless.

"Where I come from it's called money launderer," replied Sweeney impulsively. The man's eyes flashed red, but the barrel of the gun did not waver. The smile also remained unchanged. He merely shrugged.

"As you like. But since we've had to close up shop recently, I've convinced Joe here to help open a new business."

Rose paled. Here, then was the real San Francisco connection for the flow of money from Ireland. But what could he want with them? Why was he telling them this? Surely, the mere fact that they knew about the new terrorist finance point meant that they were as good as dead. She bit her lip, digging her fingertips unconsciously into her husband's arm.

Roger Sweeney continued, his tone adding no more threat to the exchange than the gun already provided. "It's very simple, really. Joe here will pick up a little mail, let a few people meet after hours, that sort of thing. Nothing for him to get personally involved with. Just provide a good, honest business location with plenty of foot traffic. And of course, he'll gain quite a bit of status once we let it be known in certain quarters that he's a fugitive hero."

"You mean to say Joe's identity is still secret?" Rose heard herself ask.

"Not from you," Roger Sweeney answered pointedly. "And not from me. Or from anyone else who chances to read this little book." He pulled out a slim black notebook and returned it to his breast pocket.

"It'll be up to me to decide who I share this fascinating little book with." He glanced over to make sure Gilmore was paying attention. Again he fixed his cruel eyes on Sweeney, sneering. "You do pretty good work, for an amateur. Too bad I didn't know about you earlier. Wouldn't have had to waste some perfectly good gelignite. You had the right idea, ole cuz. Always best to keep things quiet."

There didn't seem to be any point in arguing with this cold-blooded creature. He was as mad as Blayney now clearly had been. Sweeney could see Gilmore standing statue-silent behind the bar to the right of the man who held them prisoner, both hands still visible. Did Gilmore now believe as the gunman did that Sweeney was the killer, or was he, like Sweeney, merely listening and looking for an opening to act? And if this stranger thought he'd knifed Blayney, then why had he set things up to kill the man a few hours later? Though his brain spun like an insane merry-go-round, he managed to keep his voice steady.

"Exactly what is it you want? And what did you want with Blayney?"

"What do I want? That's simple. As to what I wanted with Blayney, well, we can't have informers littered about the place. It gives people the wrong idea."

So it *was* an IRA assassination! Or it would have been, if . . .

"I think we can do business now." The gun remained trained on the fiddler as he picked up and lit another cigarette with a practiced left hand. "Now that I know you're all in this together, I wanted you in one place to avoid any . . . misunderstandings later on. The cops are watchin' your place so we couldn't talk there, could we? Here we can all have a friendly little chat around a friendly little jar and no one's the wiser, eh?"

"You want a jar?" asked Gilmore coldly.

"Later, Joe. Plenty of time later."

"The cops?" said Sweeney evenly. "They're not watching me anymore. We weren't tailed here."

"Must've got tired of waiting for you to do something stupid. You may be an amateur, but you're not the type to kill a man and then do something stupid, are you? One thing I've been meaning to ask you, what did you do with the knife after you done in Blayney?"

"What makes you think I'd tell you?"

"Ah, well," eyes dropped for an instant to smile at the gun. "But no, whatever it was, it was clever enough to fox the bastards. As I said, nice work for an amateur."

"How do you know I killed him?"

"I didn't, not for sure. Not until I started reading this," and he patted his jacket pocket. "Michael Blayney didn't like you very much, ole cuz, did he? Not at all. We needn't go into why."

"I don't know why!" declared Rose.

The gunman merely snorted.

"This is your party," she retorted hotly. "Humor me."

"Oh come now, Mrs. Ole Cuz. A man in my profession can find out anything just by ringing up a colleague or two. I know all about Niall boy here and the pub in Clare. And Blayney wrote that you were onto him," he added, again patting the slight bulge in his jacket. "Christ, he wrote it over and over again."

Sweeney couldn't contain himself any longer. "So what the hell's in that little book that could possibly give you that idea?"

"What indeed?" With a poker player's smoothness, he opened the book one-handed and leafed through a few pages, never dropping the barrel of his gun. "First of all, here's everything the police need know about Kevin here to send him back home in patriotic glory—chapter and verse. Of course, he mightn't survive the journey . . . that's neither here nor there. Blayney's journal entries are a bit erratic but they are dated and, as far as I can tell about Kevin here, quite factual."

He turned another few pages. "Here's a few entries that might interest you, ole cuz:

> *Sweeney plagues and hounds me again. His music taunts me. He thinks he can bring me down with no one the wiser, but he is no cleverer than any of the others. I will destroy him before he can launch his spear. I will curse him so that neither he nor any other shadow from the past can harm me.*

"There's plenty more in that vein, going back more than two years. I know I wasn't the Sweeney he was writing about, so I figured it must've been you. A couple of phone calls squared it. It wouldn't take a clever man to add it all up. So don't bother denying that you knew he'd informed on Gilmore here and had taken that Brit's reward money."

If Gilmore's hair hadn't already been gray, it might have shot to gray in that instant. The man recoiled as if he'd been physically struck. From the look on his face, Joe had not known of that link in the chain connecting a dead blackmailer in San Francisco with the destruction of an innocent man two years and half a world away.

A quick glance at Annie showed her moving toward Gilmore for comfort and safety. Roger Sweeney noticed the movement, too, and spun viciously toward her, raising the pistol in a straight-arm bead directed at the bridge of her nose.

"You stay put where I can see you!" he hissed, and the terror that so clearly bathed Annie's face froze her in midstep.

Sweeney's mind continued to race in several directions at once while scattered thoughts ricocheted against each other, shouting for his attention. The thought that shouted loudest was: What sort of deranged paranoid would rave in a diary that way about imagined enemies? But this strange Sweeney had made himself clear enough. He would have to play along and do what he was told just like Gilmore, or this fellow would toss the notebook to the cops and let them both swing, innocent or not. Almost as an afterthought, he realized what Rose had known since shortly after they had arrived. This creature wouldn't be satisfied with merely handing over the notebook if Sweeney balked at complete and total cooperation. He'd have to kill them, too. Both of them.

All this time Rose assessed the situation, taking in the people, the furniture and the space, measuring, supposing, desperately searching for a way out. Her heart suddenly soared as she realized where Joe Gilmore was standing. Her eyes shot to the gunman, the juke box, to Annie, back to the gunman, to Gilmore. Yes, there was an answer! There behind the bar, Gilmore could easily reach the controls. If only he'd think to try! Desperately, she trained her eyes on the grim gray man, trying to get his attention telepathically.

Sweeney's thoughts did not paint any more pleasant a picture than did Rose's. He decided to play it along as written until he could think of something better to do.

"All right," he raised his hands slowly in a gesture of submission. "You've got me over a barrel. Sure I killed the bastard. I did you a favor, didn't I?" The other Sweeney made the slightest possible bow of appreciation. "But if Gilmore here is going to keep your little money flow operating, what the hell do you need me for?"

"Ah, that's still to be decided. Call it insurance. You can be sure that we'll have useful work for you. And for your lovely wife." Sweeney's blood surged deafeningly in his temples, but he remained still. The gunman took a final long drag from his cigarette and extinguished it in the wet bottom of one of the dirty pint glasses littering the table.

"Before leaving, I only wish to impress upon you the fact that you may be called upon at any time to do certain . . . favors for us. And should you feel reluctant about cooperating, well, then . . ." He didn't feel it was necessary to finish the sentence.

Rose concentrated on Gilmore, frozen in his vantage point behind the bar. He was so close to the tool which could free them all from this nightmare. But it was still out of reach. Were it not for the cat-like attentiveness of the man with the gun, he could slip the double-handed catch on the secret drawer and pull out the pistol which still lay there, quiet and ready. But she knew that no matter how quick he was, that succession of movements would take several seconds too long. Someone would certainly be dead before he ever had a chance to pull the trigger.

But whether in response to Rose's telepathic efforts or not, Gilmore began to move. Her eyes were riveted on him as, expressionless, he surveyed the game board before him. Directly in the center of the room stood the gunman. To the gunman's left were Sweeney and Rose, holding tightly onto each other perhaps ten feet this side of the pool table. Annie was just as vulnerable to a stray bullet as they were, standing frozen and unprotected there in the access gap between the bar and the wall. But he only needed one hand. Ever so slowly, he inched down with his left hand toward the juke box remote controls. He rotated the volume knob to full, poised his finger over the power switch and waited.

It was only a moment later that he saw his chance. The gunman reached out for the pack of cigarettes lying on the table to his left, lowering his eyes from Sweeney and Rose for a fraction of a second. Gilmore raised his right palm in warning, a motion caught simultaneously by both Sweeney and Rose. Neither of them were prepared for what happened next.

An ear-splitting scream erupted from the juke box. Roger Sweeney spun around in panic to face the new enemy just as Gilmore hurled a full bottle of whiskey over the bar. The green flash of glass caught him on the right shoulder, smashing to bits as Sweeney and Rose dove for the protection of an overturned table. The stunned man spun on his heel in whiskey and glass, grabbing at the surrounding chairs for balance. The automatic clattered to the floor and skidded to a stop against the bar.

Afterwards, Sweeney was never certain why he did what he did at that moment. Lunging up past Rose, he leaped forward at the momentarally dazed gunman, snapping his head back with a hastily-aimed punch full on the point of his chin. But rather than falling unconscious, his adversary leapt sideways with the agility of a panther, planted a fist squarely into Sweeney's stomach with the force of a cannon ball, sidestepped a second bottle launched from the bar and sprinted for the door. Without bothering to flip the bolt, he smashed through, shoulder first, into the cold night.

Gilmore was already vaulting over the bar and was halfway across the room moving at prodigious speed, followed closely by a gasping Sweeney. Rose had run over to the bar and had snatched up the gun, while Annie followed the two men toward the door, terrified and uncertain.

Sweeney reached the door when he and the others heard the sudden rising scream of car brakes and a squealing of tires. Bursting into the night air behind Gilmore he watched as Roger Sweeney somersaulted with a strangled cry high over the hood of a green delivery truck. The gunman bounced headfirst on the pavement behind it with an indescribable, sickening sound and crumpled to a stop in the cold yellow cone of the streetlight. The truck veered to the right and nosed with a tinkling crunch into a large restaurant dumpster twenty yards farther down the street. Its engine stalled and was silent.

As far down in both directions as the lights could be seen illuminating the thick, low-hanging fog, Clement Street was completely deserted.

Rose was beside him as Sweeney knelt beside the body lying in the street. The eyes were open, the neck was skewed at an impossible angle. Sweeney's stomach roiled with sharp pain and rising nausea.

There was no question that Roger Sweeney was quite dead. The coat hung open, revealing both the empty shoulder holster and the inside pocket containing the black notebook. There was no blood. Quelling his churning stomach with an effort, Sweeney knelt there, surveying the scene as if in a dream.

Annie called from the truck in alarm, "Will somebody help me? This guy's out cold."

They all ran to the driver's side of the truck, picking their way through scattered cans and hubcaps. In white on green lettering the truck proclaimed "Natural Foods Express." Sweeney gazed down into the unconscious face of the vehicle's only occupant, a skinny Rasta in a Grateful Dead t-shirt, the center of his forehead already coming up in a nasty, raised welt. He fired a silent prayer heavenward promising never to make another testy crack about New Age drivers.

Opening the door, he felt the side of the neck for a pulse, relieved to feel the answering strong, regular beat. Thank God the guy was wearing his seat belt, he thought. "I think he'll be okay," he reported to the other three, who now stood around the body of Roger Sweeney, every one of them utterly drained of energy or emotion.

They stood together in the street for a moment that lasted an eternity. It was Rose who first snapped to attention. She stepped over to Joe Gilmore and grasped him firmly by the arm. "Joe, listen! We don't have much time."

He seemed dazed. She shook his arm forcefully and his eyes cleared. "Joe, there's no time!"

She quickly crouched down and pulled the book from the dead man's coat. She pressed it into Gilmore's hand. She again locked her eyes on his and commanded, "Put this away safe and get me the knife. Quick!"

For a fraction of a second Gilmore hesitated, then realized what Rose intended. From his expression, he knew it was his only chance. He ran back into the Bag of Nails with the black notebook, emerging a moment later with a bar rag. He opened the rag, revealing the switchblade that Blayney had dropped in his first maddened attack on Sweeney. Rose carefully wiped the knife clean of fingerprints, pressed it quickly into the dead man's hand and slipped it into his pocket.

The driver began to moan. Annie seemed startled and confused about what to do. Rose came over and joined Sweeney next to the car door. She reached out and gripped the man's shoulder as he tentatively opened his eyes and gazed up into the strangers' faces.

"The man, the man!" he cried in abject alarm. "I didn't see him! He ran right out in front!" Rose assured him that they knew. Help was on the way. "Better go in and call the police, Annie. Better yet, ask for Inspector Elliot."

Chapter Eighteen

"The knife checks out as about the right size and shape, but we'll have to see what the lab boys come up with."

The flashing lights of squad cars and ambulances outside still on the street painted the frosted front windows and tinted the atmosphere inside the Bag of Nails. The Inspector paced from where Detective Leigh was taking Annie's statement back over to the table occupied by Sweeney and Rose.

"I don't bet we'll find much, though, since he's had plenty of time to sterilize it." He lowered his large frame into the slatted wooden chair opposite Sweeney. The bartender and his girlfriend had both identified the knife as the one they'd seen on the floor Friday night. If he got any other corroboration, all he'd need would be somebody who saw Roger Sweeney in the bar that night to make the story sort of fit together. But even if he wasn't seen, he could have been there in all that chaos. It paid in his business to have a forgettable face.

"You seem to know all about him, Inspector," said Rose.

"Not all. Enough. Roger Sweeney was an IRA hit man sent out to deal with Blayney. Been over here a while doing God knows what, lying low. Seems that Bernie was right after all about him setting the explosives to cover his tracks. Weird way to do it, but there's no way to ask him about his style now."

"Did you ever learn why he was after Blayney?" Rose did her best to sound innocent.

Elliot sniffed. "It seems Blayney was fingered as a paid informer and sentenced to death in absentia. We could never determine just who he ratted on, but he'd apparently been paid enough for informing to get him over here." Elliot glanced in Joe Gilmore's direction and quietly watched as the displaced man from Belfast sauntered over and unplugged the old juke box for the night.

"Blayney wasn't using a phony name or anything, though," Sweeney thought out loud. "He'd been here a while, too. Why'd they wait so long to kill him, do you suppose?"

"Search me," Elliot replied with momentary candor. "Maybe they timed it for headline value. Maybe it was meant to scare somebody else. I'll never know what makes the mind of a terrorist tick. I'm perfectly happy to box all this up and ship it back to Ireland for them to make sense of it."

Rose was only now beginning to relax a little. "And he was the man I saw watching the house."

"We think so, Mrs. Sweeney. We'd been tipped that he was in the United States but we hadn't traced him here until he made the overseas calls to the tapped lines in Ireland. We didn't find any of his fingerprints in Blayney's apartment, but we managed to get a couple of readable ones in his hotel room and found traces of explosive that matched the bomb residue in the apartment. We thought we had him on a tight lead for a while, but he must have smelled something, because he slipped us about noon today and we were still looking for him when you called."

Rose made a vague "glad to oblige" gesture with her hands. Elliot scowled.

"That reminds me. You're sure you didn't touch or move the body? You didn't take anything out of the pockets or find anything lying nearby?"

"No, Inspector, as we told you before. We just saw he was dead and went to make sure the driver was okay while Annie called you."

Right. He didn't like it, but he could devise no reason to believe they'd hide the missing notebook . . . if, in fact, it ever existed. If Roger Sweeney had taken such a book from Blayney's apartment, odds favored it being an incriminating list of IRA names or addresses for the purposes of blackmail, which the hit man would likely have destroyed immediately, having destroyed the blackmailer.

"There is something I want to know, though. Why did he call you to meet you here? And why did you agree to come at two o'clock in the morning?"

Sweeney had been waiting for that one. "The voice on the phone said it was you, Inspector. Something about coming down to identify somebody—that you'd found someone who could clear me of suspicion. Hell, I was half asleep. What was I to think? I just ran down here with Rose. Wouldn't you have done the same?" Rose reached up and quietly squeezed the back of his neck in admiration.

"Mm. But why do you suppose he called you to meet him here at the bar?"

"Protective coloration, I guess," suggested Sweeney after a pause. "Nobody notices the comings and goings at a pub, and he must have been afraid our house was being watched. Why, the poor barman and waitress were terrified. Had no idea what was going on!"

He could see Gilmore out of the corner of his eye glance over briefly with a "don't push your luck" expression and then continue polishing the bar with renewed energy.

"Protective coloration at a pub?" Elliot declared, not expecting an answer. "At two in the morning?" Sweeney and Rose made no attempt to answer the rhetorical questions.

"And he pulls a gun on you and you hit him with a bottle and he panics and runs out into the street and gets run over? Is that how it went?"

Sweeney nodded. "Joe distracted him when he switched on the juke box remote at full volume. I hit him without thinking. I mean, Inspector, how'd you like to have some clown point a gun at you?"

Elliot just snorted as Sweeney wondered if the question would sound silly to a homicide inspector.

"But why call you over here in the first place, is my question." His voice began to rise. "Since he'd murdered Blayney and knew you had nothing to do with the AdTech money laundry, what did he hope to accomplish involving you at all?"

"He wanted to frame Niall for the murder, obviously," said Rose with confidence. "He'd watched us and knew you had Niall under suspicion. He must have felt safer manufacturing a fall-guy."

"Frame him?" roared Elliot. "How? By forcing him at gunpoint to leave his fingerprints on the murder weapon and then mailing it to me?"

Rose batted her eyelashes sweetly at the helplessly reddening face of the unhappy policeman. She shrugged. "Why, Inspector, we're hardly qualified to speculate. We're just happy that you know who killed Blayney and that you know it wasn't Niall. We'd be even happier to leave all the little details up to you from here on in."

Ten minutes later they were on their way home to try to scrounge what was left of a decent night's sleep.

•

"Well, he *did* bomb the apartment, didn't he? He was going to kill him. He was paid to kill him. He probably killed other people before and he'd have done it again! What's the big problem?"

Sweeney just continued to gaze at his wife with a troubled expression. "Fine, but you forget there's still a girl running around the city who took a kitchen knife and opened up a man like a bag of rice."

"Not just any man, though. A real bastard. What does it matter what the police think? Aren't we all better off for what she did?" She regretted her last remark as it came out of her mouth.

Sweeney sighed. "I might still have a job and we might still be living the semblance of a normal life if none of this had happened."

Rose sat down gently next to him on the arm of the favorite blue chair and combed her fingers through his hair. After a nearly sleepless night and a pot of coffee, neither of them felt particularly chipper. "Okay. If you think I ought to, I'll tell the Inspector everything. The problem with coming clean, though, is that we'll have to tell him about Joe Gilmore, too."

Sweeney thought, Why? and then remembered the problem of the hidden knife. He blanched. "Yeah, he'll have to know about where the knife was that wasn't really the murder weapon but that was deliberately kept from the cops. He'll want to know who put it there and why. Hell, he'll want to know why the secret drawer was in there in the first place. And once he starts asking more than the cursory questions he'll eventually figure out who Gilmore really is. Do they really have anything on him, though? He was innocent of the charge, surely."

"In the eyes of the law, he's at least an escaped prisoner. The British prison guards may want a few more cracks at him before letting him go, or maybe they won't let him go at all. And he's in this country with phony documents. The Feds will certainly chuck him out for that, even if the Belfast charges are dropped."

Violet Reese and her mother. Vin Bowen. Joe Gilmore and Annie. And, of course, Christie Reese herself. All these lives would be forever wounded and scarred by the truth. Rose's actions had opened up an ethical can of worms, and Sweeney was equally troubled with all the options that seemed open.

"Give me time to think," he said, pulling her to him.

She could easily give him that.

•

Sweeney answered the knock on the door to find Vin Bowen standing on the stoop with his slouch more pronounced than usual and a disconsolate expression pulling down the corners of his eyes toward the ends of his moustache.

"She's gone," he said. Rose jumped up from the arm of the chair and hurried to Sweeney's side.

"Gone? Gone where?"

"She left without saying goodbye."

"You'd better sit down." Sweeney steered his friend to the nearest chair. "What happened?"

"I went over to her house this morning, as usual, and her mother said she'd left to fly back to Boston. Christie dropped out of school and she's entering a convent!" He looked up, still apparently finding the concept hard to believe.

Rose sat next to him with her arm around his shoulder to coax for details.

"Her mother wasn't surprised when Christie told her. It seems that Christie had been spending much more time with God in recent days. She said she'd received the call and her mother firmly believed that the tragedies of her life had finally brought her closer to God!" He sniffed and wiped his nose.

"Closer to God! She sure as hell wasn't getting closer to me! Why, I was being the perfect gentleman. I never even . . . She never told . . . aw, Christ!"

With comforting arms, Rose tried to soothe the disappointed romantic in the chair, though Sweeney noted the brief flash of humor in her eyes as she sat behind him. Vin sniffed again heroically and collected himself.

"Do you suppose it was me? I mean, do you think it was something I said or did that drove her to it?"

Rose found she really had to concentrate not to giggle.

"Well, Vinnie," she said with care, "going into a convent isn't like suicide, you know. It's not necessarily something you're driven to, is it? And certainly not something *you* should feel guilty about!"

"No, I guess it isn't. It's just that I'd hate to think that I'm the kind of guy that a girl dates for a while and then decides she'd rather be a nun."

Rose hugged him with genuine warmth.

"No, Vinnie, believe me, you're not! Just give it time. I'm sure you had nothing to do with it. In fact, I think I can guarantee you that nothing like this will ever happen to you again!"

"You think so?" sniffed Vin, brightening.

"Bank on it," injected Sweeney, feeling himself suddenly to be the luckiest man alive. He gazed down into Rose's eyes as if seeing her for the first time.

"Niall, is there anything else you think needs to be said?" inquired Rose.

Sweeney continued to stare into her eyes. He shook his head.

"Is there anything we need to do today? Anything important, that is?"

"No," he said, breaking into a slow smile. "I think it's been done for us."

Rose returned the smile with all the warmth she felt in her heart.

"Vinnie, I can't face the thought of another cup of coffee and it's still too early to start drinking beer." Rose stood up and stretched luxuriantly. "How'd you like a sandwich?"

As the three of them trooped raggedly up the hall to the sun-drenched kitchen, Sweeney began to hum a tune, the name of which he couldn't remember.

Printed in the United States
109346LV00004B/59/P